MIDNIGHT BLOOD

Linda Hales

Paperback ISBN 979-8-9909989-2-6

Hardcover ISBN 979-8-9909989-3-3

To my brother, Oscar, your life ended too soon, but your legacy lives on.

Midnight Blood

Chapter 1

Hailee had been down this street dozens of times, but her senses were on high alert. Usually, the streetlights illuminated the entire area, but tonight they appeared dull, making her walk to the entryway feel unsafe. Hailee quickened her pace. She pushed open the heavy, ornate door. A noise startled her; she glanced over her shoulder and quickly crossed the threshold. The door closed, leaving the night's chill nipping at her heels. Hailee breathed a sigh of relief; no one was there–this time.

The Meridian Hotel featured a regal staircase and elegant chandeliers crafted from expertly cut crystals, and its employees were professional and discreet. It was located in the heart of downtown Portland, Oregon, and just a few minutes' walk from the Portland Art Museum and the Keller Auditorium. In the lounge, she ordered a tall Greyhound; she sipped her drink and turned toward the sound of laughter. She noticed a couple in the back of the room kissing. She'd never been one for PDA and ignored them and continued to drink the smooth vodka. She twirled the ice around, watching the frozen cubes bob up and down. She scanned the room. The same old crowd filled the lounge: a few couples, some businessmen, a few single men, and her.

Portland in June was beautiful, brighter, and drier than in May, with average high temperatures in the low seventies. Portland offered a variety of events in June: the Rose Festival, Portland Beer Week, and parades. Hailee lived in Colorado; the summer temperatures were great, topping out in the upper eighties. She enjoyed spending her downtime in Portland, especially in the summer. She enjoyed the cooler weather, relishing in brisk mornings and the comfortable evening temperatures.

Hailee's relentless schedule left her with little personal time, a fact she had come to accept. She poured her heart into her work, which often left her drained. If she wasn't writing or promoting her books, she was sleeping or on her way to the next stop.

She stared into the glass, taking deep breaths to clear her mind and calm her nerves.

"Excuse me. Is this seat taken?"

She didn't look up but responded mechanically, "No."

He sat, ordered a draft beer, and laid a twenty next to his glass.

Hailee studied him from lowered lashes. He seemed eerily familiar; his toned muscles filled out his snug-fitting clothes. He sat tall on the stool; his shoulders were relaxed, and he scrutinized his drink as if it wasn't what he expected. His eyes were dark grey. His clean-shaven face, strong jawline, and prominent chin were clearly visible in the dim light. A quiet confidence emanated from him.

"Are you done," he asked?

His voice ended her reverie. "What?"

"Are you done checking me out?"

"I didn't mean to stare. You look familiar."

"Do I?"

"Sort of."

His brows arched. "Sounds like a pick-up line."

"No, I…" Her face flushed, turning a deep crimson. "Honest, you look like someone I know."

"Who do I remind you of?"

"You don't want to know." Hailee squirmed on the stool.

"An old lover?"

"No, I never slept with him."

"Ah, someone you want to sleep with."

"No, that would be impossible."

"So… he's married?"

She choked on her drink and covered her mouth with a napkin. "Not even close."

"I'm dying of curiosity; who is it?"

"You remind me of 'the perfect man,'" Hailee stated matter-of-factly.

"I'm not perfect."

"Probably not, but that's who you remind me of."

His brows creased. "How many drinks have you had?"

"This is my first one," Her eyes drifted to her empty glass; she ordered another Greyhound, "Second one."

Hailee straightened up, shaking her head; dark brown curls bounced freely off her slender shoulders. Her blue dress clung to her curves, emphasizing her trim waist. Her heart-shaped face was still hot from her embarrassing confession. Her chin jutted out to give her a permanent look of defiance. The gold flecks in her eyes sparkled when she laughed. She could feel his intense gaze on her.

"Are you done?" Hailee asked.

"Yes." He set his glass down and turned to look her straight in the eye. "I think I know you."

"Do you?"

He laughed—a deep, confident laugh. "Yes."

She mimicked his earlier movements and leaned toward him. "Sounds like a pick-up line."

She tried to keep a straight face but laughed, knocking over her glass. She jumped off the stool and frantically wiped up the spilled liquid. The bartender took over and poured her another drink, his treat.

"Do I remind you of someone klutzy?"

"Not really."

"That's too bad because I seem to be all thumbs."
She took a drink. "You know, sitting next to the perfect
man is making me a little nervous."

His shoulders stiffened. "I'm just a man."

She had offended him. "I'm sorry." How could she
tell him that he was the spitting image of her latest novel's
protagonist?

"Who are you?" he asked softly.

She took a large sip; it burned on the way down.
She stared into her glass.

"Apparently, I'm a clumsy, insensitive person."

"I don't believe that." He put his hand on her glass.
"Tell me."

"Just a woman and you?"

"Just a man."

They continued to talk and laugh. Hailee started to
relax. Tonight could really be fun: good conversation,
refreshing drinks, and the perfect man. She giggled.

A tight-lipped frown and a stern look crossed his
face.

"How many have you had?"

"Three."

"I think it's four."

"No, I spilled one. It doesn't count. Are you
policing my drinking?"

He leaned up against the bar. "'I'm the perfect man,
so I must be chivalrous."

Was he going to let that go?

He cupped her face; he bent down and brushed her
lips with his.

The bartender, Alex, cleared his throat and handed
her the bar phone. "There's a call for you."

"Hello," Hailee listened distractedly and responded,
"I'm not changing my mind. I'll talk to you later." She put
the phone down and pushed it across the counter.

"Sorry about that."

4

"Anything urgent?" The stranger asked.

"It's nothing," She stared into his eyes, "What's your name?"

"Something perfect."

"I said I'm sorry."

"I know, but I like how you blush when I bring it up," he smiled, and the corners of his eyes crinkled, "so, are you a celebrity?"

"Why would you think that," Haliee asked?

"You remind me of someone, remember?"

He bent closer and descended toward her lips. She closed her eyes right before he made contact. This time, he kissed her fervently. His arms snaked around her waist; he lifted her off the barstool and pulled her close. Their tongues danced together, and their bodies heated up. Just when she thought she would melt into a puddle of trembling flesh, he eased her down and let go.

She stepped back; her cheeks glistened with a pink hue. "I'm sorry. I—"

"Say yes."

She didn't even know his name or anything about him, and she didn't care. He lit a fire in her that had never surfaced before. Hailee's mother had never prepared her for this kind of situation. Sure, she had given Hailee 'the talk' but hadn't discussed the physical and emotional complexities of intimate relationships. She based 'the talk' on individual freedoms and doing whatever felt good at the time. And now Hailee felt insecure and unsure. She didn't know how to respond to her physical reactions. He waited for an answer, and she struggled with a decision.

She had nothing to compare this situation to. Hailee's mother's advice wasn't relevant or reliable unless you believed in the free love ideology. When Hailee was sixteen, her parents were in a fatal car accident, and she discovered that the man she had called dad wasn't her biological father. After her parents' sudden demise, and while sorting through her parents' belongings, Hailee found a picture of her parents and one of their male friends. On the back, her mother had scribbled: Mom, Dad, and Harmony's Father. Did her mother have an affair, and did her father know? How could Hailee trust anything that they had told her?

Was her first time destined to be with a handsome stranger?

Her parents had been modern-day hippies: free spirits who wore period clothes and rejected established institutions and 'the man.' As a child, her home felt like a store with a revolving door, with strangers always around. She hadn't known why they were there; she had only wanted them to leave. Her ears rang, and her head throbbed from the constant slang—'don't bogart that joint, man,' 'let your freaky flag fly,' or her personal favorite, 'turn on, tune in, and drop out.'

The parties they threw included drugs, drinking, and partner swapping. Until she found the picture, she would never have dreamed that *they* had participated in 'free love.' They'd named her Harmony, and she hated it. It had been a constant reminder of their wild lifestyle, and because of it, her classmates bullied her mercilessly. It took years of love and support from her grandmother to overcome the effects of being called 'the stoner kid.'

Hailee extended her hand, and the stranger grasped it tight as he guided her through the lobby and up the spacious, winding staircase to his room on the third floor. He threw the key on the dresser and stepped away from the door, allowing her to change her mind. She went to him and timidly pressed up against him. Her heart pounded, and her fingers trembled. She fumbled with the buttons on his shirt. His smooth flesh felt hot under her touch. He unzipped her dress and pushed it down over her hips and to the floor. Her body trembled with anticipation. He kicked his pants across the floor. His olive skin shimmered in the

6

dim light, and for a second, Hailee considered the consequences of her actions. She closed her eyes and pulled his lips to hers. He removed the rest of their clothing and eased her onto the bed. Her hair fanned over her shoulders; her skin glowed in the soft light. She moaned as his skilled hands moved across her, sending shock waves up and down her eager body…

His body shuddered, and his breathing slowed. He held her until he fell asleep.

Hailee dressed and left the room.

Chapter 2

Hailee went up the massive, winding staircase to the fifth floor. She couldn't think straight; her entire body tingled from excitement and anticipation. As Hailee entered her room, her thoughts flashed back to the stranger and how he had given her time to leave and stop it from going further; she should have run for the hills. Why did she stay? Her lips curled up into a sarcastic smile; her mother would be so proud...

As a teenager, her grandmother spent hours with her, answering questions about her parents' open lifestyle and sex life. Her grandmother assured her that the woman she had called mom was her biological mother. She loved her grandmother and craved a genuine family connection, which her grandmother provided. She had instilled confidence and strong values in Hailee, and now, Hailee wondered how she had regressed and become more like her mother.

She sat on the bed, kicked off her shoes, and turned on the TV. She flipped through the channels, and when her eyes became heavy and her mind drifted back to the stranger and his muscular body, she fell asleep watching an infomercial.

*****

When she woke, her shoulders ached. She rolled her neck several times and worked out the knot. She glanced at the alarm clock: six o'clock. She heard a news reporter on a local station mention a breaking story.

Horrified, she stared at the screen and turned up the volume. A grisly scene was unfolding on the third floor of her hotel. Housekeeping had found a pool of blood in room 312. The victim's body was gone. No one could lose that much blood and survive. A strangled cry escaped her lips. She left the stranger, and he died.

She slid into her shoes and grabbed her purse. She rushed to the lobby, pushed open the door, and flagged down a cab. She told the cab driver to hurry and take her to the nearest police station. He nodded and drove her to the Central Precinct of the Portland Police Bureau.

Did the stranger fall prey to foul play, or was he in the wrong place at the wrong time? Her hands shook, and her breath caught painfully in her chest. The cabbie stopped by the main entrance; she handed him money, jumped out, and ran to the door. Her fear and regret continued to build. By the time she reached the main door, her voice stuck in her throat. "I have, I need—"

The officer's eyes bored into her.

Hailee took a deep breath. "I need to talk to homicide; please hurry."

He picked up the phone and mumbled into the receiver. He motioned for her to sit down. She paced back and forth. What if the stranger had been hurt because of her?

"Miss."

A man who stood five ten with dark skin and a muscular build extended his hand. "I'm Detective Javon Keller. How may I help you?"

"Are you with Homicide?"

"Yes."

"I need to speak with you privately; it's urgent."

He nodded, led her to his office, and motioned for her to take a seat.

"Miss, are you feeling okay?"

The night she gives in to temptation, the man she chooses dies. No, she was not all right.

"Do you have information regarding a murder?"

"I saw the news this morning about the discovery of blood and a missing body at the Meridian Hotel. I'm staying there. I know who the murder victim is. The one in room 312."

Hailee exhaled deeply.

Detective Keller grabbed a notepad and started writing. "I need you to start from the beginning and tell me everything you know."

"My name is Hailee Hollister, and I'm here on a vacation—"

"H. Hollister, the writer?"

"Yes," She nodded. "I'm staying on the fifth floor. Last night at the bar off the main restaurant, I met a man." She cringed; shame shone in her eyes. Now, her indiscretion would be on the record. "We talked, and then we went back to his room."

Detective Keller watched her intently, no emotion on his face. "To room 312?"

"Yes. We had sex; I went back to my room. I left the man alone, and someone killed him."

"What's his name?"

Her face turned red. "I don't know."

"And you still had sex with him?"

"Not my finest moment. Yes, I did."

"You could have been the one dead or missing."

She wanted to kick herself. The stranger had repeatedly reminded her that she looked familiar. Could he have been a stalker or a rapist? Or maybe he recognized her. It had happened before: a man, pretending to be someone else, tried to get close to her and gain access to her life. Fortunately, she had seen his true intentions and had warded off an ugly scene.

She nodded her head in agreement.

"How much did you have to drink?"

"I had three Greyhounds. You can check with the bartender, Alex; he'll tell you. We were the only two sitting at the bar."

He nodded. "I need a detailed description of the man you had sex with."

She flinched; that sounded so cold, so callous. "He was six feet one, muscular, about one hundred and ninety pounds. He had olive skin, dark hair, and eyes. He appeared to be the epitome of health; he didn't smoke."

"How do you know he didn't smoke," the detective asked?

"He didn't light up at any time while we were together, and his clothes didn't smell. His fingers and teeth showed no signs of yellowing."

"Ah, mystery writer."

Hailee shook her head and said, "No, high school health class."

"What else can you tell me about him?"

"His clothes appeared to be tailored; they fit perfectly." She remembered how the stranger had teased her about not being the perfect man and how she had regretted calling him that.

"Tell me about the sex."

She gritted her teeth. "I'm not telling you anything about that."

"Miss Hollister, I'm not trying to pry or embarrass you. I'm trying to determine if he has any violent tendencies or if he has had any special...let's say, trademarks that may be useful in identifying him."

"I didn't kill him." She stated flatly.

"I didn't mean to imply you did. This is an investigation; I must get all the information."

Could this get any worse?

"I'm not sure what you want to hear. We didn't do anything kinky. We had sex once in the missionary position. He had strong hands and was a great kisser."

"Did he force himself on you?"

"No. I consented."

"After having sex, what did you do?"

11

"We fell asleep. I woke up a while later. I dressed and went to my room on the fifth floor." Hailee exhaled, "I fell asleep watching TV. I woke up and heard the news about a murder. And here I am."

She lost her virginity to a handsome stranger, and he died that same night. Was it Karma? She followed in the footsteps of her mother, and the stranger lost his life.

"Did you see him again, or did you see him leave the room?"

"No. I left, and the man was alive," Hailee's lips turned down. "I never saw him again."

"Miss Hollister, thank you for coming in, and thank you for your honesty. I hope I didn't embarrass you."

"You're letting me go without checking for evidence?"

"Evidence?"

"Yes, I haven't showered. I still have DNA all over my body. It could help you identify him."

"We haven't found a body yet; we're still looking."

"His DNA from my body could match the blood on the sheets. It's been less than twenty-four hours. What about the YSTR procedure? It might identify the victim."

Detective Keller stood. "Stay here; I'll be right back."

Hailee felt obligated to find the one who killed the stranger. She owed him that much.

Detective Keller returned and grabbed his notepad. "Detective Max Toliver will see you now. Please come with me." He took her down a long, narrow hall to a large corner office. He walked in, put the notepad on the desk, stepped back, and motioned for her to sit down.

Hailee thanked Detective Keller and took a seat. She looked up at the man across from her. The detective stared back. She jumped up, knocking over the chair. She bent down and grabbed it by the armrest. The detective rounded the corner of his desk and took it from her, setting it upright, then returning to his chair.

She shifted nervously and brushed imaginary lint from her dress.

"What's wrong?" Detective Toliver asked.

"I thought you were dead."

He raised a brow. "Why did you think I was dead?"

"The reporter said that a murder occurred in the room we were in. I thought someone killed you after I left."

"Why did you leave?"

"I felt uncomfortable; I had to leave."

"I frightened you?"

"No. I couldn't believe that I…I—"

"That you gave your virginity to a stranger."

She flinched.

"You lied to me." He said calmly.

Her eyes flew open. "I didn't lie."

"You told me that you weren't a celebrity. You are."

She glared at him. "I'm an author, not a movie star."

"Hmmm…thin line."

"No, it's not. I'm a writer who earns a living. That's all."

"You had the wrong room."

"What?"

"We were in room 321, not 312."

She shook her head. "No, 312."

He pulled out the hotel keycard and waved it in front of her.

Her eyes moved from his face to the key, "There's no number on the keycard; you can't prove to me it was room 321."

"321 is *my* room. I've had a standing reservation for years."

She humiliated herself in front of strangers and the police, and she had the wrong room. She berated herself for being so careless. Chalk it up to cardinal lust.

A crimson hue spread across her face.

"Why didn't you mention that you were a virgin? That could have been pertinent?"

"Don't be crass; that's not important even if you were the one to die. And since you're obviously not dead, we're done here." She headed toward the door.

"Wait, what about the evidence?"

"Evidence?" Her skin heated up. "You don't need any evidence. You're not dead."

"What evidence do you have?"

"Don't be naïve, semen." She stated plainly.

"You were going to submit to a thorough medical examination to assist with the case?"

"If you died and I could help, yes."

"Hmmm…"

She took another step toward the door.

"Want to make it three," he asked?

"Three?"

"You climaxed twice last night; would you like to try for three?"

Hailee glared at him and said, "If you had been this crude last night, I'd still be a virgin."

She slammed the door and strode quickly down the hall.

At least he was alive.

Chapter 3

Detective Toliver buzzed Detective Keller's office. "Bring me what we have on the Meridian Hotel victim.

At the light tapping on his door, Toliver looked up and waved Keller in.

"What do we have so far?" Toliver asked.

"CSU tore apart the room; the body's nowhere to be found. The ME stated that no one could survive losing that much blood; it looks like the vic had been killed on the bed, maybe while sleeping or passed out, then moved to another location." Keller handed Toliver the file, "I've got Henderson and Carson canvassing for witnesses. Thornton, Watson, and Hudson are searching the alleys, dumpsters, and gutters to see if they can pick up a blood trail and find the body."

Toliver glanced at the crime scene photos. He grimaced when he saw the copious amount of blood on the bed. He scanned the pictures. "Did CSU find any personal belongings, something that would indicate the vic was staying at the hotel?"

"No, they didn't find a wallet, purse, phone, or any luggage. The closets and drawers were empty."

"Have we determined who pays for the room?" Toliver asked.

"It's registered to a corporation, Natural Beauty Cosmetics. We're trying to locate the owner now."

Toliver rubbed his face; the stubble prickled his fingers.

"Late night?"

"Yeah, my first personal night in a long time, and I got dragged out of bed with our first murder in months."

"Since there's no clothes or indication that the vic had a key, maybe it was a hook-up gone wrong," Keller stated.

Toliver nodded in agreement.

"What are we going to do about Miss Hollister? She thinks she knows who died?"

Toliver chuckled. "I've already covered it with her. She's mistaken."

"That's good. Because her description of her lover, well, it fits you to a tee."

"It's a generic description and could fit me and a few hundred other men. Don't worry. She's not going to be a problem."

"Jasmine tells me that Miss Hollister has aided on at least two investigations and has been instrumental in uncovering vital information that led to an arrest."

"Your wife is a fan of Miss Hollister," Toliver asked?

"Absolutely. Jasmine has every book and follows her on Facebook and Twitter. Miss Hollister is hot right now. She's had three best-sellers in a row."

"That's impressive. However, it has nothing to do with our case. Someone is dead, and we need to concentrate on finding the body. Once we do that, we can identify the vic and a possible motive. Has anyone checked in with an update?"

"No, I'm still waiting on the team I sent out this morning. The guys are limiting the search to the immediate vicinity, including the alleys and businesses close to the hotel. It would've been hard to smuggle out an entire body without someone seeing something."

"Unless they smuggled the body out in a suitcase. Maybe the perp cut up the body, shoved it into a suitcase, and walked out as if he were a guest leaving the hotel. That could explain the substantial amount of blood on the bed."

"You mean like the Arizona trunk murders?" Keller asked.

"Yeah, if the trunks hadn't started to leak, Winnie Ruth Judd might have gotten away with murder."

"It's rumored that Winnie needed help. Does that mean we are looking for two perps?"

"Let's find some hard evidence; a body would be nice and start from there," Toliver stated.

"So, we're going to exclude Miss Hollister's statement?"

"Yes, I have it on good authority. She had the wrong room."

"What about the guy?"

Toliver shrugged. "If he's not dead, it's not pertinent."

Toliver loved his job, and he did it well. Protecting and serving meant everything to him. His father disapproved of his career choice; he had hoped Max would run the family restaurant. It would provide substantial income in a safe and familiar environment. Max had tried to convince his father that law enforcement typified a challenging and rewarding career and that he could put his intellect to good use by getting criminals off the street.

Max knew that putting the guilty party behind bars was a huge part of his job. When people grieve the loss of a murdered family member, some need to focus on something other than that loss: finding out the circumstances of their loved one's death can be the first step in the healing process. His dad hadn't understood that and had been adamant that a high-paying career was in Max's future. It's too bad he died before Max could prove he could have both.

The phone rang; Max answered, "Where? We'll be right there." He stood, holstered his gun, and said to Keller, "They found the body."

*****

Some vacation this turned out to be. Hailee had sex for the first time and with a stranger, no less, and now was

17

mixed up in a homicide. And the man she thought she would never see again was at the center of it all. She returned to the hotel and headed to the restaurant, where she ordered an omelet and a whole-grain English muffin. While Hailee ate, the hair on her arm stood up; she glanced around quickly. Sitting on the other side of the room, an older couple whispered as they stared in her direction. Perhaps they recognized her from her book jacket, or possibly they saw her leave with a stranger in the bar the night before.

After breakfast, she showered, letting the water wash over her. She took longer than usual, scrubbing her skin aggressively. Despite what her mother had done, Hailee had planned to save herself for the man she loved and would marry. It seemed silly. She had tried hard not to be like her mother. She had failed miserably. The first genuine offer of sexual intimacy, and she gave in. She closed her eyes and remembered the stranger's lovemaking; he had been tender and passionate. That all changed this morning. He had been incredibly crude. Now, she knew his name. Why did he have to be a homicide detective?

She finished her shower, combed her hair, and took a nap. She dreamed of the perfect man–his lips, his hands…

*****

The shrill broke the silence; she rolled over and grabbed the receiver. It had better not be her agent.

"Hello?"

"Miss Hollister, did I wake you?"

She leaned against the headboard. "Who is this?"

"Max Toliver."

"Who?"

He laughed. "I guess I'm not *perfect*."

"Oh, it's you. Mr. Vulgarity."

"I'm sorry about that; you caught me off guard."

18

"You're alive. That's something."

"It is." Max mused.

"I'm not interested in making it three if that's why you called."

"No, it's not. Detective Keller told me you are on vacation; when will you be leaving?"

"Why is that important?

"Someone died last night, and we haven't identified the body. I'm interviewing all the guests; do you have time tonight?"

"Did the victim have a room here?"

"We've just discovered the body. We don't know why she—"

"She?"

"Yes, a young woman. May I come by tonight?"

"Why did you have a room here last night?" Hailee asked.

"That's none of your business."

His curt tone surprised her, but what did she expect? Blaming him wouldn't ease her guilty conscience. She didn't have to say yes, even if he was on the prowl.

"I'll drop by in an hour; will that give you enough time?"

"Shouldn't I come down to the station," Hailee asked?

"I have a team interviewing a few potential witnesses at the hotel. We don't want anyone to leave before we have a chance to speak with them. It will be quicker and more convenient if I can see you there."

"That's fine. I'll be waiting in the bar."

She pulled her hair back with a gold comb, put on a green cotton dress, and slipped into her three-inch peep-toe heels. She grabbed her purse and headed for the bar.

The low lights created a relaxed, intimate atmosphere in the room. Hailee scanned it, looking for anyone who might have been there the night before; no one

19

looked familiar. She walked up to the bar and flashed Alex a nervous smile.

"May I ask for a favor?"

"Sure, Hailee. What can I do for you," Alex asked?

She squared her shoulders but couldn't meet his eyes.

"As you probably guessed, I spent the night with a stranger."

He nodded.

"And as you know from my regular visits here, I don't do that."

He nodded again.

"I would appreciate your discretion with my one-time indiscretion."

"Sure thing, I won't tell a soul."

"Thank you. May I have my usual, please?"

He poured her a tall Greyhound and refused her money. "This one's on me."

"I'm meeting the man from last night, and he should be here soon. Apparently, he's a homicide detective."

"Yeah, I thought that was a little strange, you hooking up with a cop."

"You know him?"

Alex nodded, "He comes here often; he has a standing reservation. I think he's friends with the owner."

Perhaps Max wasn't looking to hook up last night. He may have had a legitimate reason for being here. She had to stop blaming him and be accountable for her own actions. Hailee had made painstaking efforts not to fall prey to men who would see her as an easy target–always traveling and always alone. She didn't want men to see her as a barfly or available, like last night; she just wanted to unwind and relax, but she got more than she had ever expected.

She had been coming here for years, first with her grandmother and then as a home away from home while on tour, and she had never once run into Max. After choosing to write mysteries as a profession, she paid close attention to people and her surroundings. Usually, she could identify a cop in any environment. Max did not fit the stereotype at all.

"Why didn't you say something?"

"He made you laugh. I didn't want to take that from you."

Hailee sipped her drink, headed to a table in the middle of the room, and waited for Detective Toliver. She gazed into her glass, just like last night.

Alex could mix up the tastiest cocktails, and he would never reveal a confidence. She valued his friendship, and she wished she knew more people like him. Hailee glanced back at Alex, who chatted up customers at the bar. He had natural good looks, while none of his physical characteristics were dominant. His light brown hair and eyes were nondescript; he had a nice smile and teeth, and his clothes fit well and were stylish. His positivity and charm won over his customers. He stood about five feet nine and could command an audience like no one she'd ever met until Max.

She looked around the bar. No detective. He must be running late; catching killers was not a nine-to-five job.

"Is this seat taken?"

She smiled, then her lips turned down when she saw the beer. "Aren't you working tonight?"

"Not officially, why?"

"You're drinking? I thought you came here to take my statement."

"I came here to see you and ask you some follow-up questions."

"This is important. A young woman lost her life; maybe I have information that you could use." She glared at him.

"You're right," he said, putting down his drink. "My team and I are asking the guests questions regarding the victim and the possible suspect. Do you remember seeing a young blonde female in her early twenties in the hotel in the past few days?"

"I saw a young blonde in here last night before you arrived. She and a man in his late thirties to early forties sat over there." Hailee pointed to the last booth at the back of the bar.

"Can you describe the man a little better?"

She nodded. "The lights were low, and I didn't get a close look. The man had short, neat blonde hair. His skin was dark and leathery. He spent too much time in the sun or in the tanning salon. He wore dark blue jeans and a red Polo shirt."

She took a small sip and wondered if the man she saw last had murdered someone. "I didn't see a ring, and I couldn't tell if he had a tan line on his finger. He had a deep, hearty laugh. I smelled no cologne or other fragrances coming from their booth."

"Tell me about the woman."

All Hailee could think about was the man sitting next to her. He made love to her last night, and it blew her mind. Now, they were sitting together, and she had the difficult task of describing a possible murderer and or murder victim.

"She looked to be twenty-four, wore her hair in a short, angular bob, stood five feet seven inches, had smooth, unblemished skin, and her eyes were a dark hazel. She wore red lipstick and smelled of blackberries and jasmine."

Hailee remembered the night before and thought they made an odd couple, but had dismissed it. "She had on a black form-fitting dress and wore three-inch red stilettos."

She took another sip; the burning of the vodka briefly distracted her. "She wore long dangling earrings,

22

her nails were gel tips, and she wore a polish called Scarlet Red."

She felt a pang of guilt. Last night had been one of the best nights of her life, and the same night, a young, vivacious woman had been brutally murdered.

"Hailee, what's wrong?" Max asked.

"A young woman died here last night." Hailee folded and unfolded her napkin.

"Is there anything else you remember about the girl?"

"Her small oval-shaped face accentuated her overall beauty."

"Your estimation of the girl's height was that with or without shoes?"

"Without."

He smiled.

"Anything else?"

"I almost forgot she had a colorful butterfly tattoo on her right ankle."

He shook his head.

"What," Hailee asked?

"You're very observant. How could you smell the woman's perfume and not know if the man wore cologne?"

"The young woman and I were in the ladies' room together. Her sweet-smelling and overpowering fragrance filled the room."

She glared at him.

"What?" Max asked.

"Are you going to write any of this down? What if I forget something when I come in to give my official statement?"

He pulled out his tape recorder. "Don't worry, I have it all here."

"Is this how you conduct all your interviews, with a hidden recorder?" Hailee asked.

"No, I didn't want to miss anything, so I brought it just in case."

"Do you normally overlook things?"

He eyed her. "No, due to our sensitive circumstances, I didn't want anyone to doubt the validity of your statement."

"I see," she took a drink. "Are we done with my unofficial statement?"

"Yes."

"Please turn it off."

He turned it off and put it back in his jacket pocket. "May I have a drink now?"

"You should have asked me to come back to your office. That would have been the professional way to do it. It feels weird giving a statement here." Her face heated up, and she leaned in close. She whispered, "You've seen me with my clothes off."

She fidgeted with her cocktail napkin. "Where did you find her body?"

"I can't discuss an ongoing case with you. Besides, I don't want to talk about it tonight, okay?"

"Isn't that why you came here, to ask me questions about the murder?"

"No, I could have met you at the precinct. I came here to see you and used the pretense of asking you questions as my legitimate excuse."

"Why?"

"I couldn't stay away," Max confessed.

She should be angry. She knows that the first forty-eight hours of an investigation are vital. Max should be working the case, not romancing her.

"Is your first name Maxwell?"

"Maximo, it's my maternal grandfather's name."

"It's a good, strong name," Hailee stated.

He took a drink and asked, his voice barely above a whisper, "Why didn't you tell me?"

She shook her head no. Explaining to Max why she had chosen him would be impossible. She didn't understand it herself.

"Okay. For now."

She peered up at him from lowered lashes, "So, do you come here often?"

They laughed and finished their drinks. Hailee peeked over at Alex and pursed her lips together. *One more?*

"Let's go."

"Go?" Hailee asked.

He held out his hand.

Haliee's relaxing vacation started to feel like a whirlwind romance. Other than her writing, she didn't have a life. Maybe it was time to start enjoying life. Uncertainty tugged at her conscience.

She grabbed her purse and held his hand. They climbed the stairs to her room, where he took her in his arms and kissed her.

Chapter 4

Hailee ran her hand across the warm sheet. The sound of running water made her smile; she stretched, pulled the sheets over her breasts, and waited for Max to emerge from the shower.

"Good, you're up. I didn't want to leave without saying goodbye. And I didn't want to wake you."

"Busy day?"

He frowned. "I don't want to talk shop with you. It's not always pleasant, and it's never pretty."

"I know, but it's right up my alley."

"Hailee, writing murder mysteries is different from solving real-life murders."

"Maybe I can help some more."

"I don't want you anywhere near this. I don't need an amateur sleuth interfering with my case."

"I'm a professional writer. And I wasn't interfering last night when I gave you a detailed description of the couple at the bar."

"The detailed information you shared helped immensely, and I'm grateful for that. You're on vacation; why don't you relax, have a good time, and let me solve this case?"

He finished dressing and headed out the door. He grabbed the door handle and turned back to look at Hailee. "I want to be crystal clear. You are not to go near anyone or anything remotely related to this case, do you understand?"

"Yes. Rest, relaxation, and no investigating."

"Good." He closed the door and pulled on it.

Hailee crawled back into bed, closed her eyes, and drifted off to sleep.

She woke up at ten o'clock, took a shower, and dressed comfortably: black slacks, a blue long-sleeve blouse, and ankle boots. She had worked up an appetite, so she went to the restaurant.

She ate and went up the elaborate staircase. Her curiosity got the best of her, and instead of going to the fifth floor, she turned right toward the third floor. Hailee couldn't resist inspecting the crime scene; she headed to room 312. Crime scene tape blocked off the hallway, and an officer stood stoically on the other side. Maybe she should turn back. What if that had been her friend or a family member who had been murdered?

She approached the tape and the officer with caution; he frowned as she drew nearer.

"Hello, I'm a friend of Max Toliver; he asked me to meet him here. Has he arrived?"

"The detective is around, but this area is for police personnel only."

"I can wait here until he's done. Is he checking on the crime scene? Is it that door over there?" She pointed to room 312. "Was the murdered woman a guest here? Have you found the murder weapon? Do you have any leads?"

"Miss, I can't discuss that with you." His hand went to his earpiece, and he nodded. "Miss, I'll have to ask you to leave."

"Sure, I'll wait at the bar."

Hailee headed down the stairs, took a right on the second floor, and waited two minutes before returning to the third floor. The officer had gone. She ducked under the crime scene tape and approached the door. She stared at the door reverently; a woman had lost her life here. She reached up to grab the handle.

An angry male voice boomed. "Don't touch that door."

Hailee whirled around.

"I thought I told you to stay away from here."

"I wanted to pay my respects."

"Contaminating the crime scene is how you pay your respect?" Max's words echoed in the barren hallway.

"Someone needs to mourn for her."

"Then do it somewhere else."

She stepped away from the door.

"I can't have you or anyone else interfering with my investigation."

She didn't know the victim but felt compelled to investigate. Max had told her to leave. Hailee knew she should, and she tried; her legs wouldn't move.

"This is my crime scene. Go."

"As you wish." Hailee's step faltered as she headed toward the crime scene tape.

"Wait." He turned to face her. "Do you want to have dinner with me tonight?"

"You don't think I'm smart enough to assist with your case, but you want to date me?"

"We're not colleagues–you are not law enforcement." The intensity in his voice softened, "I'm a man who wants to date a woman, so yes, will you go out with me?"

"I'd think you have better things to do, like catch a killer." Hailee's response sounded bitter even to her.

His eyes were mesmerizing; her body tingled. She felt like a naïve schoolgirl. She never realized how strong the sexual pull could be.

"I don't know. You're busy."

"I need to eat."

"You can eat at the station while trying to catch a young woman's murderer."

"Don't be mad. I know you want to be involved, but you can't be."

"I can, and I have in the past."

"You are too close to this, and you are not a homicide detective. You need to eat, too. Say yes."

Apparently, she would never be able to say no to Max. "What time?"

"Be ready at seven; I'll come to your room."

"Seven then."

This vacation felt different. Hailee had stayed at the Meridian numerous times and had always enjoyed her time here. Her grandmother started bringing her here after her parents died. It served as a home away from home, where they could be together, make new memories, and try to deal with the heartache from the past. It had worked. She loved this place, and now that her grandmother had passed, she would come here every chance she could.

Hailee's book tour, her battle with her agent, and her grandmother's passing had left her emotionally overwhelmed and physically drained. When she met Max, she had just started to relax. Hailee wondered if her weakened condition had been the reason she had succumbed to her attraction to him and if that was why she felt oddly protective of the victim.

She went to the lobby and spoke to the concierge, Carrington. Hailee tried to get him to tell her why Max had a key to room 321. He politely declined several times and wouldn't budge. She was prying. She didn't care. How could she get answers if she didn't ask questions? Hailee apologized for being pushy and left him to handle his guests.

When she traveled, she typically carried extra author copies of her latest novel, but this time, she had left them at home. She headed to the nearest bookstore to buy Carrington her latest novel and sign it for him.

When Hailee entered the bookstore, an enthusiastic mob of fans descended on her. She signed about ten books and shook hands with twice as many people. She loved her readers. They were passionate and enthusiastic.

Once her fans had gone, she bought a copy of her book and asked the cashier a few questions about the hotel,

Max, and the murder. No one seemed to know the victim's name, where she lived, or anything about her. How could the police solve her murder if they didn't know the identity of the victim? What about the victim's date? He seemed to be as elusive as the murdered girl. Perhaps he killed her and then left town. Even though Hailee had given Max a detailed description of the man, she had never seen him at the hotel before, and as far as she knew, Max and his team hadn't found him yet.

Hailee thanked the clerk, signed a few books, and headed to a small café off the main road from the hotel. She ordered a walnut chicken salad sandwich on pumpernickel bread and three pickles. She laughed inwardly. She wouldn't eat a cucumber to save her life, but she loved pickles. They were crisp, juicy, and tangy. They were a perfect complement to any sandwich or burger.

While waiting for her food, she wrote a personal note for Carrington. She signed: *I didn't mean to put you on the spot. Your discretion is appreciated—your number one fan, Hailee Hollister.*

He should get a kick out of that. Hailee ate her lunch and did some shopping. She visited a dress boutique and purchased a red dress and matching shoes. She went back to the hotel and gave Carrington his book. He laughed when he read the inscription. He assured her that their friendship remained intact. Carrington considered her a friend; she smiled inwardly. She asked him to give her a wake-up call at five thirty, returned to her room, and napped.

The phone ringing woke her up.

"Max?"

"It's Carrington. It's five thirty."

"Thank you."

"Have fun on your date with Mr. Toliver," he chuckled and hung up.

She liked Carrington. When she first met him years ago, he reminded her of a stuffy Englishman—all manners and no personality. After getting to know him, she found him fascinating and that he had quite a sense of humor.

She showered, dressed, and, after using hot rollers, pulled her bangs back on one side and secured them with a large red comb. Her new dress accentuated her fair skin and dark brown hair. The halter top emphasized her small, delicate shoulders and gave her breasts a soft, sensuous look, and the hem of her dress swirled around her knees as she walked. She put the essentials in her purse, touched up her makeup, and sat on the edge of the bed.

After hearing the rapping on the door, she opened it. Max wore a light blue, long-sleeve shirt and black pants. The blue softened his dark features. She let him in and turned to retrieve her coat and purse.

"Are we going downstairs?"

"I'm taking you to one of my favorite places. I hope you like Italian."

He held the passenger door open, and she slid into the seat. She didn't know much about cars, but recognized the emblem as a Cadillac CTS. It had four doors, and the silver exterior had a sleek, shiny finish. The tan leather seats were slim and comfortable. The controls were large and well-lit and didn't monopolize the entire dashboard. The screen located just below the vents made it easier to read. She settled in and wondered where they were going.

They headed down SW 4th Avenue, and she watched the hotel fade into the distance. They continued, turning onto SW Jefferson Street, heading toward the Willamette River. There were only a few cars on the road, and they arrived at their destination in less than ten minutes. Max parked nearest the main entrance, and Hailee glanced up at the red and white lighted sign, Felicità Ristorante. Her stomach grumbled. She loved Italian food.

The red canopy with gold trim hung over the black-and-white checkered chairs. The outside tables were covered in a solid red tablecloth. They were adorned with short, clear vases with white, flickering candles. Two golden columns supported the stone archway. Hailee couldn't wait to taste the food.

Max opened the door; she stepped inside. The walls were embellished with pictures of cathedrals, churches, and tiny old-world homes. They took her breath away. She wished she had paid more attention in her art history class. She walked up to a large picture of a Grand Cathedral and lightly touched the frame. "Do you come here often?"

"A couple of times a month."

She caressed the frame, admired the craftsmanship, and whispered, "Do you think the owners would mind me touching their artwork?"

A quiet, hearty laugh echoed down the hall. "No, Dear. Feel free to touch, to smell, to taste. It's what life is all about."

A short, shapely woman with a friendly face, dark hair, and eyes came from around the corner and gave Max a big hug and a kiss on the cheek. "You're right; she is beautiful and smart."

"Oh, Mama." He kissed her on both cheeks.

Hailee tensed. Max's mom?

"Mama, this is Hailee Hollister. Hailee, this is Sophia."

Hailee went to shake her hand, but was caught in a big bear hug.

"She has good, strong bones and soft skin. She's a keeper." Sophia laughed; Max rolled his eyes.

Hailee smiled. Max squirmed.

"Stop embarrassing her; you'll scare her away."

"She doesn't look like the type to run away, and you're embarrassed, not her."

She liked Sophia. Her short stature and sweet demeanor were a ruse for a strong personality, and she packed a mean punch.

"Can we eat now?" He asked.

She led them to a private dining area. "Max tells me you write books for a living."

"Have you read any of them?"

"When Max called to tell me you two were coming for dinner, I rushed out and bought one: very interesting and provocative." She winked and elbowed Max.

He shook his head.

Poor Max, Sophia seemed to enjoy giving him a hard time. "When you finish it, let me know if you like it."

She nodded and sat them at a table for two. She smiled at Hailee and left.

"I like her; she's a riot."

"She likes you, too."

"How do you know that?"

"Look at her; she's on cloud nine. She's already chosen you as my wife and the mother of my children. So, watch out."

Hailee giggled.

"Don't laugh; she's hard to resist, especially when her mind is made up. Trust me."

She swallowed hard and stared at the table.

"Hailee, what's wrong? I won't let her bother you. Don't worry."

"Your mom is great. She made me remember my parents," she looked up into his eyes. "They died in a car accident when I was sixteen." The guilt and sadness of her parents' passing overwhelmed her. Her eyes glistened.

"I'm sorry; I didn't mean to make you cry."

Unsure of why she told him that, she quickly responded, "You didn't."

Sophia returned carrying a large basket of bread and a bottle of wine. She put them down on the table and glared at Max. "I leave you alone for two minutes, and now she's crying."

"It's not his fault. My mother passed away; I'm sad."

Sophia hugged Hailee. "Don't worry, dear; I will be your mama soon. I will ease your pain."

Max groaned. "This is our first date. Give her a break."

"You be nice to her; she is mourning the loss of her mother."

"Can we have some food now?"

Sophia huffed and headed toward the kitchen.

"I love her to pieces, but this is why I only come once or twice a month. All my brothers are married, so she has no one to marry off except me. I'm sorry if she embarrassed you or hurt your feelings."

"Don't be silly. I like your mom." Hailee's eyes twinkled.

"Great…"

Sophia returned with a large platter of lasagna and a wooden bowl containing a garden salad. She winked at Hailee and left without saying a word.

Hailee stuffed herself. The hot, flavorful food paired well with the Pinot Noir. She felt giddy.

"Did you enjoy dinner," Max asked?

"Yes."

His hand touched hers; tiny shivers of pleasure ran up her arm.

She pulled her eyes away from his. "So, have you read any of my books?"

"I don't have much time to read." He answered quickly.

"You mean you don't have time to read my books: fiction books about amateur sleuths."

"No, I don't have much time to read anything unless it's job-related."

"I have a copy of my latest book, *Doppelganger*, in my room. You could read it when we get back.

"If you think I'm going to waste time reading a book, you are out of your mind."

"It won't take long; it goes fast, and I'm sure you'd like it. It's interesting and provocative." Hailee winked.

"Are you ready to leave?"

"Aren't we going to say goodbye to your mother?"

"No, if we do, we'll never get out of here. I'll call her from the car."

"That's rude, don't you think?"

"It's necessary."

He led her to the car and held the door for her. He pulled out of the parking lot and dialed. "Mama, we had to leave. Sorry, we couldn't say goodbye. I'll call you tomorrow." He hung up.

"That would have been sweeter if we hadn't just dined and dashed."

"Trust me. I had to do it, or we'd still be here until two in the morning."

Chapter 5

Hailee stretched and turned toward Max. He had woken up first, showered, dressed, and turned on the TV. He stopped at Channel 8. The reporter stood at the entrance of the Meridian Hotel, and the cameraman panned the area to show the police cars and the bystanders gathered there. Max turned up the volume and listened. The investigator reported that another brutal murder, the second one in one week, had taken place at the Meridian Hotel.

Max pulled out his phone and dialed. He paced, and while he listened, his demeanor changed from lighthearted to gloomy.

She bolted up; there had been another murder here at her hotel. She watched, her eyes wide, her heart beating wildly. Max stood stiffly by the window, speaking quietly on the phone.

She continued to watch the newscast. Hailee reached for the remote and cranked up the volume. She caught the last of the report: another young woman, a guest at the Meridian Hotel staying on the 4th floor, was bludgeoned to death.

She stood up and stared at the screen. "What's happening here?"

"Keller confirmed that there had been another murder, another young female."

"He's moving up to my floor?"

"What?"

"The blonde died on the third floor, and now another woman died on the fourth floor. Is he going to kill someone on my floor?"

"Hailee, I don't know if the murders are related," he grabbed her shoulders and turned her toward him, "I won't let anyone hurt you."

"Do you think that he's coming after me?" She hadn't even considered that.

"No. I don't want you to worry."

"I'm not worried about me; what about everyone else? Who's going to protect them?"

"We'll be vigilant and watchful now."

"Maybe I should leave, return to my book tour, and let you concentrate on your work."

"Is that what you want, to leave?"

"No. There is a killer on the loose, and you have work to do."

"I want you here where I can protect you."

Hailee squared her shoulders. "I can take care of myself."

Two girls have been murdered; their lives snuffed out for no reason. "Are there any similarities between the women or the way they were killed? Have you found any witnesses? What about the murder weapon—"

"I don't want you anywhere near this investigation."

"I write about murder all the time. I base my stories on facts. I've done my research."

"Damn it, Hailee, I said no." He glared at her. "I'm the detective in charge of this case; I'm telling you, stay out of this!"

She recoiled.

"If I can't assist you, why should I stay?"

"Do what you want; that's up to you, but stay away from my case. Is that clear?"

Hailee nodded, sat on the bed, and turned toward the window. She heard the door slam.

She should have her head examined–picking up a man in a bar, sleeping with a stranger, a homicide detective. Self-recrimination overwhelmed her. *So...she was just like her mother.*

Hailee showered, dressed, and went to the elevator. She denied her writer's curiosity and continued to the

37

lobby. She went to the restaurant, had breakfast, headed toward the main lobby's entrance, and then turned back to the bar. Hailee hoped to see Alex. He worked the afternoon and evening shifts, and she might get lucky.

She approached the bar and asked the bartender on duty when Alex would be working next; he told her that Alex was out back checking a delivery and should be done in a few minutes.

While she waited, she ordered a screwdriver. Orange juice energized her in the mornings. Typically, she drank Greyhounds; she enjoyed the grapefruit juice's tartness.

Alex came in with a handsome guy in a uniform. They spoke, and Alex signed a receipt, which he then gave to the uniformed man. He looked up, saw Hailee, and came over to him.

"Hey, what are you doing here so early?" Hailee asked.

"Doing inventory and helping Simon with our delivery."

Simon's blue eyes, spiked hair, full brows, and goatee gave him a roguish quality. He came over when Alex mentioned his name.

"Hey, aren't you that mystery writer," Simon asked?

"Yes." Hailee extended her hand, and they shook. "You must be Simon."

"That's me—the Ice Guy. My old man owns the company. I guess I have a job for life." He laughed and tried to smile, but it didn't reach his eyes.

Hailee examined Simon; he didn't seem happy. Maybe working for his dad wasn't what he had planned for his life. Although obligation and responsibility appeared to be important to him.

"So, what brings you to the bar this early," Alex asked.

"I'm hoping to get some information. Have you heard about the second murder?"

"Yeah, I couldn't get in the front door; the media has clogged up the entranceway, so I came in the back way and found Simon getting ready to unload the ice."

"Last night, did you see or hear anything that might identify the victim or find out why she was at the hotel?" Hailee asked.

"No, I didn't hear anyone talking about a murder or wanting to commit one. I could barely keep up with the demand; the tables were swamped."

Simon chimed in. "There have been two murders?"

"Yeah, someone died last night," Alex replied.

"Bummer." Simon waved goodbye and headed out the back way.

Hailee watched as Simon sauntered out. He seemed a little detached and apathetic, which was not to her liking. Someone had died, and he didn't react or stop to reflect. Alex seemed to like him. She might be overly cautious because of the two murders, and she wanted to shield Alex. He made her travels to Portland fun, and she felt safe with him.

"What about my first night here? Did you see the blonde girl with the older guy in the corner? Did they get their drinks from you?"

"No, Kelly White waited on them. I guess he tipped big, probably trying to impress his date. She was way out of his league.

"They were an odd couple. Did you see if they came together, or did he meet her here?"

"I'm not sure; they could have come together. Ask Kelly, she might remember."

"Is she working tonight?"

Alex pulled out a sheet of paper and read through it. "No, she'll be in tomorrow."

39

"I would love to speak with her. Can you give me her number?"

"I can't give out her number, not even to you. Sorry." Alex feigned regret. "The tables were jam-packed; she probably doesn't remember any of the patrons anyway. Besides, I think the police have questioned her about the couple. You could ask them."

Hailee left a five under her glass and nodded. There wasn't a snowball's chance of that happening. If she asked Max about Kelly's statement, he might lock her up to keep her away from his case. She would need to find another way to get more information, but right now, she just wanted to get out of the hotel. The news reporters had descended on the hotel, trying to get a scoop on the latest murder.

Dozens of cops and reporters gathered at the lobby entrance. The cops lined up, keeping the reporters at bay and guiding the guests in and out. She squeezed through the line of cops and reached for the door handle.

A reporter yelled. "Hey, there's Hailee Hollister." The other reporters turned and headed toward her. She looked back; she would never reach the elevator before they descended on her. She exited the hotel, letting the door bang shut.

The reporters ran down the sidewalk shouting their questions; she turned, stepped into the street, and hailed a cab. Any other day, she would have had three by now.

The media continued their relentless pursuit. They stopped on the sidewalk, pointed their microphones at her, and asked questions simultaneously.

She turned away and waved her arm frantically. A cab slowed, then sped off, leaving her frustrated. What a horrible morning! First, her fight with Max, and now the reporters swooped down on her like an eagle on a mouse.

She kept her head down and stepped back onto the sidewalk. They continued their barrage of questions, and their cameras flashed. She felt lightheaded from the bright lights, the car noise, and the relentless questioning. She spun around a few times, trying to find an escape route.

One of the reporters pushed his way to the front. He pointed his camera at her and shoved his microphone in her face. "Hailee, are you here to help with this case?"

"No, I am not here in any official capacity. I am a guest at the hotel." She tried to push past them. They huddled close and moved slightly forward.

"Are you afraid to stay at the hotel now that two women your age have been brutally murdered?"

His question shocked her. "No, the police are working diligently to solve this case and will take every precaution necessary to protect the hotel's guests."

She leaned sideways, put her hand on the back of a female journalist, and gently pushed; the crowd leaned forward, and she ended up back in the street. She crouched down slightly and squeezed past two of the persistent reporters. She looked up and realized her efforts were wasted. She stood in the middle of them; their cameras continued to flash, and the crowd surrounded her. Their questions came fast; she couldn't hear, think, or concentrate. She pressed firmly this time. The mob refused to budge.

Trying to be heard above the noise, one reporter screamed at her. "How do you know that?"

In her confusion, she asked, "Know what?"

"That the police are working diligently on this case and will try to protect the hotel's guests?"

In her haste to answer the question and get away, she had repeated what Max told her this morning. It wasn't an official statement. She had to fix it.

"The police are working hard to solve these heinous crimes. It's their job. It's also their job to protect this city and its citizens."

She exhaled. She wanted to scream. She should have let Kat, her friend and faithful assistant, hire a bodyguard. Their persistent bombardment of questions annoyed her. She pushed frantically at the crowd.

"Are you dating Max Toliver, the homicide detective on the case?"

Had someone seen her with Max? She cringed and struggled to see who asked the question. She decided not to answer and concentrated on her getaway.

"Is it true? Are you dating him?"

Hailee stopped and took a deep breath. "Young women are dying right here, a few feet from where we are standing, and you want to know if I'm dating Detective Toliver. What's wrong with you?" She shoved past them, heading away from the crowd.

Her strides were long and determined. Her frustration had turned to anger, so she kept walking. She lost track of time and direction and didn't care. She wanted to get as far away from the hotel, the reporters, and the murders as possible.

If she had known she would be walking, she would have worn comfortable shoes. She walked for what seemed like hours. Hailee's anger had taken over, and she marched hurriedly down the streets; she had no location in mind; she just wanted to get away from the chaos. She didn't want to be followed, so she turned frequently. She walked in circles and ended up in the middle of nowhere, unable to return to the hotel.

She swallowed hard; her dry throat ached for water. Hailee stopped to look around and studied the buildings, trying to remember if she had been there before. In her frustrated and depleted state, they all looked the same. She checked the street signs and realized she had unconsciously headed toward SW Yamhill and that the Felicità was just down the block. She quickened her pace and stood outside under the golden columns. She'd found something familiar amid the morning's chaos, and she needed a moment to gather her thoughts.

She walked hesitantly to the front door and pulled on it. It opened. She walked in cautiously, thinking she could get something to drink and call a cab.

She stood near the entrance, wondering what to do next. She looked at the picture of the cathedral, which she had seen with Max.

"*Figlia*–what's wrong?"

Sophia, Max's mother, came over and hugged her. "Come sit down." She led Hailee into the main dining room. Several people were sitting at a large, rectangular table watching the news. Hailee looked up; Max appeared on the screen.

She sat down and watched the press conference. Max loomed over the pulpit and answered questions; most of them were about the murders and specific questions about the girls who were killed. And then, a reporter asked him a personal question about her. She held her breath. He professionally sidestepped all intimate questions.

Another journalist interrupted one of his answers. "Is it true that Hailee Hollister is missing and that she hasn't been seen since this morning after out-of-state reporters had accosted her?"

He hesitated and recovered quickly. He told the press that he would look into Miss Hollister's whereabouts, but he was confident that she would return unharmed. He ended the press conference and headed back into the hotel.

The people at the table turned to look at her. She stared back at them, her eyes wide with anxiety.

Sophia came over. "Are you all right, dear?"

Hailee shook her head. "Yes, may I have some water?"

Sophia took her to the kitchen and poured her a glass of cold water. Hailee sat down at a small table and took a large drink. She felt safe and welcome here; she didn't want to leave.

"Does Max know where you are?"

"No, I got lost."

"You should call him; let him know where you are."

"I don't know. Max is angry with me, and he's trying to solve two murders."

"*Figlia,* he needs to know. Trust me, he will not stay mad for long."

Max said that, too–trust me. Hailee wanted to, but trust didn't come easily for her. Sophia convinced her to call. She pulled out her cell phone and stared at it.

"I don't have his number."

"Things will get better." Sophia gave Hailee the number and then left.

Hailee dialed his number; would he be mad?

"Hello," he answered.

"Max?"

"Hailee, where are you? Are you hurt?"

"I'm okay. I'm at your mother's restaurant."

"What are you doing there?"

"The reporters trapped me in the street. I broke away. I walked for what seemed like hours and ended up here?"

"Why didn't you call me?"

"I didn't have your number."

"Stay there, I'll come get you."

"You're working."

"I'll be there in twenty minutes."

She returned to the dining room, sat at the rectangular table, and glanced around. Everyone seemed happy. Why did she feel so alone? Max left work to get her; he must care, or did her celebrity status warrant his interest and concern?

She writes for the pure enjoyment and thrill of shaping characters into a logical storyline with twists, turns, and murder. Murder—

"Is he coming to get you," Sophia asked?

"Yes."

"It will all work out."

"I've made quite a mess of things. I'm not sure it can be fixed."

"Max is a complex man; you two belong together. I can feel it."

Sophia *was* hard to resist.

Sophia introduced Hailee to the others at the table, and they talked and laughed while they waited for Max to arrive.

The door burst open, and Hailee stood up. Her heart pounded in her chest. She waited as Max made his way across the room. They stared at each other, and she leaned in and wrapped her arms around him.

Chapter 6

Max and Hailee got into the car and headed back to the hotel. Max had his hands full; he didn't need the drama currently surrounding her. A deranged lunatic preyed on young women, and Hailee felt she would be a valuable asset to Max and his team if she stayed. He didn't want her involved, and she couldn't convince him otherwise. Hailee looked out the window, trying to come to terms with what she actually wanted. She had been thrown into the middle of a homicide and had landed in Max's arms. She didn't want to leave, and if she stayed, she would have to find a new hotel room. The Meridan was a dangerous place to be, and she might feel safer somewhere else.

"Hailee, are you listening?"

She turned to look at him. "What?"

"How are you feeling?"

"Today's been hell."

"I know," He watched her as she listened, "You did a wonderful job with the press today. You sounded like our PR guy, Pete."

"You must have missed the part where I almost knocked someone over trying to escape."

"I saw it. You were great," Max grinned. "Are you hungry?"

"I'm tired. Is the hotel still under siege?"

"Not really; most reporters have gone for the day."

"Are you keeping some of your men at the hotel for the night?"

"We are posting a few undercover men throughout the hotel to keep an eye on things."

"Are you staying the night?"

"Do you want me to?"

"Yes."

At the elevator, they waited while several people got out. Hailee looked around.

Max observed while she inspected the room. "You shouldn't be able to tell who they are."

"Don't underestimate my power of observation."

She continued to scan the room. An undercover cop stood casually by the lobby desk; one hovered by the elevator, and the other two were 'patrolling' slowly from the lobby to the restaurant and back.

"I see four."

Max glanced around and frowned, "That's right," he whispered.

She noticed his frown, "What's wrong?"

"If you can tell, then the perp can too."

"I know what to look for; maybe the killer doesn't."

"There's a maniac on a killing spree. I'm not going to underestimate him." He scolded her.

"You don't give me enough credit."

Max nodded to the man standing by the elevator.

"Max, what about the descriptions I gave on the first murder victim? I was dead on." She cringed at her own pun.

"How many times do I have to tell you? Stay away from my investigation."

"I guess a few more. I'm not trying to steal your thunder."

He shook his head, took her key, and let them in. He put the key on the dresser.

"Do you think he's making his way up the hotel? Is my floor next?"

"Hailee, I don't think so. We don't have enough evidence yet."

"Have you talked to Simon yet? He may not have been here while your team interviewed the guest."

"Who's Simon?"

"He's the ice guy. He works for Glacier Palace. They deliver ice for the bar and the hotel."

"How did you hear about him? Have you been investigating my case?" He scowled.

"I am on vacation; I'm not investigating. Alex and Simon had finished a delivery and came over to the bar. Alex said he had to come in the back way this morning and found Simon in the back unloading the ice."

Max pulled out this phone and dialed. He left a message to have Simon looked into and brought in for questioning. Max hung up and stared down at her.

Max looked furious. She stepped back.

"The police use outside sources all the time. I might find something your team missed. Or maybe—"

"I can't have a civilian involved in this. You're just a woman who writes for a living."

Hailee faltered. "That was mean."

"It's the truth. Why are you fighting me on this?"

"Women are dying. I have to do something."

"Why can't you just let me do my job?"

"I don't want to fight anymore. Go or stay; I don't care."

She went to the bathroom, shut the door, and locked it. She came here for some much-needed rest. Her tour would resume in a week, and she would prefer not to spend it fighting with Max.

She turned on the water and let it heat up, then added some lavender bath beads. Her clothes fell to the floor; she eased into the tub and leaned back. She closed her eyes and wondered how she got here, in the middle of a murder investigation and in a sexual relationship with Max. She retraced her steps and considered her physical and mental state–reasoning that her exhaustion made her vulnerable to Max's charms and good looks. She then realized that in any condition, she would have succumbed to him; his confidence and sex appeal intrigued her from the moment she heard his voice.

The phone ringing jarred Hailee from her thoughts. Max answered on the second ring. She listened intently; she couldn't hear what he said. It was probably the precinct calling. She pondered the events that had brought her here, and then she heard Max laugh. Who called–a friend?

The hot water worked; the stress from the day floated away. When the water cooled, she pulled the drain and dried off. She put on her robe and turned off the light. She headed for the bed and stopped when she saw Max in it; had he fallen asleep?

She tiptoed to his side of the bed. His eyes were closed, and he breathed slowly in and out. She walked around to her side of the bed. Underneath her cell phone, she found a note from Max. It read: *Call Kat – it's urgent.*

She sat on the bed and dialed Kat's number. Kat picked up on the first ring. Kat wore many hats: friend, assistant extraordinaire, and public relations guru, and what a character…

"Hailey, are you all right?"

"I'm fine, Kat."

"I saw the news; you gave me such a fright."

"I can handle pesky reporters–you know that."

"I would normally agree with you, but what a nasty business, two girls getting murdered."

"It's horrible."

"So, who's the yummy guy who answered the phone, Max?"

"Yes, please tell me you didn't hit on him."

"I did; he sounds delicious."

"He is. He's taken–I think…Anyway…Why are you calling?"

"It's Rex."

"What did he do now?" Any news about Rex troubled her.

"He's in a tizzy. He's sending more inappropriate emails, and they're getting more demanding."

"Forward them to Carl and copy me. What's his problem now?"

"You know. I love you; marry me, or else… Rex wants you to come back right away."

"I don't have time for him. Kat, I need you to get him off my back, okay."

She thought a moment; she had to find a way to keep Rex busy, or he would continue to harass her until he got what he wanted.

"If you can keep him away from me for two more weeks, I'll give you anything you want." Hailee needed something to motivate Kat to pull out all the stops. "I'll give you my Corvette, you know, the convertible you like so much. What do you say?"

"How am I supposed to do that?"

"I don't know. Ask Rex out on a date. That'll throw him for a loop."

"I have standards."

"Kat, I need your help," Hailee pleaded.

"I'll try. Why don't you ask Max? He sounds strong and capable."

Hailee wanted to laugh, except this was serious. "I can't. He's working on solving murders. Besides, I'm not going to mix him up in Rex's drama."

"Too late."

"What do you mean, too late?"

"I told Max about Rex."

Hailee gasped.

Kat ignored her and continued. "Don't get mad; we had a long conversation while you were in the bathtub. Is he protecting you?"

"You told Max." Her voice went up two octaves. "Are you crazy?" Hailee's heart raced, and she heard herself screaming. Max didn't stir.

"Rex is a scourge on this planet and a huge pain in my butt, so I told him."

"Max is trying to solve two heinous crimes and prevent anyone else from getting murdered."

"I didn't mean to upset you. Rex needs to be stopped."

"Kat..." Hailee closed her eyes, "I know you were trying to solve a problem, but Rex is my problem. I can handle him. Keep him away from me for two more weeks, and I'll give you my Corvette–okay?" Hailee hung up.

She paced back and forth. Could this day get any worse? She walked over to Max, who looked exhausted. She pivoted. Max grabbed her arm and dragged her to bed.

He opened his eyes and smiled.

*****

She woke up to the phone ringing; she looked around for her phone. She picked it up; it wasn't ringing. She staggered out of bed and pulled the phone from Max's pocket. Hailee shook him, handed him the phone, and glanced at the clock radio: ten.

Max pulled on his pants when she emerged from the bathroom.

"What's wrong?"

"I have to leave; it's about the case."

He finished dressing and secured his gun.

"When did you start carrying a gun?"

"I always carry a gun."

"I've never seen you with a gun, and I've seen you naked."

"I always carry my weapon. I have to–especially now. You don't pay attention when we're together."

"I always pay attention; as a woman, I need to be aware of my surroundings."

51

"Hailee, I've had my gun since we first met. You've been a little distracted lately."

Had her attention been solely on him? What about Max? Could his concentration be suffering because of her?

"If I've been preoccupied, your focus could be compromised, too."

"I'm very good at multitasking. I assure you that no one will prevent me from finding the perp."

Hailee hoped he could; she didn't want to be the reason for someone else's death.

"Are you coming back?"

"I don't know. It may take the rest of the night and into the morning."

She nodded and watched as he headed for the door.

He reached the door and stopped. "Hailee, don't leave, and don't let anyone in."

"I'm going back to bed."

She slid under the covers and closed her eyes. Max turned off the light and closed the door.

Chapter 7

Max headed toward the stairs, then took two at a time. He met Keller in the lobby.

"Where is she?" Max demanded.

Keller shook his head. "Don't know. Dispatch said she would be waiting in the lobby near the concierge desk. "I've already checked the lobby, the restaurant, and the bar. I don't see anyone fitting the description dispatch gave me."

"Check with dispatch; verify the caller said it was the Meridian. Maybe the witness didn't want to show up here."

Keller nodded and pulled out his phone.

Max made a quick tour of the main areas. Did the potential witness bolt or change her mind? Maybe she didn't want to get involved. That happened all the time. People want to do the right thing only if their actions don't put them in danger. His friend Jake quoted books and movies all the time, and it annoyed Max to the point of frustration. However, one quote that kept coming to mind went something like, 'Evil triumphs when good men do nothing.' He hoped the witness didn't give in to fear.

Keller waved Max over. "You're right. The witness called back and said she got the wrong hotel. She's at the Sumpton on 5th."

Max and Keller sprinted out the door toward 5th Street.

*****

What the hell? Hailee rolled over and checked the time: ten-thirty. She listened hard. Her heart pounded. She blinked to focus. A scream–a blood-curdling scream. She called nine-one-one and stated that a woman was in distress and screaming.

She put on her robe and cracked open the door. A young woman was fighting with someone dressed in black. Blood stained the young woman's nightgown.

Hailee sprinted toward the struggling duo. "Fire! Fire!" The person in black looked up. The woman pulled free and ran toward Hailee. The woman hit the floor. Hailee yanked her up. The assailant grabbed the woman's ankles. The woman flailed wildly. She clawed Hailee's arm. The woman hit the carpet. Hailee crashed into the wall and crumpled to the floor. Her head throbbed. Hailee lay gasping. White spots blurred her vision. The attacker dragged the woman toward the back stairs. Blood smeared the carpet. The woman's high-pitched scream echoed in Hailee's ears. Hailee stumbled, then charged the person in black and kicked hard. The aggressor flew back. The injured woman convulsed, and her sobs pierced the hallway. Hailee pulled the girl toward her room.

Someone grabbed Hailee from behind; their fingers dug into her flesh. She screamed and swung hard.

"Miss, it's okay. I'm Officer Thornton. I've got you."

"She's bleeding. The one who attacked her is wearing all black and is getting away. I'll stay with her. Please hurry."

Hailee bent down and gently rolled the girl over. Hailee gasped. The woman's flesh had been sliced, and blood oozed from her upper body. Hailee whispered words of encouragement and pushed down hard on the pressure points. Blood continued to flow. The red, thick substance covered Hailee's fingers and palms. The woman tried to speak; she coughed and made a gurgling sound as blood spurted from her mouth. The injured girl's eyes, wide with fear and pain, beseeched Hailee.

The flow wouldn't stop. Hailee pressed harder. Hailee's head pounded, and nausea overwhelmed her. The medics arrived and took over. They stabilized the young woman and wheeled her to the elevator.

Blood covered Hailee's robe, and a knot swelled on her forehead. Her thoughts were jumbled; her arm and shoulder ached.

Officer Thornton came back and asked. "Were you stabbed?"

"No—" She leaned against the wall and slid down.

Officer Thornton called for a second ambulance. They put Hailee on a gurney and took her to the hospital. They rushed her to the emergency room. Several police officers were there. She recognized them from Max's office.

Where was the girl? Did she make it?

The paramedics wheeled Hailee into a stall and transferred her to the bed. Hailee blushed and pulled the robe closed.

A nurse came in and checked her head, arm, and vitals. She asked the usual questions: Did she have any allergies? Did she have any pre-existing medical conditions? Was she pregnant?

Pregnant...Hailee never had to consider that before. She'd only been having sex for a couple of days. She answered no.

The nurse methodically cleaned the blood off. Hailee didn't realize she had the young woman's blood on her robe; her stomach did somersaults. The nurse finished, threw the bloody rags into a plastic bag, and left them on the floor near the bed. The nurse gave her a few more blankets and told her a doctor would be in soon to see her.

"What about the injured girl? How is she doing?"

The nurse gave her a weak smile. "I don't know she's in surgery. Her condition is critical."

"Will you let me know when she gets out? I want to stay with her."

"I'll see what I can do." The nurse pulled the drapes closed.

Hailee lay back on the pillow. She closed her eyes and tried to rest. She should call Max.

She sat up and pressed the call button for the nurse, but no one came, so she called out for help.

A young male nurse came in. "Do you need assistance?"

"Yes, I need to make a call; it's important."

"I'm sorry. You need to stay in bed until you see the doctor."

"I need to call my...um...boyfriend. He'll be worried."

"I'm sorry."

"May I use your cell phone? Please."

The nurse opened his mouth to respond, and Detective Keller came in. She pulled the blankets up around her shoulders.

"Miss Hollister, are you all right?"

"I think so; have you called Detective Toliver?"

"He's on his way. Do you feel up to answering a few questions?"

"I'm okay."

"Can you tell me what happened? Start from the beginning."

She didn't know whether to mention Max. She decided against it.

"While sleeping, a high-pitched noise woke me up. I couldn't make it out. I waited and listened, and I heard it again. A woman's scream."

Hailee rested her hand on her stomach. The night's events were catching up to her. She might hurl. "I called nine-one-one and peeked out my door. I saw a woman fighting with someone. I started screaming 'fire' and ran down to help her."

She closed her eyes and touched her head. The throbbing increased, and so did the pain.

"Are you feeling sick?" Detective Keller asked.

"My head hurts."

She heard the curtain open…good, the doctor.

"What the hell do you think you're doing?" Max boomed!

Hailee opened her eyes and smiled; at least he wasn't mad at her.

Keller whipped around. "I'm getting her statement; she's a witness."

"She's hurt. Get out."

Keller excused himself and left.

Max closed the curtain. "Where are you hurt?"

"My head is pounding; stand back, I might throw up."

He pulled down the blankets and saw her blood-covered robe. His face paled; he covered her up and left.

She stared after him; what did she do? The curtain opened up again. She looked up anxiously. Max didn't return; it was the doctor.

The doctor, a short, round man with thick-rimmed glasses, had a kind face.

He looked at her chart and said, "It looks like you might have a concession; let's take a look."

He flashed lights in her eyes, asked her to follow his finger, and had to endure the pain when he pressed on her head.

"Do I have a concussion?" Hailee winced. Concussion or not, it hurt.

"It doesn't look like it. I want to do a CAT scan to be sure. It says here you're not pregnant, is that right?"

"Um…Probably not."

He looked at her and shook her head, "We'll take precautions just in case. I'll send an orderly to wheel you down to X-ray." He looked down at her chart. "Are you hurt anywhere else? What about your stomach?"

"I have some cuts and bruises. I hit my head; it's painful, and I'm nauseous."

"That could be from trauma or from the head injury or both. I'll get you a pan to keep by your bed." He wrote on her chart, nodded, and left.

So, the doctor wanted her to stay here, naked in a bloody robe, until who knows when.

She lay back down on her pillow and closed her eyes.

She heard the curtain moving, and she opened her eyes. Max held a bedpan. She laughed and then moaned. He put the bedpan at her feet and sat down.

"Does it hurt?"

"A little. Is the girl out of surgery yet?"

"No."

"Have you heard anything about her condition?"

"No. I need to concentrate on you right now."

"I have a bump on the head, and I'm going to hurl, but she's the one fighting for her life."

"What did the doctor say?" Max asked.

"I need a CAT scan and a bedpan." She swallowed back the bile building in her throat.

An orderly came in and took her to the X-ray department. After the X-ray, he wheeled her back to the ER. When she arrived, the stall was empty.

She waited and waited; no one came back to check on her or to release her. Did they forget about her? She rang the nurse, but no one came. She swung her feet off the side of the bed and wondered if she could stand unattended.

"Where do you think you're going?" Max asked.

"I'm leaving."

"Did the doctor say you could go?"

"I haven't seen anyone in a while. I'm going back to the hotel."

"In that?" Max pointed to the bloody robe.

She pulled it closed. "It's all I have at the moment, so yes."

He handed her a hospital gown. "Put this on."

"No thanks."

"I need your robe. It's evidence."

He watched her shrug off her robe and put on the hospital gown; she could feel his gaze on her naked body. "I didn't have time to dress–I heard screaming."

She handed him the robe. He bagged and sealed it. He picked up the bag of bloody rags the nurse left on the floor.

"I need a ride back to the hotel and a shower. I'm tired."

He shook his head. "The doctor must clear you to leave, and you can't return to your room; it's a crime scene."

"Why is my room a part of the crime scene? No one entered it."

"The hallway and the back stairs are the crime scene, so you can't get to your room."

"I'm sure Carrington can find me another room. I haven't seen the doctor in a while. I don't know where he is; as far as I know, he could have died from old age."

"I don't think the good doctor has died; he's busy. I'm not letting you go back to the hotel. It's too dangerous."

Her feet hit the floor; she winced. "Won't let me?"

"That's right." He stood tall, towering over her.

They were in the middle of a stare-down when the doctor returned.

"Is there a problem?" He asked.

They both answered no.

"The CAT scan confirmed there is no concussion. Here is a prescription for pain. Take it as needed, and no driving. And no strenuous activity for a few days."

"Strenuous activity?" Hailee asked.

"He means no sex. Can she leave?"

The doctor handed Haile the paperwork. "Let me know if you continue to experience nausea or dizziness. And I'm *serious*; no strenuous activity."

He looked straight at Max, then left.

Chapter 8

Hailee slipped Max's coat over the hospital gown, and while she checked out, Max pulled the car around.

"Where's your car?"

"I have more than one."

"Why are you driving this one?"

"I heard you like Corvettes, so do I."

"Who told you that?" She thought a moment, "Oh, blabber mouth, Kat." She shook her head. "Kat talked me into buying a Corvette; she's the one who likes them."

"So, you're not a car fanatic?" He feigned disappointment. "Are you really going to give her your car?"

"What?" She turned toward him. "Have you spoken to her again?"

"No, I heard you two talking last night."

"Great," she mumbled. "What else did you hear?"

"Everything."

"You were eavesdropping?"

"We were on the same bed; it's not my fault I heard everything you said."

"I thought you were asleep."

"I know."

Hailee wondered about the young woman in surgery, fighting for her life again for the second time tonight. The thought sickened her and evoked horrific memories of screams and blood. So much blood...A woman, someone who looked to be her age, had been brutalized and had fought for her life. "When do you want me to give my statement?"

His fingers tightened on the steering wheel, and he focused on the road. "I don't want to talk about it tonight."

She nodded; she had all she could handle for one night. Max seemed visibly upset. He must be furious that

61

he had been called away moments before the murderer showed up on her floor?

"Just one question, okay?"

He nodded.

"Don't you think it's strange that right before the attack, you're called away to meet with someone about the case? Someone who didn't show up and that you couldn't find?"

"Who told you that?" Max asked.

"I heard some officers talking about it while waiting in the ER."

"What I think is not relevant. I can't discuss it with you."

"The other detectives let me in on their cases and were appreciative. I assisted with leads, and arrests were made."

"In those cases, did you come in direct contact with the suspect?" He demanded.

"No, but I aided in getting dangerous people off the street. The police appreciated my support."

"This time, it's different. You witnessed a crime and were a victim of a crime. You can't get involved. It will only jeopardize the case. And I won't stand for that."

"But—"

"Tell me about Rex."

She looked out the window. She hoped Max would tell her something about the case. Anything would be better than reliving the bloody scene in her hallway or discussing Rex.

"Hailee, who's Rex?"

"An idiot." That was Rex in a nutshell.

"Who is he?"

She wanted to divert the conversation away from that topic, except that her head throbbed and prevented her from speaking.

"I'm waiting."

"Rex wants to marry me; I said no. Now he's trying to blackmail me. That's all–end of story." She said flippantly.

Hailee snuck a peek at Max from under semi-closed lashes. His lips were pressed into a thin line.

"How can you treat this so dismissively?"

"I'm not. Kat and I can handle him."

"You and Kat are going to handle a blackmailer?" He grunted. "No offense to Kat, but seriously, you're joking, right?"

"I have to handle it diplomatically. I still have a year on my contract."

"Contract?"

"He's my agent. I want to get out of my contract without ruining my reputation."

"Your agent?" Max's shoulder tensed, and he gripped the wheel tighter.

She turned to look at him. His face turned red, and his brows pinched together.

"I have been working with my lawyers for over a year. He'll be off my back and out of my life in no time."

"What does he have on you?"

She stared out the side window. "I'm not going to tell you."

He shook his head. "Well, it can't be anything to do with sex partners or sex." He thought a moment. "Did he take suggestive pictures of you?"

"Oh, for Pete's sake. I waited until my late twenties to have sex. Do you think I would be dumb enough to pose for compromising pictures?"

"Sometimes people do things because they're afraid."

Frustrated and annoyed, Hailee blurted it all out. "Rex knows a secret I don't want to be told, and I'm doing everything I can to prevent him from leaking that information. Regardless of the situation, I would never allow him to take pictures of me that he could hold over my head for the rest of my life."

Max pulled up to a towering wrought iron gate. He pushed a button on his dashboard, and the large metal gates swung open. He parked just outside the garage door.

It was the largest and most extravagant house she had ever seen. The two-story Italian mansion's awe-inspiring beauty intimidated Hailee. The manicured lawn spanning at least five acres surrounded a massive marble fountain. Hailee could see the crystal chandelier hanging from the second-floor ceiling.

"You live here?"

"Yeah." He walked around the car and eased her out.

"You must make a lot of money solving murders."

"I own a couple of businesses; they're quite lucrative."

"I'd say." She shook her head and followed him to the door.

Max unlocked the door and disarmed the alarm.

It surprised Hailee that Max would choose a beautiful Italian chateau to reside in. In the few days she had known him, he seemed to be a no-nonsense guy who enjoyed whiskey, getting justice for crime victims, and loved his mother.

The elaborate entryway decorated with pictures and furniture similar to those at his mother's restaurant welcomed her. Max's choice of décor clearly defined his heritage.

Hailee had money, clearly not as much as Max. Her writing allowed her to enjoy both financial and emotional rewards. It made the pain and guilt of losing her parents almost bearable.

Max watched her as she took it all in.

"Your mother is Italian, but not your dad?"

"That's right."

"Where is he?"

Max stared reverently at his father's picture.

"He passed away a few years ago."

Her heart went out to him; she knew the pain of losing a parent. Only in her case, she had been the cause of their demise, and it would haunt her for the rest of her life.

He led her up the spiral staircase and down the main hall to the master bedroom. He then went into the closet at the end of the hall, returned with a woman's robe, and offered it to her.

She declined. Hailee wasn't about to wear a previous lover's robe.

"What side of the bed do I get?" Hailee asked.

"Whatever side makes you happy."

She walked over to the bed and slowly eased herself down. Inhaling, she gently rolled over onto the other pillow. She rolled back over to the first side. "I want this side."

"That's my side."

"I know." She moaned.

"Are you in pain?"

"Some."

Max pulled out a lightweight blue shirt and handed it to Hailee. She dropped her gown to the floor and pulled the shirt over her head.

"Let me see your shoulder." He pulled the shirt back over her head and examined her shoulder. A massive purple bruise covered her entire shoulder blade and the left side of her back. He examined the scratches on her arm. "Who gave you these?"

"The girl. The ninja person tried to pull her down the back stairs, so the girl clawed me in an attempt to hang on."

"Does it hurt?"

"Not much. I'm going to take a pain pill, just in case. What does *figlia* mean?"

"It means daughter. Did Sophia call you that?"

"Yes, she's very kind."

"And pushy, you two will get along famously."

Hoping to steady her throbbing head, Hailee sat on the bed. "I'll be leaving soon."

"I know." He walked out of the bedroom and down the stairs.

She pulled the shirt gently down over her shoulders and followed Max down the stairs and through two large rooms, where she ended up in the kitchen. He had the latest state-of-the-art kitchen appliances, including a convection oven.

"You don't cook; yet you have all of this?"

"I upgraded the kitchen to make Sophia happy. If she thinks I'm planning for the future, for a family, she backs off for a while."

She understood the value of loyalty and the importance of pleasing others. "I don't want to leave; I have to. You know that, right?"

Max turned away. He dug around in the refrigerator, pulling out some cheese and grabbing a box of crackers from the pantry.

The night's events had taken a toll on her physically and emotionally. Seeing the girl savagely attacked and knowing that Rex couldn't wait to pounce on her if she refused him was too much. Hailee started to shake.

"What is it?"

Rex would ruin everything: her life, career, and future. Her fear, anger, and frustration boiled over. "He's making me leave!"

"Who?"

"Rex... I hate him."

"What is he making you do?"

"He wants to own me. He's not going to stop until he has it all."

Max tensed.

Her body went limp; she felt drained. Every ounce of energy she had left had been used in her declaration. It felt good to vent, but by the look on Max's face, she had said too much. "You have enough to deal with. I'm being selfish."

"You need to tell me what he has on you so I can stop him."

"I can't."

Frustrated, Max exhaled. "I know you're afraid, but he needs to be stopped. I won't ask again for a few days, then I'll expect an answer."

She stared at him with flushed skin and furrowed brows. Her guilt and pain consumed her.

Silence engulfed the room; Max plated the cheese and crackers, and they began to eat.

"What are we doing," Hailee asked?

He looked puzzled. "Eating...does your head hurt?"

"No. What are we doing, you, me, the sex?"

"I'd like to get to know you better. Is that what you want to know?"

"What should I tell Detective Keller when I give my statement? Do I tell him about us, about you being there before I called for nine-one-one?"

"Yes, you'd better. I think the cat's out of the bag."

Her eyes widened.

"At the hospital, I yelled at Keller; he's going to know something's up."

"I don't want to risk your professional reputation."

"What about your reputation?"

"Mine was shot to hell the day I thought you died."

He nodded, and they continued to eat.

"Would you have looked for me if I hadn't come to your office?"

"No," Max stated.

She stared curiously at him. "No?"

67

"I already knew who you were; I didn't have to go looking for you."

"When did you know?"

"Alex confronted me on my way out the next morning." Max took another bite. "He told me in no uncertain terms that I had better not hurt you. He's extremely brave, considering he knows who I am and that I carry a gun."

"He's a nice boy. He told you about my books?"

"No, I found out from Keller after he interviewed you. You can imagine my surprise when I found out *you are* famous."

"Not famous, easily recognizable."

Hailee took a few more bites and looked down at her plate. Her head started to spin, and bile built in her stomach.

"What's wrong?"

"I'd better go lie down; some water would be nice."

Hailee headed upstairs, and Max brought her a bottle of water. While she took a pain pill and snuggled in, he sat on the recliner, turned on the lamp, and began reading the first page of Hailee's latest book:

I wiped the blood from the knife and returned it to its sheath. I looked around slowly for any movement or sign of life–good, no witnesses. I walked away and didn't look back…

*****

A ripple of pain woke her; she moaned.

"Good morning; how did you sleep?" Max asked.

She slowly raised her head from the pillow. "Your side of the bed is extremely comfortable."

"How's your head?"

"It hurts, and it feels huge–like a watermelon."

68

Hailee noticed that Max had dark circles under his eyes and was wearing yesterday's clothes. She hoped he got some sleep last night. He needed to be alert; she imagined they would be in for a long day.

"Am I going to give my statement today?"

"I think we can wait until tomorrow until you feel better."

"I have important information that may turn the case around."

"It can wait one more day."

"It's a woman."

"What?"

"I don't know if she is the one who killed the first two girls, but the person I fought with last night was female.

"Are you sure?"

"Absolutely. Right before I kicked her in the chest, we locked eyes, definitely a woman."

Max didn't seem convinced.

"I didn't have shoes on, and I made contact with her breast."

"She saw you?"

"Yes, and she has a star-shaped birthmark in the middle of her left eye."

"You kicked her; why did you get that close," Max asked?

"I had to." Hailee took a breath, "They're fake."

"What?"

"She has breast implants."

He rubbed his forehead.

"Do you want to hear all of it?" Hailee asked.

"Why don't you rest, and I'll make some calls?"

Her shoulder ached, so she decided to take a bath. The two-person tub had strategically placed jets. She returned to the bedroom to get a robe and noticed Max standing in the doorway. She walked past the recliner, and

69

she saw her latest book on the table. Her eyes narrowed, and a wide grin spread across her face.

"What," he asked?

"Did you like it?"

"Not bad."

"Liar."

"I enjoyed it. So, tell me," Max started, "How did you make the love scenes come to life when you hadn't had any sexual experience?"

"Ah...*Fiction is* where fantasy meets reality," Hailee winked. "May I take a bath?"

He entered the bathroom, turned on the water, and adjusted the jets.

Hailee eased her aching body into the hot water. The jets pulsed gently on her bruised skin. Hailee wondered what it would take to get Max to believe in her. She knew she would never have the same level of experience as law enforcement. However, she had been a valuable asset to them in the past, and she believed she could still be of assistance now. Hailee was the only witness, and her description of the assailant could narrow the list of suspects.

She had never been in a fight before. Her body hurt from head to toe–her head throbbed, and the scratches on her arm were raw and tender. The hot water reduced some anxiety and deepened the pain in her exposed skin.

Chapter 9

After the water had cooled, Hailee put Max's shirt back on and went to the kitchen. Max sat at the counter, talking on the phone.

She opened the refrigerator and found ingredients to make a Denver omelet. She looked through his cabinets for a skillet, a bowl, a knife, and a cutting board. While heating the pan, she mixed the vegetables, eggs, and cheese. She toasted four pieces of bread and covered them with butter and blackberry preserves. She kept busy, trying not to listen to Max's conversation. She didn't want to eavesdrop.

When he ended the call, Hailee said, "I made enough for two."

"Good, I'm starving."

They sat down and ate in comfortable silence.

"I'm surprised; you can cook."

"Not really; I only make four or five things–that's the extent of my cooking expertise." She laughed. "Your mom, now she *can cook...*"

"She really likes you."

"I like her too," she said, sipping the coffee. "When can we return to my room and pick up my things?"

"The entire floor is a crime scene; it will be that way, possibly for days."

Memories of the young woman fighting for her life, first at the hotel and now at the hospital, dominated Hailee's thoughts. The young girl had fought valiantly, and Hailee hoped she would continue to fight to save her life. Hailee knew her injuries were severe; she had lost so much blood, and her upper body's skin had been sliced and torn and, in some areas, had been completely severed. The scene was grotesque, and the pain must have been unbearable. Still, Hailee imagined fear had motivated the girl to fight back more than the excruciating pain.

"Have you heard any news on the girl from last night? Is she okay?"

"I'm not going to discuss the case with you. Stop asking."

"I'm involved whether you like it or not. The attacker saw me–I probably hurt her. She's going to be mad."

"You're a witness, and I can't discuss the case with you."

"I'm not asking about the case. I'm asking about the condition of a scared young woman who is fighting for her life. I care about what happens to her. I told her that everything would be okay. Please, tell me."

"I haven't heard anything yet."

She winced and gently touched her head.

"Do you need a pain pill?"

"I could use something for my headache."

"Stay here." Max went upstairs and brought down a large bottle of over-the-counter pain medicine.

"Do you get a lot of headaches," Hailee asked?

He shrugged. "It comes with the job."

"Why do you do it? It's dangerous?"

"It's rewarding and challenging."

"Is that why you're not married?"

"No, why would you think that?"

She locked eyes with him. "It takes a secure and brave woman to love a man who puts himself in constant danger."

She left the kitchen and returned to the master bedroom.

Hailee stared at the mirror. She balked. Her hands hung at her sides–clumps of blood and hair were knotted together. She turned on the shower faucet, stepped in, and recoiled. The water scorched her torn skin. After adjusting the temperature, the water flowed gently over her body, stinging the tender and inflamed skin. She quickly washed her hair, relishing the warm, delicate spray. She heard a knock on the bathroom door and shut off the water.

"It's a little late for modesty, don't you think?" Hailee asked.

"But not too late for good manners."

"Please hand me a towel."

The doorbell rang. Hailee peeked out from behind the curtain.

"It's mom. I called her earlier and asked her to bring over a few things." He headed toward the front door. "Oh, and if she tells you how many grandchildren she wants, just smile and ignore her."

She quickly dried off and pulled on his shirt. She suddenly felt very self-conscious. She put on the robe Max had offered her earlier, which she had refused, and went down to greet Sophia.

Hailee waited near the bottom of the staircase. Max carried large pans of food and other miscellaneous bags and put them on the kitchen counter. Sophia came in, pointing and giving orders.

Sophia walked over to Hailee, inspected her injured head, and asked, "Oh, *Figlia,* are you all right?" She hugged her gently.

"I'm fine," Hailee blushed.

Sophia looked Hailee over again, smiled, and winked at her. *She knows…*

"Max, I told you that robe would come in handy one day."

He rolled his eyes.

"You bought him this robe," Hailee asked?

"Yes, he never wants to prepare for the future; he's always waiting for things to fall into his lap. He doesn't bring women here; you're the first." Sophia beamed.

Hailee watched as Max and his brothers brought in bag after bag. It looked like Sophia had cooked enough food to last through a long, cold winter.

"So *Figlia,* how are you holding up? Is my son treating you well?"

"I'm doing very well. You did a great job raising Max."

Sophia brushed off the compliment. "He should be giving me grandchildren, not grey hair."

"Hailee has been through a lot these past few days. Please not now."

"She's a strong one; she will have to be to be your wife."

Hailee stared at his mother. She'd already made up her mind.

"Max and I are still in the first stages of our relationship. It's a little early to be talking about marriage and kids, don't you think?"

"He should have thought about that before he took you to bed."

Hailee's mouth dropped open, and Max crushed a bag.

His eyes darkened; anger flooded his face. "That's enough!" Max boomed.

"See, he loves you."

Max put the rumpled bag on the counter.

Hailee probably imagined it, but she thought she saw steam coming from Max's ears.

"I think you're being too hard on Max; maybe you could let it go for a while."

"She loves you, too. Well, I should leave now and let you two talk." She winked and walked out with a knowing smile.

They heard the car start. Hailee and Max stared after her.

Hailee continued to stare at the door. Sophia seemed confident that they loved each other. They'd only known each other for less than a week, and most of that week had been spent having sex. Sophia wanted so badly for him to settle down that she was projecting her desires onto them.

Hailee had too much to worry about: the murders, her tour, Kat, Rex, and her lawsuit. She didn't have time for romantic fantasies. She moved slowly, as if in a trance, methodically unpacking the bags.

Max came in and asked, "Hailee, are you okay?"

"I'm fine."

He walked over and grabbed her hands. "She didn't mean to upset you."

"I'm not upset," she looked around, "Where do you want me to put these?" She held up two five-quart pans.

He took the pans from her, forcing her to meet his gaze. "I'm sorry if she hurt your feelings. She wants her kids to be happy, and to her, happiness means being married. Ignore her."

A wave of nausea erupted, and she hurried up the stairs. She hovered over the bowl and waited for the inevitable; thankfully, it never came. Wrenching over the throne could have been extremely painful. She took a pain pill and climbed into bed. She closed her eyes and drifted off to sleep.

*****

Max shut the water off and wrapped a towel around his waist. He rummaged through the closet and chose a dark suit and a light-colored striped tie. He dressed and approached the bed, gently shaking Hailee. She was sleeping and groaned when he tried to get her up.

"Where are you going?" She asked.

"We're going to my office. You have to give your statement, and I need to do some things."

Max combed his hair and tugged on the bedspread. "Time to get up."

Hailee showered and dried her hair. She dressed, slipping into a yellow dress with blue flowers and pumps with a two-inch heel. She let her hair flow straight around her shoulders and followed Max to the kitchen.

"Is that what we're having for breakfast, warmed-up food?"

"Sorry, it's the best that I can do."

They began to eat. "That's a great color on you."

She looked down at the dress. "Thanks," she said, taking a bite and chewing. "Why did Sophia buy me new clothes?"

"I asked her to."

"Why?"

"Your clothes aren't available yet, and I didn't have anything for you to wear."

"How much do I owe you?"

"You don't owe me anything."

"I have money; I can buy my own clothes."

Max moved toward the door. "Are you ready to go?"

Hailee guessed he wouldn't answer. She refused to accept charity; she would remind him later about buying her own clothes. "Sure."

The drive to his office was quiet. Hailee remembered the first time she entered the police station. She went to identify Max as the possible murder victim, and her civic duty had cost her dignity, having to retell her first night with Max.

Max interrupted her thoughts. "Don't be nervous. Javon, Detective Keller, is a stand-up guy and a consummate professional."

She visibly cringed. "He knows everything about my first night with you and how I jumped into bed with a stranger. Can't I leave you out of it? There's no reason we both should go up in flames. Your professional integrity needs to remain intact."

"Let me worry about that," Max led her through the station and into Detective Keller's office. She hesitated at the door. "I'll be right here. It'll be fine."

She entered slowly.

Detective Keller looked up and smiled, "Have a seat, Miss Hollister."

She smiled politely and sat in the all-too-familiar chair.

"May I ask you a favor before we begin," Keller asked?

"Sure," her voice squeaked a little. She looked behind her. Max stood in the door jamb, nodding encouragingly.

"My wife is a huge fan, and she threatened to divorce me when she found out I met you and didn't get your autograph. Would you mind signing your books for her?"

"It will be my pleasure, what's her name?"

"Jasmine. She's one of your biggest fans."

Hailee looked at the stack of books on the table; his wife had all six books. She looked up; he shrugged. She signed them all, adding a personal note to each one. "So, are you a fan?"

He laughed, "I like whatever my wife likes."

"Smart man."

"Let's begin, shall we? Please tell me what happened the night of the tenth."

Hailee glanced toward the door; Max was in deep conversation with another detective. Her head ached, so she gently massaged her temple.

"Miss Hollister, are you okay? Does your head hurt?"

She cleared her throat. "May I have some water?"

Keller frowned and looked concerned. "Sure, I'll be right back."

He came back with a bottle of water. Hailee opened it and drank most of it.

Max walked in. "How's it going?"

Hailee looked up and smiled weakly. Max frowned and glared at Keller.

Keller shifted under Max's glare. "She hasn't said anything yet. I don't think she feels well."

"Are you feeling okay?" Max asked.

"I'm fine."

"Do you want to try again later," Keller asked?

"No. Reliving what happened is going to be harder than I imagined."

"Just tell him what happened. If he needs you to elaborate, he'll let you know."

"I don't know where to begin."

"Why don't you start by telling him what you were doing before you called nine-one-one?"

"I went to bed—"

"No, before that." Max urged.

"It's not relevant to what happened."

"Yes. It is."

"No. It's not." Hailee snapped.

Keller cleared his throat. "Would you like to take a break? I could come back when you're ready to give me your statement?"

"See, he already knows; don't be embarrassed."

Max seemed determined to get it all out; Hailee had no choice but to start at the beginning. "About ten, Max's phone rang; he told me he received a call about the case and had to leave."

She stopped and looked up at Keller. "Max told me not to leave or let anyone in and then left. I lay back down. I heard a noise. I couldn't identify it, so I closed my eyes and tried to go back to sleep. Then I heard it again. The hair on my arm stood up. It was a woman screaming."

Max stood behind her, his hand resting lightly on her shoulder.

"I called nine-one-one. The screams pierced my heart. I had to do something. I ran out and saw a woman in her nightgown fighting with someone in black. I yelled, 'fire'—"

"Why did you do that?" Keller asked.

"In my high school self-defense class, the instructor told us that if you scream fire, you'd have a greater chance of getting help–especially if others felt they were in danger too."

"Did it work?"

"No, no one came. I don't know if any of the rooms on my floor are occupied. Anyway, the person wearing black looked toward me when I screamed 'fire,' and the girl pushed her down and ran towards me."

"Her?"

Hailee nodded. "The girl fell; I ran to her and yanked her up. We headed to my room; we were pushed down. I crashed into the wall and hit my head," she touched her forehead. "My head spun, and a sharp pain shot through it. The person in black tried to drag the woman back down the hall. I ran up and kicked her in the chest." Hailee felt dizzy. "I got a good look at her eyes. They were green, and she had a star-shaped birthmark on her left eye."

She took another drink and took a cleansing breath.

"The woman in black fell and landed on her back. I clutched the girl and dragged her to my room, and then Officer Thornton shook me. He ran after the lady in black; I stayed with the injured girl. She had deep cuts in her chest and throat. One of her breasts had been almost completely severed–the blood gushed out."

Hailee's heart rate increased, and panic enveloped her. The shrillness of her voice echoed in the room.

"I held her hand, and I whispered words of encouragement. I put pressure on her wounds to slow down the bleeding; I couldn't stop it. It wouldn't stop." Hailee gasped.

"Do you want to stop?" Keller asked?

Stopping would only interrupt her flow. She wanted to get it all out.

"The paramedics came; the color had drained from the girl. She wouldn't let go of my hand. She needed me. They took her away and wouldn't let me go with her."

She stared at her books sitting on the desk.

Max followed the direction of her stare. She looked scared and confused. "Did you remember something else?" He asked.

"No. I'm wondering why people write or read about murder. It's horrific."

"What happened next?" Keller urged.

Hailee shook her head, dispelling the feeling of despair consuming her. "Officer Thornton returned to see how I was; I fell, and he called the paramedics. I went to the hospital, and you know the rest."

Hailee felt a tiny weight lift from her shoulders. She told the story of a young woman's fight for survival, but Hailee didn't know how it would end.

Keller continued to take notes. " How do you know that it was a woman, and can you describe her?"

"Before I kicked her, I looked into her eyes. She wore black mascara and eyeliner. As I said earlier, she has a birthmark in her left eye. When I kicked her, my bare foot came in contact with her breast. Instead of squishing flat, it separated into two pieces. She has breast implants." Hailee slowed to let Keller catch up. "She stood five feet seven inches, weighed one hundred thirty pounds, and had an olive skin tone. I can't be sure. It might have been a foundation."

She stopped to catch her breath and to steady her aching head. "She had on one of those black TV Ninja outfits. I didn't notice her shape until I kicked her. The only visible part of her skin was a small, rectangular area above her nose, which exposed her eyes and a small portion of her skin. I couldn't see her face or her hair. Sorry."

"Don't be sorry. You did a courageous thing."

"Are we done?" Hailee asked.

Keller stood up and offered Hailee his hand. "Thanks for signing the books."

"Anytime."

Max and Hailee returned to Max's house; Hailee went straight to bed.

*****

Max was not easily impressed, and he was amazed at how bravely Hailee had relived her terrifying encounter with danger. Not only did she recall specific details, but she also did it all while suffering through immense physical discomfort. When Max first met her, he never realized that she would have such a profound impact on his life. That could be why he felt so uncharacteristically protective of a woman he had just met. Blackmail could lead to more severe problems if not handled delicately. Hailee had proved to be intelligent and intuitive. It would take finesse and experience to neutralize Rex. If that didn't work, Max knew how to handle a creep like him.

If Rex thought he could intimidate or scare Hailee, he had another thing coming. Max had cultivated friendships with men and women in agencies worldwide and could, if forced to, put a stranglehold on Rex's attempts to blackmail Hailee.

Law enforcement was a tight-knit group that supported one another and stood together. Max joined the force for several reasons. He wanted to be part of something bigger than himself, and he hoped to prove his father wrong, showing that he could have a rewarding career while still caring for his family. He wished his father had lived long enough to see it. Max's mother overlooked his successes; she wanted him to quit and start a family. She didn't understand his resolve to prove to his dad's memory that he made the right decision for him and that his family would have to learn to accept his choices.

Max glanced toward Hailee; she slept peacefully, oblivious to his inner turmoil.

Chapter 10

Hailee slept most of the day, and when she woke, she felt rejuvenated. She stretched and climbed out of bed. She combed her knotted hair, straightened her dress, and went downstairs.

Max wasn't in the kitchen, so she headed to the front portion of the house. He wasn't in the formal sitting room, so she searched the adjoining rooms, the den, and the library. Hailee headed back down the hall and through the kitchen. It led out to an enormous yard.

Large shade trees, rose bushes, and a multitude of plant life garnished the grand gazebo in the center of the backyard. She could see a silhouette of a man. Hailee strolled to the gazebo and watched Max take in the picturesque sunset. He looked like he wanted time alone, so she turned to leave.

"Join me."

They watched the sun disappear from the sky. Hailee enjoyed the beauty and warmth of the sunset. She snuck a glance at Max and remembered the night she met him. She knew then that he would be different from anyone she had ever met, and his passion, his desire for her, set her on fire. She was lost in thought when Max laughed.

"Hunter?"

"What?" Hailee asked.

"I remind you of Hunter?"

Her cheeks reddened. "Yes."

"If you had told me that I reminded you of a character from one of your books, I would have thought you were off your rocker."

She smiled. "Ignorance is bliss."

"Why did you have sex with me," Max asked?

"I had my reasons."

"Tell me."

"Does it really matter?"

"I would like to know."

"It's hard to explain." Hailee still hadn't come to grips with her decision; it had completely changed her life.

"It's important."

"You were open and honest. I felt safe and desired." She walked the perimeter of the gazebo, running her fingers lightly over the robust, intricate design.

"Why didn't you tell me you were a virgin?"

"I didn't know what you would do if I told you."

Max nodded, and they continued watching the sunset. Yellow, orange, and red hues signaled the end of the day.

After dinner, they settled in on the large sectional.

"I wonder what Sophia thinks of Hunter."

"I don't want to talk about her right now." Max scowled.

"Don't be mad; she loves you."

"She crossed the line."

Hailee would stay away from that topic for a while; he wasn't over it yet.

"When can I get back into my hotel room?" Hailee asked.

"I'll check and let you know when I can get your clothes and things."

"I'm not allowed to go back to the hotel?"

He looked up from the newspaper. "I don't want you anywhere near there; you witnessed a crime and were in contact with the perpetrator. You're not going back."

"If I'm not safe at the hotel, the other guests aren't safe either."

"They've been relocated. We're shutting down the entire hotel."

"Shutting down the hotel; what about Carrington?" Hailee jumped up. "I need to call him."

"He's fine. I spoke to him earlier."

84

"That hotel has been his whole life, and now it's been shut down. I need to speak with him. He's my friend. What about Alex?"

"Here." Max handed Hailee his phone; she dialed frantically.

"Carrington, are you okay?"

He chuckled. "I am. I have been moved and am vacationing at a suitable hotel."

"Really–you're fine? The hotel is closed."

"I am doing rather well. I am being treated like a king."

"Do you need anything? Do you need money?"

"Miss Hollister, I assure you, I am truly and honestly fine."

"Let me know if you need anything. I won't have my phone for a few days. You can leave me a message, okay?"

"There is no need to worry, my number one fan. I am wonderful. Good night." Carrington hung up.

She called Alex and grilled him to ensure he didn't need anything. He laughed at her and said he could take care of himself.

Hailee hoped she didn't offend them. Ever since her grandmother died, she had no family, and her career made making and keeping friends difficult. This situation made her appreciate Kat even more. Kat could be a handful. Hailee truly cared about her.

"All done," Max asked?

"No, those are the only two numbers I have memorized." She couldn't think of anyone else and didn't want to overlook anyone.

"Hailee, I promise. They're safe."

She handed him his phone. Hailee wanted to believe him.

"How are you able to relocate the guests," Hailee asked?

85

Max put the phone on the table and said, "I told you that I own several businesses and that they are quite profitable. My father bought and remodeled The Meridian Hotel, and when he passed, he left it to me."

"Is that why you have a permanent room key?"

He shook his head yes, "When I need an escape from my loving but ever-present family, and if I need a break from everything, especially work, I stay at the Meridian and relax. I also use my time there to check up on the employees and see how everything is running. Of course, Carrington is meticulous, and the hotel runs like a well-oiled machine."

"So the employees know you own the hotel," Hailee asked?

"Only Carrington. I don't want them to treat me differently when I stay there."

Carrington had proven time and again to Hailee that he was loyal to a fault; no wonder he guarded Max's privacy with great care. He wasn't just a guest; he owned the hotel.

"Have you heard anything about the woman's condition? Is she okay?"

Max stared at his silent phone. The grave look on his face said it all.

Hailee sank on the sofa. "She didn't make it, did she?"

Max shook his head no.

Hailee remembered seeing the terror on the young woman's face. She never imagined how much it would affect her. The young woman had sustained fatal injuries and continued to fight like a survivor. What raw courage it took to endure the savage attack on her body, have her skin cut and shredded, and never give up. To lose someone so young, so strong, broke Hailee's heart. When Hailee intervened, the young woman must have thought that she would escape; she must have believed, if only for a few seconds, that she was safe, only to lose in the end.

Hailee lay her wet cheek on Max's chest and closed her eyes.

*****

Max disconnected the call and angrily shoved the phone in his pocket.

Hailee stared at him, sleep still in her eyes.

"Did I wake you?" Max asked.

"Rough morning?"

"I had to make a few phone calls; the last one was unpleasant."

"Do you want to talk about it?"

"No," he said curtly.

"Do you want breakfast?"

"No, I have to go to the office. I'll be gone all day. I have a lot of work to catch up on."

"Is your work suffering because of me," Hailee asked?

"No, there's just been a lot going on."

"When can I pick up my phone and the rest of my things. My flight is in a few days, and I have to catch up with Kat."

"You won't be leaving."

"My tour resumes in a week."

"You're staying here under my protection until I arrest the psycho who's been killing the women at the Meridian."

"I need to finish my book tour, or Rex will ruin me!" Hailee screeched.

Max balked. "I don't care what Rex wants."

"I can't stay." She glared up at him.

"Hailee, you're a witness. You're staying."

"You're just making things worse for me. I have to go."

Max looked at this watch. "I'm late."

"I don't have my laptop or a car. What am I supposed to do all day?"

"Get some sleep or explore the grounds. I'll call you later."

While Max drove, he thought about Hailee. Her frantic behavior when confronted with staying convinced Max that Rex must have something personally incriminating on her. What could it be? If Max knew what it was, he could get Rex off her back. She would have to trust him with information. But that would have to wait; he had three murders to solve and one witness to keep safe. He would protect Hailee first and deal with Rex later.

The murders had everyone on high alert. Even Max's unshakable secretary, Erma, was feeling the pressure. Max could feel the tense, frenzied atmosphere. He headed to his office, and Erma met him halfway. He greeted her; she smiled back. Her frazzled state spoke volumes.

"What's wrong?"

"The phones are ringing off the hook. Everyone is calling about Miss Hollister."

"Who's calling? What do they want," Max asked?

"Literally everyone, her fans, friends, and agent. They saw the news and the pictures of Miss Hollister at the hospital. They're upset and worried."

"What pictures?"

"A reporter took pictures of her arriving and leaving the hospital; they're all over the news. I guess this guy has been following her around her whole visit."

"Following her? Can we ID him?"

"No, I checked. The news stations won't give us the identity of the photographer; they say the pictures are being sent anonymously."

"Damn," he thought a moment, "Rex called here. What does he want?"

"He's boiling mad. He wants to know how you plan to protect his star writer."

Max scowled. "Give me his number. I'll call him. Come see me after you speak with Pete about releasing a formal statement."

He closed the door to his office and dialed Rex's number.

"Rex Chandler."

"This is Max Toliver; you called and left a message regarding Miss Hollister."

"Where is she–is she safe?"

"She's safe; she's in protective custody."

"I need to speak with her; she has a book tour scheduled to resume next week. This is important."

"What's more important, the safety of Miss Hollister or her book tour?"

"Hailee's safety, of course, but I must speak with her. It's urgent."

"I'm sorry. Miss Hollister is not available for phone calls. And we have to keep her location secret; she is our only witness to one of the murders. I'm sure you understand," Max's words dripped with sarcasm.

Frustration and annoyance laced Rex's tone. "This is of a personal nature; I must speak with her."

"I'm sorry, Mr. Chandler. Until this matter is resolved, she will not be available for phone calls or visitors. Your urgent personal matter will have to wait." Max slammed the receiver down.

Heat penetrated Max's face and neck. Rex had some nerve; he wanted Hailee to resume her book tour so he could strengthen his hold on Hailee. Well, too bad. Hailee would stay until he could be sure she was safe.

Max sifted through the phone messages; there must be fifty of them. He pushed them aside. Max would let Pete handle the influx of calls and the public fallout. He had more pressing matters to attend to.

Max opened the file of the first murder victim, the blonde killed on the third floor. The partial file listed her statistics: name: Ashley Thomas, age: twenty-five, and education: a recent graduate of California State University. She lived in Portland with her college roommate and secured a job as a paralegal at a small law firm. She died in a room registered to a local company. They were still trying to locate the owner to get the information on who had access to the room. She had no police record, and her friends, the ones who were interviewed, said that everyone loved her and couldn't believe that someone would want to hurt her.

He flipped through the crime scene photos. They were gruesome. The victim had been decapitated. Her body and severed head had been moved to a different location; the crime scene, the hotel bed, was covered in her blood. He hated this part of the job, examining the remains. He tried not to think about the victim, the girl. He had to concentrate on the evidence, the facts, or he wouldn't be able to do it.

The detectives found no indication of family or relationship problems or work-related issues. The Medical Examiner reported that she had been in good health: she didn't smoke or drink in excess and had no medical conditions. He listed the time of death as midnight, blood type as O Negative, and, other than the cause of death, she sustained no other injuries.

What a horrible way to go...

Karen Striker, the second victim, a brunette, was murdered on the fourth floor, and she, too, was twenty-five years old. She had been staying at the hotel for a couple of weeks while attending a work convention. Like the first victim, she had no entanglements that might have led to murder. The ME's report showed that she had been bludgeoned to death; the weapon had yet to be determined or found. Blood type, O Negative, and TOD midnight.

Two young women, the same age and, other than having O Negative blood, had nothing in common except for the fact that they were both dead and killed at the same hotel.

His mind kicked into overdrive, two grisly murders in one week, at the same hotel and under his watch. He closed the folder, tapped a pen on the desk, and dialed.

"Toliver residence," Haliee answered in her most professional voice.

"I called to see how you are feeling."

"I'm fine. How about you? You sound horrible."

"It's been rather hectic here."

"Did you talk to Simon or Alex? Simon's demeanor feels unnatural. Something rubs me the wrong way. I'm not sure what it is. You should check it out."

"Hailee, stay out of it."

"I have a great eye for details and—"

"Stop questioning my detectives and me, and stay away from potential witnesses."

"You sound depressed."

"Murder and death are depressing!"

"Okay." She hung up.

Max didn't mean to snap at her. He called to see how she felt; she had been distraught when he left. Now, he had hurt her feelings.

Dread enveloped him as he opened the last file; it was tragic that the others died, and it troubled him how much this young woman's death had affected Hailee. Her personal connection to the third victim rattled him. She could have been the one to die.

Brenda Jacobs had black hair and was twenty-five years old. She did not register at the hotel and didn't appear to be dating or visiting anyone who was. She wore a sheer nightgown; she must have been staying with someone...

The third victim had died from multiple stab wounds, and it looked like the perp had tried to amputate one of her breasts. Bruising appeared on both arms just above the elbows. The bruises looked like handprints. The ME could not determine which wound caused her death. The damage to her organs had been substantial; she had been gutted like a fish.

Max closed his eyes and thought of Hailee. She stepped up when no one else did. Her actions put her in direct contact with a killer. He shuddered at the thought. She could have been seriously hurt or even killed. He had to stop thinking about it; it didn't happen. He wouldn't let it happen.

He had to concentrate on the case and focus on the third victim. Why did she have bruising on her arms? Did someone hold her down while someone else tried to remove her breasts? The time of death and blood type were the same as those of the first two victims. Would she have anything else in common with them? Max thought it strange. The assailant attacked the third victim, and a fight ensued; she, too, died at midnight. How could that have been planned, or had the perpetrator planned on torturing her, delaying death to match the others?

None of the young women looked alike, and as far as he knew, they were from different walks of life. The common factors of the crimes were the Meridian, the time of death, age, and blood type. What did these four items have to do with three distinctly different women? For a moment, his mind went to a frightening place. Serial *killer.*

A primary characteristic of a serial killer was absent. There had been no cooling-off period. Serial killers typically want to bask in the kill. There had only been a day between each killing; it didn't fit.

He would wait until he had more information before he would identify the killings as the work of a serial killer–
no need to throw everyone into a full-blown panic.

Chapter 11

Hailee spent the morning exploring the vast garden and plush landscaping; it felt good to be outside soaking up some sun. She wondered if Max had found any leads. Even though he refused to discuss it with her, she knew the investigation had just begun, and the police were still collecting evidence. It felt like every day since her first night with Max, a woman had died. She wondered if the victims had anything in common other than staying at the hotel where they died. She heard from the news reports that all the women were about the same age. Max wouldn't deny or confirm it. Hailee paused and considered the worst-case scenario. If there was only one killer, it could be the work of a serial killer...

She didn't have much experience writing about serial killers. The thought alone scared her from doing the research. She didn't want to delve into the mind of a murdering, antisocial, animal-killing predator. She would let the police handle those types of menacing killers.

She went inside, made lunch, and settled on the living room sofa. She flipped through the channels and stopped at a local news station. A man named Peter Stallings, from the 63rd precinct, was making an official statement:

"It has come to our attention that there are rumors that Miss Hailee Hollister's safety and health are being threatened. That is not true. She is doing well and is currently in protective custody. I am not at liberty to say anymore." Pete looked directly at the camera and said, "Due to the grave and sensitive nature of this case, we ask that only calls that pertain to the recent murders be directed to the precinct and any calls regarding Miss Hollister be directed to her publishing company or agent, Rex Chandler. Thank you."

Her mind raced. Who called about her? Hailee rushed to the phone and dialed star six nine.

"Max Toliver."

"Do you have a minute?" She asked breathlessly.

"Hailee, what's wrong?"

"I just saw Pete on the news; what's happening?"

"I had Pete make a statement so we could get back to work. Apparently, your fans saw the pictures of you at the hospital, and they were frantic, so they called here."

"What pictures?"

He exhaled. "A reporter or freelance photographer took pictures of you at the hospital in your bloody robe, and they were shown on the news. We received dozens of calls inquiring about your condition."

Did someone follow her and take pictures of her at the hospital? Hailee always made every effort to be aware of her surroundings. Her first night back in Portland, she had thought someone had been lurking in the dark following her. She had dismissed it, blaming it on jetlag. One never knew when an excited fan might pop up. Now, she knew someone had been tailing her and had sold gory pictures of her. No wonder her friends and fans were upset.

"Something frightening occurred to me. I know that you are just starting your investigation and still collecting evidence, but all three women were killed at the Meridian and are about the same age—"

"Who told you that?" Max ground out.

"About the age? The day after the second murder, the day I got lost, one of the reporters asked me if I was scared to stay at the hotel when women my age were dying. Why?"

"That information hasn't been officially released. We hold pertinent information back so if we get a confession, we can verify that specific details weren't splashed all over the news."

94

"I don't know how he knew or if he was just speculating. Anyway, if the three women are related by age and the Meridian, maybe they have more in common than those two items, and if they do," she swallowed hard. She didn't want to say it out loud. "It could be the work of a serial killer."

The line went silent. Did Max hang up?

She waited; she thought she heard quick, angry breaths.

"There is no evidence to back up your claim. I do not want you to breathe a word of that to anyone, not even me. It could send the entire city spiraling into a frenzy of uncontrollable hysteria." Max ground out. "Do you understand?"

Hailee's mouth went dry, and her heart raced. "Yes."

She used to react this way, with a dry mouth and racing pulse, when she considered writing about serial killers; the implications were terrifying. The thought of an antisocial lunatic roaming the streets and targeting young women sent chills down her spine. If a serial killer was stalking Portland, she would stay out of Max's investigation. She had enough to worry about, and her biggest problem was Rex.

"You're right. We are still gathering evidence; it's too soon to draw any conclusions. Pete will handle the press."

"Kat must be frantic. I'll call her. Are you coming home soon?"

"I don't know when I'll be finished; it will be very late."

Kat's flustered cell phone messages confirmed what Hailee knew. When Hailee didn't call back, Kat contacted Max. Kat seemed to trust Max. Hailee called Kat and told her she didn't know when she would be ready to return to her book tour. She asked about Rex; she knew he would be furious.

"Girl, livid doesn't even come close. After Max called Rex, he ranted about going down there and dragging you back here."

"Max called Rex?"

"Max told him you weren't available for the phone; Rex was fit to be tied. Max is my hero."

"Oh, no. Max shouldn't have done that. Rex will take it out on me. Kat, you have to fix this. Please."

"There's nothing to fix. Rex can't blame this on you, and you now can spend more time with Max."

"I can't take that chance."

"Max knows what to do. It'll all work out."

Hailee knew Kat meant well, and she appreciated all the advice Kat so openly imparted. If the circumstances weren't so dire, she would be willing to let Max step in. "I miss you."

"Sure, you say that now, but wait until I'm driving your Corvette."

They laughed, then hung up. Kat had this inherent talent for putting even the scariest of situations into perspective. Her positive outlook rubbed off on everyone around her, and they seemed to start thinking and behaving differently, better, and happier. Even though Kat's instincts were typically spot on, when it came to Rex, she had blinders on. Rex had to be handled just right, or he would destroy Hailee and everything she cherished.

She had only a few days before she was due back, and Rex would not tolerate any more excuses. He would torpedo everything she worked so hard to build if she didn't do as he asked. He would expose her sin and relish in it.

Hailee called her attorney, Carl Langston, and left a message regarding her case against Rex Chandler, asking him to return her call. She hoped he had enough evidence to break her contract and permanently get her away from Rex.

Hailee hung up, feeling more anxious than before. Carl had been working with her for over a year. They had been gathering evidence and biding their time until Rex slipped up and did something so blatantly wrong that she could escape his grasp and move on with her life free from fear. Rex hadn't made any flagrant mistakes yet; Hailee would have to wait until he did. She had one opportunity to get him off her back; she didn't want to blow it.

She considered going back outside, but she couldn't shake the feeling that something big was about to happen. Max had his hands full. Rex annoyed and harassed everyone, and Max didn't need the added pressure of dealing with him.

Hailee dialed, hoping Alex would pick up.

"What's up, dude?"

"Alex? It's Hailee. How are you?"

"Oh, sorry. I thought you were someone else."

She laughed, "No worries. I wanted to know if you needed anything?"

"No, I'm good. The Meridian owner is handling everything."

"That's great. Speaking of the Meridian, has a detective interviewed you regarding the murders?"

"Yeah, just the basic questions. Where was I? Can anyone verify my whereabouts? Did I know any of the girls? Did I see anything suspicious?"

"Did you see or hear anything unusual during any of the murders, or did you see anyone that seemed out of place?" Hailee asked.

"Just like I told the cops, the night shift is the busiest shift, and one of the bartenders didn't show, so I wouldn't have noticed anything out of the ordinary if it happened right in front of me. Are you working the case?"

She didn't want to admit she was snooping in case it got back to Max; he would blow a gasket. "No, I'm just curious. It keeps me at the top of my game as a writer."

"That's good. It's probably best to stay out of it. Especially since you came face-to-face with someone who murdered the last girl. Did you get hurt?" Alex asked.

Hailee touched her head; it hurt. "No, I'm good. I'm angry that I couldn't save the girl. That's why I want to do whatever it takes to get her killer off the street." Her shoulder throbbed painfully when she switched the phone to her other hand. "How well do you know Simon? Is he a friend?"

"Even though we both work a lot, we hang out once in a while. I mostly see him when he comes in for deliveries. Simon told me that he got into some trouble as a teen and that his dad cracks the whip at work and keeps him constantly on the go so he won't repeat his past behaviors."

"Did Simon tell you what type of trouble he had gotten into? Was it criminal?"

"No, he only said that his dad freaked out, and to keep the money flowing, he had to buckle down."

Hailee felt something might be off about Simon, but she couldn't put her finger on it. Delivering ice didn't appear to be his passion, nor did it seem to be a suitable job. It may be the family business. Still, Hailee could tell he was bored and distracted by his responsibilities.

She thanked Alex for the information and hung up. Hailee would call Kat and see if she could check Simon's juvenile records. He might be a viable lead for Max.

*****

Max entered Hailee's hotel suite and packed her clothes and toiletries. He cleaned out her nightstand and packed her phone and laptop. He locked the hotel door and put her suitcases in his trunk. Good thing Max brought his sedan; Hailee didn't pack light.

He pulled into the driveway; the lights were out. Max carried Hailee's suitcases in and left them in the entryway. He headed upstairs, loosened his tie, and ran his fingers through his hair. What a day.

Hailee slept soundly on his side of the bed. Max put his gun in the nightstand drawer and undressed. He slid under the comforter, curled up against her, and fell asleep.

Max woke and headed to the kitchen. He made a pot of coffee and sat down with the morning paper. Most people prefer to use their phones to stay informed about the news. However, he loved the entire process of reading the paper, from turning the pages to folding it. It was comfortable and familiar. He had finished the business and the editorial sections and had started on the feature articles when Hailee entered the room. He'd hoped to finish the paper in case there were any articles about Hailee or the murders. Max didn't want her to feel threatened or pressured. He had to keep her safe; if that meant keeping her in the dark, so be it.

He poured her a cup and handed it to her. "How'd you sleep?"

"My shoulder still hurts, so I took a pain pill–it did the trick," she sipped her coffee. "I'm leaving. If I don't get back, Rex will cause problems for me."

"I don't think that's wise; I need you to stay until I make an arrest."

"I know that my problem can't compete with your job of solving murders. Still, my life, as I know it, is at stake. I have to get back to work, back to my book tour."

Max rinsed out his cup and turned to face her. "You're right. I am trying to solve three heinous murders, one of which you witnessed. I can hold you here as a material witness."

"Please don't do that."

"I'm tired of discussing this."

He brushed past her toward her suitcases, which he took upstairs to the master bedroom. He hurried down the stairs, where she waited by the door.

"This is extremely important to me; I won't let you boss me around just because we're sleeping together."

"Whether you sleep with me or not is your decision. You're staying, and that's final." He slammed the door.

Max headed to the Meridian; he hated laying down the law. Rex frightened her, and she seemed terrified of what he might do. Max won't let her leave until he finds a way to make her safe and free her of Rex's hold.

Max pulled into the hotel parking lot; Keller and the ten-person forensic team were waiting near the front entrance. A thorough search of the crime scenes had been performed after each murder. Now that all the guests had gone, he and his team could conduct a comprehensive sweep of the entire hotel and its surrounding areas. Max greeted them and handed out the assignments. Max and five members of the forensic team were tasked with searching the hotel's interior. Keller and the remaining team members would take the pool, grounds, dumpsters, and parking lots. They were instructed to search every inch *again* with the same zealousness and thoroughness as the first time. If they didn't find the murder weapon or weapons, they would expand their search to the surrounding businesses and streets.

They geared up and entered the hotel. Max and his team headed for the bar and the restaurant. Max headed toward the back of the bar, to the booth where Hailee saw the first murder victim and her date. After the first murder had been discovered, the booths, tables, and bathrooms had all been dusted for fingerprints. Nothing much turned up except a couple of partials from the hotel staff; the rest of the prints had been wiped clean by housekeeping.

Hailee had given a detailed description of the man the first victim was with. Still, they have not been able to locate him. None of the first victim's friends recognized the description of the man, and they said she didn't have a steady boyfriend. The hotel staff didn't recognize him. If he did frequent the hotel, he did so discreetly. If only they could find him, he would be a solid lead and maybe even the murderer…

After hearing his name, Max scanned the bar area of the restaurant for Keller. Keller escorted a young man across the room and stopped a few feet from Max.

"Who's this?" Max demanded.

"I found him loitering by the back entrance. He told me he'd arrived a few minutes ago to make an ice delivery for the bar."

Max scrutinized the young man. He wore a Glacier Palace shirt and navy pants. He shaved the sides of his brown hair and styled the top in a textured, spiked look. His thick brows and disconnected goatee matched his hair color. They gave him a devilish quality offset by his intense blue eyes.

Max snatched the plastic badge clipped to his pocket and studied it. "Is this your badge?"

The young man nodded.

"Have I seen you here before? What's your full name?"

"I'm Simon Adkins. My dad and I have been servicing the hotel for ten years. You may have seen me; I deliver ice for the bar daily. What's wrong?"

"The hotel is a crime scene. You're not supposed to be here. Keller, take him downtown. Get his prints and see if he will agree to provide a DNA sample. Let's see if we can eliminate him from the suspect pool."

Keller directed Simon toward the door, answered his phone, and looked back toward Max.

"Do a full background check on him; see if he knew any of the vics. The murders have been plastered all over the news. Find out why he showed up today."

Keller nodded to Max and led Simon to a cruiser.

After the second murder, Max had men watching the hotel round the clock, and they continued to watch even though the hotel's guests had been relocated. He hoped someone would return to the scene to try to remove evidence or admire their handiwork. So far, no one other than Simon had shown up. Max would wait for Keller to eliminate or confirm Simon as a suspect; until then, he would continue his search.

Max's team worked their way up the second and third floors. Max looked at his watch and decided a break was in order. He told the rest of the team to take lunch and to return at one-thirty sharp.

Max went back to the bar and called his house. Hailee didn't pick up, so he tried again. She might still be angry. Perhaps she left. The gates would only open with the remote or once the correct code was entered, and she had neither. He looked up the number on his cell phone when she called him from the restaurant. He dialed, and she picked up on the first ring.

"Where are you," Max asked?

"Having another bad day?"

"No, you didn't answer the phone."

"I'm outside enjoying your garden."

"I thought you might still be mad about this morning."

"I'm not mad. I can't see how we will work this out. I don't want to fight with you. I have to leave, and I will."

"I won't let Rex endanger you or your life for a stupid book tour."

A long, tense pause hung in the air.

"It's not stupid. It's my life, and I love it."

"I'm trying to protect you, don't you see—"

"I'm perfectly capable of taking care of myself; I know you believe you are doing the right thing—"

"It's imperative that I keep you safe."

"You have a job to do, and I have mine." Hailee disconnected the call.

*****

Max called off the search at six and headed back to the precinct. His eyes were stinging, and he was jonesing for some hot, black coffee. Max needed a jolt to tackle the mound of paperwork on his desk. He walked past Detective Cory Thornton's desk, and the stern look on his face stopped Max cold.

"Thornton, why so grim?" Max cringed. "Another murder?"

"You have a visitor. He's waiting in your office."

Max looked over his shoulder toward his open door. A tall, heavy-set man with graying hair and thick glasses stood in the door jamb, tapping his right foot.

Max gestured back to the door, "Who is it?"

Thornton grinned. "The high and mighty Rex Chandler."

"Good, I have been waiting to speak with him." Max strode confidently to his office.

Max pointed to the chair directly across from his desk. "Mr. Chandler, please sit down."

Rex glared at him. "Where is she?"

"Miss Hollister?"

"You know damn well who."

"Mr. Chandler, there is no need for vulgarity."

"Oh, cut the bull. Where's Hailee?"

Max walked over to his desk and sat down. "Have a seat and tell me what the problem is."

Rex sat down and leaned forward. "You told me that Hailee wasn't hurt and that she is safe, even though I haven't been able to reach her. What have you done with her?"

"I assure you, Mr. Chandler, I have done nothing to Miss Hollister."

"I want to speak to her. Now!" Spit sprayed the files on Max's desk.

Disgusted, Max looked down at his files. "You are not in any position to demand anything," Max leaned back and took a slow breath, "As I told you before, she is a witness to a murder, and she will be released when I see fit." He leaned forward and locked eyes with Rex.

"If you need to relay an urgent message, I will happily pass it along. Is there anything that you want me to tell Miss Hollister?"

Rex shifted in his seat. "I need to know that she is okay, and I want to know if I should reschedule the last half of her tour."

"She is safe. I promise. And as for the tour, you should probably postpone it until further notice."

"Indefinitely? Are you kidding me?"

"Mr. Chandler, I wouldn't joke about something this serious. We are investigating a murder, and then there will be a trial. We will need her testimony; she is our only witness."

"NO!"

Max hid his smirk and asked, "Is there a problem?"

"I won't tolerate this grandstanding. I want to know where Hailee is!"

"No."

"We're done here."

Max stood up and met his stare. "Yes, we are."

Chapter 12

Max approached his front door, and all the lights were off. He grabbed his briefcase and coffee and pushed open the door. He dropped his case and sprinted upstairs to the bedroom. She was gone.

Max searched the closet and drawers. Hailee's clothes, laptop, and cosmetics were missing. His heart pounded in his chest. He pulled his phone out and dialed.

"Keller."

"I want a BOLO out on Hailee Hollister."

"What for?"

"She's a witness to a murder, and she's missing. Do it now." Max swore under his breath and threw the phone down on the bed.

He went downstairs and paced back and forth. How did Hailee get the gates open? He hurried to the kitchen, opened the knife drawer, and reached back. The remote was still there. He rubbed his neck. Damn...

*****

Hailee exited the plane, walked through the tunnel, and scanned the area near the gates. The Denver International Airport had a steady stream of travelers heading to the gates and gift shops. Hailee searched the area again; she caught a glimpse of pink and knew Kat was nearby. Kat stood patiently in the Starbucks line. Hailee walked up behind her and asked, "Is there room for me?"

Kat spun around, wrapped her arms tightly around Hailee, and squeezed. She shook her head disapprovingly. "I was getting worried. You're never late."

"Well, I wasn't flying the plane, so..."

Kat flicked her tongue over her teeth. "You look good. Your clothes need a serious overhaul. How's Max? Is he still yummy?"

She hesitated. "He's fine."

Kat waved a disapproving finger at her. "Oh no, you didn't. You left without a word. What's wrong with you? How will you hold on to him if you take off like that?"

Hailee stopped to order a caramel cappuccino. "He doesn't understand what a pain Rex can be. I had to do it this way." She paid and moved away from the counter.

"He seems reasonable to me."

"It's complicated."

"What's so difficult? He's hot. You're single—"

"But—"

"Don't go there. Stop dwelling on Rex and your past."

"Did you bring my car?"

"You mean my Corvette." Kat smiled smugly.

"That's right. You earned it."

They exited and headed toward the short-term parking. Kat glided over to her new red convertible. Her olive, sun-kissed skin shimmered against her waist-length, carnation-pink hair. She waved her bejeweled, razor-sharp stiletto nails toward the car and asked, "Where to?"

Hailee threw in an overnight bag in the back. "Tony's. I'm starved. After lunch, I'll bite the bullet and see Rex. Maybe I'll be able to smooth his ruffled feathers until Carl can get me out of my contract."

Kat offered her a gentle smile and glanced to her right before punching down on the gas.

It felt good to be back. Hailee closed her eyes, leaned back against the seat, and let the brisk wind whip through her curls. Her stomach tightened when she thought of Max; he would be mad. Maybe he would even miss her a little. No time to think about that now. She had to divert disaster by speaking with Rex, or there would be hell to pay.

Tony's was crowded as usual. They slipped in unnoticed, and the wall separating the dining rooms kept them from prying eyes. Tony's, the best Italian food in town, known for its fresh ingredients and unique sauces, had always hit the spot, yet still somehow paled in comparison to Sophia's, Max's mother's, cooking. Maybe it was her spunky attitude and 'hot' son that evoked memories of—

Hailee sighed and moved the last piece of grilled chicken around the plate.

Kat eyed her and said, "Don't stuff yourself, girl; you have to stay fit for your new man."

"I don't think he's mine. We've just hooked up a few times; his mother is great, except for her one-track mind, getting Max married off to a nice girl. Besides, he doesn't have time for anyone or anything except his career. He has an important job, and I'm just a welcome distraction."

Hailee shifted nervously in her seat and stared out the passenger window as they drove to Rex's office.

"Do you want me to come in with you?" Kat asked.

Being in the same room with Rex gave Kat hives. This was Hailee's bittersweet comeuppance, and she would have to bear it alone. "That's sweet, but no."

Kat pulled into the front parking lot of Chandler Literary Agency and came to a stop. Hailee grabbed her purse and gave Kat a wistful glance. Kat smiled reassuringly.

"Call me in exactly thirty minutes, and if I'm not out in four minutes, start honking the horn and call me again."

Kat flipped open the vanity mirror, pushed back a stray hair, and nodded. "You go, girl." She gave Hailee a thumbs-up and floored it.

Hailee brushed invisible lint off her floor-length skirt and played with the suffocating collar of her long-sleeve blouse. She tucked a stray curl behind her ear and ran her hand over her tight spinster chignon. Her cheeks were darkened with rouge; her eyeliner and eye shadow were a metallic blue. She had caked on her foundation, and her fingernails were adorned with fluorescent lime-green polish. She walked past the receptionist and headed straight for the elevator. Hailee hit the button and braced herself for the worst. Max did his best to ward off Rex and his attempts to get her to come back early. One can't fight fate. She must face Rex. If anyone intercedes, Rex would know that her secret was out.

Every day, Hailee suffered the shame of her questionable parentage. Hailee had convinced herself that if her parents exhibited immoral behavior that led to her conception, that somehow diminished her worth as a person, as a woman. It had been one of the reasons she waited so long to have sex. This was her destiny: to pay for the sins of her parents or pay the ultimate price. Her parents weren't the only ones who had committed sins. Hailee's attorney claimed she did nothing illegal. Lying is wrong; she lied, and now she must suffer the consequences: the total annihilation of her career and her life.

She knocked on Rex's door and swallowed hard. He should be surprised; she had that going for her.

"What?"

She squared her shoulders and kept her eyes on the ground. She walked in.

Rex slammed the phone down, crossed the room in three giant strides, and engulfed her in an awkward and unwanted hug.

"Hailee, it's so good to see you. I've been worried sick. Come sit down."

She twisted out of his grip and sat across from him. She crossed her legs and sat tall in the chair.

"How did you get free from that horrible Max Toliver?"

At Max's name, her chest tightened, and butterflies danced in her stomach.

"I," she stopped and looked down at her lap. She had to pull herself together, or Rex might pick up on her emotional vibe and contribute it to Max. She took a breath. "I convinced Detective Toliver that I had to resume the book tour. I did promise him that I would be able to testify anytime he needed me." She lied. *Oh, how easy it was. She was just like her mother.*

Rex left his chair and knelt beside her. "Oh, Hailee, my love. When I heard you were in danger, I rushed over there. That Neanderthal, Toliver, wouldn't let me see you or tell me where you were. I'm sorry. I tried."

He revolted her, and she wanted to hurl.

"Rex, I was being protected by the police."

"You were hurt and went to the hospital."

Exasperated, Hailee blew out a long, heavy breath. "I had to do something. I ended up with a bruise or two." Tears welled up in her eyes; she couldn't stop them. "A girl had been brutally stabbed and then died."

Even though the pain went deep, Hailee didn't want to show weakness in front of Rex. She wiped away the tears and continued. "I'm back now. Kat told me you are pushing for more dates for this stretch of the tour. I can't do it. I'm not ready for more work given what's happened. I won't cancel any dates. However, I don't want you scheduling any more." She stopped and looked him in the eye, a scowl hovering on her lips.

He walked back to his desk and took his seat. "I understand. I'd hoped to capitalize on the tour to generate more sales. They're looking a little sluggish."

"Are you kidding me? I checked last week's sales, and they have skyrocketed. The sales have tripled since the photos of me at the hospital were released. So don't try to feed me a line of bull, Rex. I won't stand for it."

"I need you here."

"Cut the crap." She knew she shouldn't push Rex. She had had it with his bullying tactics. She shifted in her seat. Her phone rang; she jumped to her feet.

"I'm on my way," Hailee said, then hung up. "I'm tired, and I have to go." She grabbed her purse, took a few steps, and reached for the doorknob.

"Hailey, I'm glad you're home and safe; it's not enough. We need to talk about the future, our future."

She stopped but refused to face him. "Not now, Rex."

"When?"

She whipped around. "When I'm good and ready, that's when."

She shut the door and hurried out of the building. As promised, Kat waited by the front entrance. She buckled up and glanced at her friend, "How's the car working for you?"

Kat's smile lit up the darkened sky.

"You earned it. Anyone who has to put up with Rex deserves something special."

"Did he give you some dribble about how worried he was?"

"Yes. Rex blubbered on about how much he missed me and how scared he was. He hated that he didn't have complete control, and it annoyed the hell out of him."

"Well, better you than me. I've had all I can take of Rex." Kat eyed her. "Did the outfit and that glob of makeup work?'

"Like a dream." She leaned back into the seat and enjoyed the cool breeze.

"When will we be free of him?"

"Soon. I hope."

Chapter 13

The following day at the office, Max snapped at everyone. Hailee had left without a word. His work didn't allow for long-term relationships, and he had, until now, accepted that. Not only had Hailee captured his complete and undivided attention, but she had witnessed a murder. She was his only witness. He would use that to get her back. First, he had to find the fiend killing women on his watch.

Max stared at the files of the three dead women. His stomach turned. Did he have a serial killer on the loose, slaughtering young women? Were there enough similarities? Hailee thought there might be, and she didn't have all the information. The MO differed in each case. A nagging feeling gripped him tight. What type of person was he dealing with, a psychopath or a sociopath? Psychopaths lacked remorse and were skilled manipulators. They were methodical and calculated in planning their crimes. Sociopaths were erratic and more emotionally volatile, and were capable of experiencing some remorse. Both were extremely dangerous. Did the murders have enough in common, and if they did, what type of serial killer was he dealing with?

Max dialed.

"Hall."

"Jake, it's Max Toliver. How are you?"

"Better than you, my friend."

"That's why I'm calling. I hate to admit it. I could use backup and fast."

"What can I do for you?"

"I have a lunatic running through my town killing young women."

"What do you have so far?"

"The TOD, age, blood type, and murder location are the same. They all come from similar backgrounds, upper middle class, none of them were sexually assaulted, and they were all slain violently with different weapons."

"Any suspects or leads?" Jake asked.

"No, and my only witness bolted."

"Ah, the writer. Has the BOLO located her?"

"Not yet. Miss Hollister seems to be flying under the radar. I'm checking the obvious. She has a few places she calls home, so finding her is just a matter of time."

"Kind of risky putting out a BOLO on her, don't you think?"

"She's a material witness. I need her back here."

"I'll call my friend at NCIC and see if he can come up with any hits. He owes me a favor and can get what you need ASAP." Jake paused. "'…But have I not heard you say often that to solve a case a man has only to lie back in his chair and think?'"

"I've never said that." Max glanced down at the files and shook his head. "Oh, for Pete's sake, is that a quote from another movie?"

Jake laughed. "No, it's from *Murder on the Orient Express* by Agatha Christie. Don't you read?"

"Not unless it has to do with a case or new procedures. Besides, that's a really old book."

"It's a classic. This particular book is filled with suspense, red herrings, and intrigue. I highly recommend it."

"Maybe I'll read it after this case is solved, and then, oh yeah, after the next one."

"It could make you a better detective."

"What I need is some information from the NCIC and a prayer so that no one else gets killed."

"I'll have my friend put a rush on it. If anything is out there, he'll find it. Good luck, Max. If you need anything else, call. When this is over, we should get together and chill out for a little while."

"Thanks, Jake. We'll do that."

Max felt a little better; Jake has always come through for him. Still, none of the murder weapons have been found yet. What type of weapon did the perpetrator use, and where did he hide them? Hailee felt sure the person who attacked the third victim was female. Most serial killers are male in their late twenties to early thirties, from the lower to middle class, and come from broken homes. Are there two of them? Are they working together?

Max opened the first victim's file, reread the crime scene report, and re-examined the photos. He knew the pictures held the answer; he just had to find it. His pulse quickened; Max saw something. He checked the second and third files.

He rang the intercom. "Get in here."

Keller knocked and went in. He sat across from Max and waited.

"I've found something interesting in the vics' files; something else links them together." Max handed Keller the files. "I don't know how we missed it."

Keller read the first, the second, and the third. "I don't see it."

"Look closely at the pics, where the vics' bodies were found. What do you see?"

Keller studied the photos one by one.

"Water stains?"

Max nodded, "Weapons made of ice. That's why we haven't found any of them. Now we have something to go on other than the hotel and the vics' stats. This is our first big break."

Keller handed the files back to Max, "Is it possible for ice to stay hard enough to kill or decapitate?"

"I've done some reading on it and have seen some websites where you can make ice daggers; if done correctly, it's a long process. I don't know what damage they can do or how effective they are. It doesn't seem probable, but it's our only lead on the weapons."

"I'll look into ice sculpting companies, ice manufacturers, their customers, and employees."

"When you brought in Simon, the kid from the ice company, did you process him?" Max asked.

"Yeah, he submitted voluntarily. Come to think of it, he remained calm the whole time and chatted me up like we were best buds. I ran his prints. They were clean."

"Keep an eye out for him; right now, he's the only one we know of with a connection to ice," Max said, studying the photos again. "I called my friend Jake, who is contacting a friend at NCIC. We should have an answer later today or early tomorrow. I don't want anyone else getting killed."

"Have you heard anything about Miss Hollister?"

"No, I'm still looking."

Keller went back to his office.

The quote that Jake previously cited haunted Max '...To solve a case a man has only to lie back in his chair and think.'

Max had always kept his distance and maintained a clear head. A possible serial killer and accomplice were on the loose, and Hailee might be in danger and couldn't be found. He closed his eyes and leaned back in his chair. He tried to concentrate on the new lead. If they can find at least one person who knew the victims or had reason to harm them, it would be a step in the right direction. Thankfully, no one else had been murdered in the past couple of days.

A loud rapping on his door pulled him from his thoughts. "Come in."

A blond man of average height, in his late thirties, with a faux tan and adult, clear braces, hovered near the door. "My name is Dr. Alfred Swisher. I'm here about the murders."

The doctor looked familiar. "Please sit down." Max pulled out his notepad and his recorder. He nodded towards the doctor. "Do you mind if I record this?"

The doctor looked toward the door and back. He shook his head no.

The doctor looked familiar because Hailee had described him so well.

"Why did you wait so long to come forward?"

He stared at his shoes and wiped the sweat from his brow. "I'm married, and my wife freaked out when my patients started dying. I didn't want to upset her by coming in."

"Ashley Thomas was your patient?"

"Yes, a surgery patient."

"What kind of surgery did she need?"

"An eye and brow lift and a nose job."

"Plastic surgery? Why would she need work done?"

"Her mother and I are old college friends, and I did some work for her. When her daughter complained about a few issues, she sent her to me."

"Did she really need plastic surgery?"

"I didn't feel that she needed any; she inherited her mother's good looks and strong bones; even so, Ashley refused to listen."

"The room where Miss Thomas was murdered, is it registered to you?"

"Yes, I own a small, natural cosmetics company; I listed it under my company name. I didn't want my wife to find out."

"There were no signs of sexual activity found; are you telling me you two had sex?"

"Even though I wanted to, Ashley wasn't into me; I felt a little guilty, knowing her mom and all. So, I let her stay in the room and went home to my wife."

"Do you have any information on the other two girls?"

"They were my patients, too. And it scares the crap out of me. All of them were murdered the night before they were scheduled to have surgery."

The link. Max's face turned red, and his eyes narrowed. "Why the hell didn't you come in after the second girl died, after you knew they might be connected?"

"I told you. My wife freaked out, and I was scared out of my mind."

"We may have been able to save the third girl if you had spoken up. Did you ever think about that?" His voice held no hint of compassion.

"No…"

Max balled his fist; it took every ounce of restraint not to pop the guy in the face.

The intercom interrupted him. "Not now, Erma."

"Max, it's Miss Hollister."

"I want to see the files on all three girls. I want them tomorrow," he stood up and glared at the perspiring man across from his desk. "I'm not done with you."

The doctor nodded and hurried out.

Max picked up the receiver. "Hailee, where are you?"

"Hailee, are you there?"

"Hello, Max."

"Are you alright? Where are you?"

"I'm sorry."

"Tell me where you are. I'll come get you."

"No. You don't need me there to distract you."

"You're a witness; you need my protection."

"I'm home, and I'm safe. Kat is here with me. We'll be fine."

"Is Rex there?"

No answer.

"Hailee, is he?"

"We can handle Rex. You need to find the one who killed those girls. I just wanted to let you know I'm okay."

"Don't go. I need—" Max stared at the receiver; the dial tone echoed in his ear.

He grabbed his jacket, slammed the door, and hurried out. Walking past Erma's desk, Max didn't hear her calling for him. He had to get out. Clear his head. Maybe Hailee was a hindrance.

Max jumped on the back roads and headed west out of town.

He had no destination in mind; he kept driving and drove for hours. Hailee's celebrity status made her an easy target. She could be the next victim, if not from a lunatic, butchering young women, from Rex. Hailee shook every time Rex's name was mentioned. What had she done? He can't believe she did anything that would warrant blackmail. Her fans loved her, and her friend, Kat, showed fierce loyalty and protectiveness. He wanted to dig deeper, and he would when he got the time.

He dialed Jake.

"Do you know what time it is?" Jake yawned.

"Ten o'clock."

"Not here, it's one."

"Sorry, Jake. I've had an important break in the case, and I wanted to update you so you can call your friend at the NCIC."

"What kind of break?"

"All three vics were patients of the same plastic surgeon, Dr. Alfred Swisher. And they were all murdered the night before having surgery. I'm having the doc bring in the vic's files tomorrow."

"You think it might be another patient or someone who works at the office?"

"Or maybe the doc's wife got tired of him sleeping with his patients. It's too early to tell. I also came across an interesting piece of evidence. In the crime scene photos, there were large water stains at all of the scenes—"

"Water stains?"

"Two of them were in the rooms with the vics, and the third was down the hall near the exit stairs. I need to find a weapon. I have to stop this creep before someone else gets killed."

"Do you think the author is in danger? She is your *only witness*."

Max's stomach contracted painfully. "I don't know."

It's crunch time, and his father might have been right. What if he couldn't keep his friends and family out of harm's way? Law enforcement can be a dangerous and stressful profession. Maybe he should've taken the easy route, taken over and managed his father's businesses, and been stuck in a room with expensive furniture and cigars with stuffy, greedy CEOs? If he couldn't protect Hailee, he would have failed, which would be his ultimate failure for him, her, and his father.

"She's going to be an easy target. Everyone saw the shots of her at the hospital, and I hear her fan response was overwhelming; if they saw it, so did the perp."

Max squeezed the steering wheel tight. "Call your friend, give him the update, and see if anyone in the database has medical experience or a similar MO. I need the information ASAP."

"You've got it," Jake yawned again, "did I tell you about the movie I just saw—"

"Just get me the information." Max hung up.

Chapter 14

At home, Max paced around; he never really noticed how empty it was. Hailee had been the first woman he had invited to his home. Now that she was gone, the deafening silence grated on his last frayed nerve. He stripped off his clothes and slid under the covers. He could still smell her, still feel her. He tossed and turned. His concern turned into an unfulfilled desire. He could deal with that.

He woke at seven, showered, grabbed some coffee, and headed out the door. His cell phone rang.

"Toliver."

"Hey, Max, it's Jake. Sam had a couple of hits from the database; I'm faxing them. They should be at your office when you get there."

"Any leads?"

"There are a couple of repeat offenders with medical training or connections, though I'm not sure how it fits into your case. It's a start."

"I should have the vics' medical files today; I hope I'll find a viable lead. Thanks again, Jake."

"Do you know why blondes make the best victims?"

"What?"

"'They're like virgin snow that shows up the bloody footprints' and 'there is no terror in the bang, only in the anticipation of it.'"

"What movie is that from?"

"They are quotes from the late, great Alfred Hitchcock."

"Goodbye, Jake."

Max headed toward his office. Erma held the receiver to her shoulder and flagged him down. He waited by her desk, and she put her call on hold.

"You have a visitor."

"Dr. Swisher?"

She frowned. "Mr. Chandler."

Great, just what he needed. He breathed in a long, slow breath. He had to stay calm and not throttle Rex. He pushed open the door. Rex spoke quietly into his cell phone and looked out the window. Max slammed the door shut. Startled, Rex looked up.

"Mr. Chandler, I don't mean to be rude," his jaw twitched. "I'm working on a murder case. What do you want?"

"I want to know what you did to my Hailee."

"Your Hailee?"

"Yes, Miss Hollister. She came to my office yesterday. She looks terrible. And she's scared. Tell me what happened to her."

He clenched his hands. "I assure you, Mr. Chandler, we took exceptional care of her. She witnessed a murder that would frighten anyone."

"There has to be something else. I can feel it."

"Have you witnessed a crime or someone being killed?"

"Well, no, but—"

"Then you don't know what she's going through. She risked her life to save another, and you come here while I'm trying to apprehend the murderer and waste my time. Get out!" Max stood up. His entire body shook.

"I never—"

"Get out and don't come back."

Rex shuddered, exited, and closed the door behind him.

Max dialed Erma.

"That man is not welcome here. Keep him out of my office." He slammed the phone down.

Max stared at the phone; his pulse returned to normal. He picked up the receiver, "Did Mr. Chandler leave his card?"

"Yes."

"Bring it to me."

He didn't need this complication. His door opened, and Erma poked her head in. Max waved her in. She gave him Mr. Chandler's card and Jake's fax. He nodded, and she left.

He thought about ripping the card to pieces, but instead, he shoved it into his wallet. Then he reviewed the NCIC data, cross-referenced it with evidence from the crime scenes and information from his interviews, and picked up the receiver.

"Has Dr. Swisher called?"

"No, do you want me to call him," Keller asked?

"Yes, thanks."

He continued studying the fax; something wasn't right about this whole bloody mess.

The door flew open; Keller burst in. Max looked up.

"Another DB has been called in."

Max's throat tightened. "Another woman?"

"No, the doctor."

"Where?"

"His head nurse found him in the patient's file room at his office."

"Damn. The doc pulled the files I requested and was murdered for them. Get a warrant for the doc's patients' files and his employees' records. I want to search all of the employees' homes and cars. Once the warrant has been issued, have the guys rip apart the doc's office, home, and his cosmetic company's files."

Keller nodded and left. Max put the files and the NCIC fax into his drawer and locked it. He stopped by Erma's desk, and she gave him the doctor's office address.

Max sped away.

Max reached Swisher's office, signed in on the crime scene log, and put on his gloves. He followed the voices to the file room, where he found Detective Phillips.

Detective Phillips waited for the Medical Examiner to clear the body to be moved and watched as her team processed the scene. She looked up when she heard her name.

"Toliver, what took you so long?"

"I had an unexpected visitor. What happened?"

"It looks like the perp came in, stabbed the vic in the right kidney and the neck–hitting the jugular, and the doc bled out. The poor guy didn't even see it coming."

"Did you find the weapon?"

"Not yet."

"Did you find a water stain near the vic?"

"Water stains? No."

"Were any of the files taken? Is anything missing?"

"Keller called to see if the files on the murdered girls were still here. It looks like they're gone. We don't know if the perp took them or if they're just misplaced. We're still looking."

Max shook his head, "Damn."

"What?"

"I instructed the vic to come to my office this morning with the files, and now he's dead. My first real lead in the case, and now it's gone."

"Tough break."

"Yeah."

Max left the file room to speak to the nurse who found the body. She appeared anxious and had little information to share. He gave her his card and asked all the employees to call his office upon arrival.

The CSU team processed the scene, and Max waited in the hallway to see if anything jumped out or if they found anything to indicate that other files were missing. He didn't want any more patients to die. His phone rang; he looked at the number and answered.

"Not now."

"*Figlio*, don't be mad," Sophia pleaded.

"You let Hailee leave, and now I can't find her."

His mother's sobs muffled her words, "I'm so sorry. What have I done?"

He blew out a tired breath, "Don't cry. I'll find Hailee."

"It's all my fault."

"Do you know where she went?"

"She said she wanted to go home. How could I not help her?"

"Did she say where home is?"

"She was upset about meeting a man. What have I done?"

"Please try to remember. Did Hailee go home where she grew up or home where she lives now?"

"Her home now. I think."

"Did she say where that was?"

"She wanted to leave. I kept thinking she was leaving my son and that she was happy. You are a good man, a loving man. Why would she leave?"

"I have to go."

Max drove straight to headquarters, his mind whirling with the latest developments. Was the alleged, elusive witness a member of the doctor's team or a frightened patient? Why did she call to meet, then disappear the same night that the third victim died? Did someone target the doctor or his patients?

Max had Erma hold his calls. He studied each file and compared it to the data on the fax. The second look didn't reveal anything new. Now, the doctor was dead, and Max had no viable leads.

He called Keller to get an update on the search warrants. Keller told him he was waiting for the judge to sign off on them and should have them by morning. Max picked up the receiver and dialed Tom Wilson.

Tom, a retired police detective and good friend, owned a private investigation firm and enjoyed his semi-retirement and new financial stability. Tom had been Max's first partner; he taught Max everything that the academy didn't, the things that made him a better cop and kept him alive. Max waited for Tom to pick up.

"Toliver," Tom asked?

"Yeah. How's your knee?"

"My knee's doing better than your case."

"It's not as cut and dry as one would think."

"How so?"

"All the vics have a connection to the same plastic surgeon. However, they don't have a connection to each other. They were all young and beautiful, and they all died on the eve of their surgeries. They all died at the same hotel, and they all had different reasons for being there."

"What about the weapon or motives?"

"That's all I have so far. That's why I'm calling. I need your advice."

"Sounds like it."

Max laughed. Tom said he would always be the better cop, smarter and faster than anyone on the street. "I need your help on a personal matter."

"You have a personal life, since when?" Tom asked.

"It's complicated."

"It always is. What do you need me to do?"

"I need you to locate an eyewitness to one of the murders. She left town without notifying me and won't answer her phone."

"I thought you said this was personal."

Max knew how it would sound. "It is."

"Damn it, Toliver. I taught you better than that. What the hell is wrong with you? Are you willing to jeopardize the case to sleep with some broad?"

124

"It's not like that. Besides, I slept with Hailee before the first woman died."

"Is that supposed to make it okay? Once she became a witness, you should have backed off."

Max knew Tom would be mad and disappointed. Tom had spent their time together teaching him how to be the best and to stay on top. "I tried to protect her. The perp can ID her; she might be next to die."

"Did she leave because she was scared or because of you?"

Tom always asked the tough questions—ones you dreaded and knew he'd ask. They made you think and get your act together. "Both."

"I'll find her, and when I do, I'm going to be the one to keep her safe until you close the case. And Toliver, you know the drill. It's a need-to-know basis."

"And I don't need to know."

"That's right."

Tom's annoyance didn't surprise Max. Tom had always been a straight arrow, always by the book. And until now, so was Max. Hailee came into his life and turned it upside down. Max didn't want or need any attachments or distractions. He had one priority: to apprehend the one preying on young women and stealing their futures.

Max's stomach grumbled. Times like these forced him to strike a balance between work and health. If he didn't watch it, the case would run him into the ground, and he would lose momentum and focus. On his way home, he stopped by Sal's Deli and picked up a Reuben sandwich and Sal's famous garlic onion rings.

At home, he walked up to the black double-entry wrought iron door and had to squash the flurry of emotions that had flooded him since Hailee had left. He lived alone and enjoyed it. After spending just a few days with Hailee, he became acutely aware that he needed more.

Max cracked open a domestic beer and flipped through the news channels. A local reporter recapped the news about the gruesome Meridian Hotel murders. As the reporter spoke, he flashed his perfectly white and straight teeth. The sparkle in his eye made Max's stomach turn. Don Henley's song *Dirty Laundry* came to mind. Either the reporter enjoyed acting or relished in other people's pain. Max shook his head; he started to think like Jake, constantly comparing real life to some form of entertainment. Max finished his beer, tossed the remote onto the cushion, and headed upstairs.

Max lay in bed and wondered what kind of maniac would brutally mutilate a young woman. None of the victims were sexually assaulted, and the only injuries they sustained were fatal ones. Even though the third victim fought back, there were no other injuries other than the stab wounds and the attempted removal of her breast. What kind of psycho would try to remove a woman's breast? Was she stabbed to subdue her, or did she get stabbed because she fought back? There were no drugs found in the victims, so other than the first victim, who died instantly with one powerful blow, they all suffered intense pain and terror before they died. The perpetrator grew more confident with each kill and became increasingly deviant. How does the perp that Hailee fought fit into this? Was she the mastermind behind all of this or a willing accomplice? Max's questions swirled around in his head.

The beer did nothing to relax him. He padded down to the kitchen, popped open another one, and headed back upstairs. He checked his phone. Damn, he missed a call. Adrenaline pulsed through his veins as he listened to the voicemail. His mother invited him to a family dinner at the restaurant. He checked the time; he could still make it if he wanted to. His family would still be there until two in the morning. He put the phone down by his Glock. He hated being angry at his mother for putting Hailee in danger.

Right now, he didn't want to face his mother's questions or her tears. He leaned back against the headrest and crossed his legs at the ankles. He took a deep breath and gulped down the last of his beer.

The phone shrilled, sending chills down his spine. Max grabbed the phone. He hated this part of the job.

"Toliver."

"I found her."

The line went dead.

Chapter 15

Hailee brushed her hair until it was soft and smooth. She put on her favorite jeans, Levi's straight-leg, and a blue sweater, tucked her spinster outfit in the bottom drawer, and kicked it closed. Hopefully, she won't need that again. She dialed her attorney, Carl Langston, private number.

"Hailee, hold on." Carl covered the mouthpiece and yelled. "Jason let go of the puppy's tail." Hailee heard Jason's giggles and the yelp of a scared puppy. "Jason, go find Mommy."

"Sorry about that. Are you in town?"

"Yes, I arrived yesterday. I went to see Rex."

"I thought we agreed that you wouldn't make any contact with him unless it went through me first. I don't want you doing anything that will jeopardize your case."

"Rex has been harassing a police detective. I had to assure him I would return, or he might have done something I'd regret."

"Hailee, why don't you just come clean. It's not as bad as you think."

"I can't. It'll ruin me. No one likes a liar."

"You'd be surprised how forgiving people can be."

"My whole career is built on a lie. How can I expect my fans ever to trust me again?"

"You think you did something wrong, but you didn't. What you did was all by the book, pardon the pun."

"It might be legal, except it's not ethical. I deceived my readers." Hailee closed her eyes; memories of her mother's sin and betrayal filled her with anguish. "I can't tell the truth now. It's too late. I'll lose what I love most in this world."

"You'll feel better if you confess."

"No." Writing meant everything to her. It saved her from a life of complete and utter despair.

"The kids are out of school today. I'll call you later. Jason. No!" The phone disconnected.

Hailee knew Carl meant well. He didn't fully understand how lies had devastated her life.

She powered up her laptop and checked her emails. Rex sent her fifty of them in the past two weeks, and twenty of them were sent after she met with him. She forwarded them to Carl and filed them in a folder labeled 'creep.' Hailee updated her Facebook and website and answered several panicked messages from her fans. She had tried several times to explain this to Carl, the symbiotic relationship she enjoyed with her fans; they needed her, and she needed them. Her shoulders sagged; how could she have lied to them for so long? Her stomach constricted, mother-like daughter.

She sent Kat a quick email and pulled up her current manuscript. Hailee's fingers hovered over the keys and refused to type. She was too close to it this time. Murder and death took on a whole new meaning. Real people did die horrible and painful deaths. The image of the hotel victim flickered across her mind—a pain shot through her chest. The memory of that night would haunt her forever. The girl fought so hard to stay alive, and although Hailee knew she was not to blame for the girl's death, she wished she had been able to save her.

Hailee couldn't save the girl or her parents. They betrayed her, but didn't deserve to die. Their blood stained her hands. The sounds of The Cranberries' *Animal Instinct* interrupted her self-recrimination.

Hailee answered the phone.

"What's the matter?" Kat blurted out.

"Hey, Kat. What makes you think something's wrong?"

"You know, Rex, Max, and that pathetically desperate email you just sent me."

"Pathetic? I just asked if you wanted to go to dinner."

"It's more than that. You know it, and I know it. Spill."

"I spoke to Carl, and he said I might have jeopardized my case by visiting Rex without telling him. He wants me to come clean," she waited. When Kat didn't respond, "I can't do it. I'll be finished." She glanced down at the screen. "Kat?"

"It's eating you up, and it's why you're manless."

"I can't."

"Forgiveness is for everyone, including the sinner–"

"I'll call you later."

"Wallowing in self-pity isn't doing you any good. Do you want to go to Tony's or maybe somewhere new?" Kat asked.

"I'm not hungry anymore."

Hailee stared at the laptop screen. The words were blurred; she strained harder. She hunched forward and forced her fingers to type. They soared across the keys. She pounded faster and harder. Her bent-up feelings for Rex, Max, and her parents spilled onto the page. She reveled in the freedom. Writing has always been cathartic, and she needed it now more than ever.

As Hailee typed the last word, she held her breath and let it out gradually. A loud, confident knock startled her. Her pulse quickened. Oh, no. Please, not Rex. She peered out the window and breathed a sigh of relief. A tall, mature man in a grey suit stood in her entryway. Since Hailee lived off the main road, she didn't get many visitors or solicitors. She was surprised to see someone at her door. The stranger knocked again, this time louder. She hurried to the front door and waited. Why won't he leave? The knocking grew more insistent, and the doorknob turned. Hailee ran down the hall to her bedroom. She dialed nine-one-one.

"Miss Hollister, don't be frightened. My name is Tom Wilson. I'm a friend of Max Toliver."

Hailee locked her bedroom door and hunched down in the bathroom. The emergency operator took her information and told her to stay on the line.

"Miss Hollister, Max sent me here to keep you safe. I can show you my ID."

Hailee called Max's private line; he picked up on the first ring."

"Hailee, I'm so glad—"

She whispered, "Max, there's a strange man outside my door—"

"Call nine-one-one."

"I did. The police are on their way. He says he knows you."

"The man at the door?"

"Yes, he's a tall, older guy wearing a gray suit. His name is Tom. Did you send him?"

"Put him on the phone."

"I don't think that's a good idea. He looks mad."

"It's okay. Go get him."

Hailee peeked out the window. The stranger, Tom, was down the path speaking to a patrol officer. She opened the door and stepped out into the entryway. The patrolman and Tom headed toward her. She handed Tom the phone.

"Toliver?"

"You should have called first," Max stated.

"I didn't want her to bolt."

"I should have warned you."

"Thanks for the heads-ups," Tom said sourly, handing Hailee the phone.

"Max, why is he here?"

"I told Tom you might be in danger, so he volunteered to be your bodyguard."

"I don't need one."

"Well, it's a little late for that. Tom's not going to take no for an answer. He's going to keep an eye on you whether you like it or not."

"Tell him no thanks."

"It's out of my hands. You'll be safe. Tom is a retired law enforcement officer."

"Mr. Wilson, I appreciate your efforts and your concern. I don't need or want a bodyguard."

"Miss Hollister, four people are dead—"

"Four?" Hailee let her arm drop to her side; she squeezed the phone.

"Yes, Miss Hollister, a man came forward with some information regarding the Meridian Hotel murders and was killed."

"Max, is that true?"

"Yes," he paused. "Just do as Tom tells you."

Hailee bit back a retort. She didn't like to be told what to do. "It sounds like you need Tom more than I do."

"I can handle the case."

*****

After Hailee hung up with Max, Tom invited himself in. She did her best to convince Tom she didn't need a bodyguard, to no avail. She watched Tom's hands move in unison as he pieced together his phone and surveillance equipment; he closed his steel case, checked, and secured the doors and windows.

"Is this really necessary," Hailee asked?

"Yes."

"I don't understand why it's important to secure my house. I'm leaving in three days to resume my book tour."

"If things get dangerous, we need a home base. We're coming—"

"We?'

"Yes."

"You're going with me on tour?"

"Yes."

"Wait a minute. I don't want you to upset my fans, and I don't want them to be in danger."

"Cancel it."

"I won't."

"Your choice."

Hailee blew out a loud breath. "We need to set some ground rules."

"Yes."

"If you must come, I want you to be invisible—"

"Or…you do what I tell you to do when I tell you to do it."

"Seriously?"

"Yes."

Hailee's mouth dropped open. She watched Tom stash his equipment case in the coat closet, unpack his duffel bag, and spread blankets on the sofa. Although he looked like he'd been doing it a while, his speed and efficiency surprised her. He laid out his laptop and electronic gadgets on the coffee table.

Tom glanced up and asked, "Do you have any coffee?"

"No." Hailee hurried to the bedroom and locked the door. She dialed and spoke in a low tone. "Carl, it's Hailee."

"Why are you whispering? What's wrong?"

"One of Max's old cronies is in my living room. He has decided to be my protector whether I want him to or not. How do I get rid of him?"

"Stay put and call the police."

"I did. The two officers who were here left because their captain vouched for him, so they didn't do anything."

"Did Max send him? Are you in danger?"

"There was another murder. No threat has been made against me that I know of."

"Maybe it wouldn't hurt to let him tag along for a while."

"My fans have been through enough. The bloody pictures of me at the hospital were horrific and really upset them. I don't want Tom around, causing my fans unnecessary grief."

"People are dying. I'm sure your fans want you to be safe."

"He wants to go on tour with me. That's absurd."

"Hang in there—oh, damn. I have to go. Stay away from Rex."

A knock on the door, a quick swooshing sound, and a low moan jolted Hailee into action. She ran into the living room to see Kat against the wall, hands behind her back.

"Let her go!"

Tom released his grip.

Kat rubbed her wrists.

Kat glanced toward Tom and back to Hailee. "Who's the goon?"

They glared at Tom.

"He's Max's friend from the police department."

"Are you in danger?"

"I don't think so; I guess they do."

Hailee waved to Kat, urging her to follow. Kat stopped in the bedroom door jamb, and Hailee yanked her all the way in and closed the door.

"What's going on?"

"Tom just showed up, no warning from Max, and he's been barking orders since he arrived."

"So, Max hired him to protect you. See…he cares."

Hailee rolled her eyes. "That's not the point. He doesn't think I can take care of myself. Either he believes my life is in danger and the killer might be after me, or that I can't handle Rex, or both."

"Just tell Max. He'll understand. Your fans will understand. You are not to blame for what happened to your parents."

Hailee whispered, "Yes, I was."

"There's nothing you can do about that now. Stop pouting and tell me about the prehistoric brute. Is he as old as he looks?"

"I'm not sure how old he is; I know he's older than Max. Besides, you're nineteen; everybody looks old to you."

Hailee went to the door and shook the handle. Tom was here to keep her safe, but who would protect her from his zealousness?

"What," Hailee asked?

"I asked you again about the caveman in your living room."

"Oh yeah, Tom and Max worked together on the force. Tom retired a few years ago and started his own security business. Max told me he's a good guy and will keep me safe."

Hailee waited at the end of the bed. Kat plopped down beside her and put her arm around Hailee's shoulders.

They sat in silence.

Hailee wondered how she would work this out and keep her fans safe.

A loud rap on the door startled them.

"Miss Hollister, we need to go over your tour schedule."

Hailee opened the door, "Can't we go over it in the morning?"

"It needs to be done now."

Hailee led the way. They entered the living room and sat together on the couch. They stared at Tom and waited.

"Your friend isn't invited."

"She stays. Besides, she knows more about my schedule than I do."

"Fine. What's your full name and address?"

"Why?" Kat asked.

"I need to check you out; if you don't pass, you're out."

"Fine. My name is Catalina Sanchez, and I live at 4389 E. Hershey Street, Ashland."

"How did you meet Miss Hollister?"

"We met five years ago at a Portland bakery."

"Are you employed by Miss Hollister?'

"Yes, I'm her executive assistant *and*," Kat said, flicking her wrist upward, "wonder girl extraordinaire."

Tom glared at Kat, "What exactly do you do for Miss Hollister?"

"Anything and everything."

Tom tapped his pen on his notepad.

"I book her signings, make hotel and airline reservations, watch her house and cars when she's out of town, monitor her website and emails—"

"You check her emails? Do you ever respond on her behalf?"

"I just make sure she's not getting bombarded with spam or receiving threatening emails."

Hailee glared at Kat.

Kat continued. "I never respond unless she tells me to."

Tom leaned forward. "Has she received any threatening or strange emails lately since the murders began?"

"Well… There has been—"

"Kat, no!"

Tom put his pad down. "Miss Sanchez, tell me about the emails."

"Kat, don't. My emails are private, and my attorney has advised me not to divulge their contents to anyone."

"Miss Hollister, I can't protect you if you don't tell me everything."

"Forget it. I don't want your protection anyway. My emails have nothing to do with the murders," Hailee's eyes narrowed, and she glared at Tom. "And don't think for one minute that you can intimidate my friend or me. She'll die before she tells you." She headed toward the kitchen, with Kat following close behind.

"Die?" Kat asked breathlessly.

"I am trying to make a point. I don't want Tom harassing you to get information that you will never give him."

"I shouldn't have mentioned the emails. I'm sorry."

"It's not your fault. Tom's glare is daunting." She put her cup down and gripped Kat's shoulders. "I need you to promise me you won't tell Tom anything. Carl will have my hide if we jeopardize my case at this late stage. He's almost ready to make his move on Rex."

"I won't say anything," Kat promised.

"Good. I need to distract Tom, so he doesn't snoop into my affairs."

Tom entered the kitchen. "So, no coffee?"

Hailee smiled. "I have black or green tea."

"No thanks. Miss Sanchez, I need Miss Hollister's itinerary."

Kat winked at Hailee and headed to the living room. "Sure, I can print it out for you."

Hailee watched from the kitchen. Kat chatted on and on about the tour, her schedule, and the details of the book signings. She didn't miss a beat or give Tom a chance to ask any more embarrassing questions. Hailee had enough to worry about without Tom interfering with Rex.

Hailee slipped by them and into her bedroom. She sent out a couple of emails and decided to make a call. She waited anxiously while the phone rang and rang.

"Yes, my number one fan."

"Carrington. It's so good to hear your voice. How are you?"

"It's good to hear your voice, too. Your abrupt departure had us worried."

"Us?"

"Yes, Alex, poor fellow, was beside himself. Mr. Toliver called and asked if we knew your whereabouts. We were quite shocked to find out you left without saying goodbye."

"I'm sorry. I had to get back to work. I won't do it again. I promise."

"Very good."

"Carrington, um, how is Max?"

"Busy."

Carrington wouldn't tell her more about Max; then again, Carrington had always been the epitome of professionalism and discretion. She counted on his loyalty more than once; he had always come through for her. Hailee cracked open the door; Kat sat uncomfortably close to Tom. Hailee knew she did it on purpose.

She entered the living room; Tom looked relieved. Kat smiled.

"How's it going?"

"We're done."

"Tom, I didn't go over the next tour. After the next eight cities, Hailee only has three weeks to herself, and she's back on the road."

"Maybe later." Tom packed up his laptop and notepads. "What's for dinner?"

Kat threw Hailee a knowing glance. "Sushi."

Chapter 16

With search warrants in hand, Max, Detective Keller, and the forensic team headed to Dr. Swisher's office. While the forensic team searched the filing room and reception area, Max and Keller searched the doctor's private office. Patients' files, surgery schedules, emails, vendor and pharmaceutical company information, and all other pertinent evidence were tagged and bagged. Even with ten people, the office sweep took eight hours. The forensic team left for the lab; Max and Keller returned to the precinct.

Sitting at his desk, Max studied the surgery schedule. He found three new names. None of them fit the killer's MO. They were all older than the victims, and their surgeries were for medical, not cosmetic reasons. And only one of the patients had type O-negative blood. He breathed a sigh of relief. Since the doctor was dead, Max hoped the killings would stop. Max ran his fingers through his hair. Where were the missing files? Max hurried to Keller's office.

Keller sorted the boxes containing the patient files, which were piled shoulder-high. Max made his way past the boxes to Keller's desk.

"Any luck?"

"I'm still sorting them." Keller surveyed the room and shook his head. "Are all these patients potential vics?"

Max's lips pressed into a thin line. "Yes.

Max spent the night in his office. It wasn't the first time he'd done an all-nighter, and it wouldn't be his last. He hoped to come up with a new lead or angle to make his sacrifice worthwhile. He continued to rifle through the evidence seized from the doctor. The surgery calendars, the doctor's day planner and little black book, and the doctor's emails for the last six months yielded nothing new. Max's neck and back ached, and his stomach growled incessantly.

*****

The following morning, Erma knocked and peeked in; Max waved her in. Erma closed the door.

"You look like hell."

"Thanks, Erma, it's wonderful to see you too."

"Well, your morning has just taken a turn for the worse. You have a distraught woman in the lobby demanding to see you. She won't tell me her name and says she's not leaving until she sees you."

"Please bring me some coffee. Make sure it's black and hot. Give me five minutes and bring her back."

Max straightened his shirt and tie, ran his fingers through his unruly hair, put the evidence back in the box, and pushed it under his desk. Erma returned in precisely five minutes, coffee in hand and a flustered woman in tow.

His visitor, a well-dressed and manicured woman in her mid-thirties, thrust her hand at him.

"I'm Doreen Swisher. My husband was murdered yesterday. I want to know what you're doing to find my husband's killer."

Max pulled his hand from hers and waved it toward the chair. "Please have a seat," Max said, "I'm sorry for your loss. I know it must be a great shock, but it's only been one day since he was murdered. We are still gathering evidence and setting up interviews. Rest assured, we will investigate this thoroughly—"

"What does that mean? Are you even trying to solve this case?"

"I know this is an upsetting and frightening situation. We are gathering information—"

"What information?"

"This is an ongoing investigation; I am not at liberty to—"

"If you already gathered evidence, why are there men destroying my home? What are you looking for?" Doreen asked.

"As I said, we are following up on every lead—"

"Am I a suspect?"

"We are checking everyone out."

She huffed and folded her arms across her chest. She squinted, and her lips sagged into a thin frown.

"For us to eliminate someone, we have to investigate everyone."

Her cold stare didn't faze Max; he met her gaze and sipped his coffee.

"This is ridiculous."

"I'm sorry. It has to be done. I need to ask you some questions; they will be personal and possibly upsetting."

Max took another drink. Mrs. Swisher fidgeted in the seat and played with her purse strap.

"Where were you Tuesday night between six and ten?"

"Home alone; I'm sure you already guessed that."

"I had to ask. Just because your husband was at his office doesn't mean you were alone."

"Well, I was."

"How often did your husband stay out late?"

"Two or three times a week."

"Did your husband's work keep him out late?"

"Work," she snickered. "What he did couldn't be called work. He lured young women to sleep with him. He had a love nest at the hotel where the three girls were murdered. Did you know that?"

"Some of these questions may be offensive, but I have to ask."

A tiny laugh rumbled in her throat. "Everyone knew my husband was a man whore, including me."

"If you knew he cheated, why did you stay with him?"

She leaned forward and stared Max in the eye. "Money, and that's why I didn't kill him. All his money and shares in the cosmetic company go to his kids from his first marriage. I get nothing." A smug smile crossed her face, and her eyes twinkled. "Am I in the clear now?"

Max pressed the intercom button. "Erma, bring me more coffee and a bottle of water for Mrs. Swisher. We're going to be here a while."

*****

Max rubbed the base of his neck and his temple. He opened the door and shook his legs. The interview with the doctor's wife took three hours. One minute, she played the grieving wife; the next, she scrambled to find the right words. He knew Mrs. Swisher lied about her relationship with her husband and his money. She had no verifiable alibi; she stayed in and thought the doctor had gone out on one of his trysts. Her demeanor didn't sit well with him; Max had questioned hundreds of victims and persons of interest, most of them stuck to one point of view: the victim or the liar.

Keller knocked and came in. "You look beat. How did it go with the doc's wife?"

"Long and tedious. She's not a good liar and not as innocent as she claims. She's hiding something."

"Did she knock off the doc to get his money?

"Mrs. Swisher says she doesn't get any of it. She said they had an understanding; the doc could screw around discreetly, and she would have full access to a bank account."

"Maybe she stepped out too, and the doc found out. He might have cut off the money."

"The doctor told me he didn't want his wife to find out about his hookups. And that he was afraid she had found out, so he didn't come forward after the second girl died.

"If the wife didn't know, how could they have an arrangement?" Keller asked.

"Exactly."

"I'll check and see if she has any hidden assets."

"We've been at this all day," Max checked his watch, "Go home. We'll start fresh in the morning."

Keller nodded and left. Max put his feet on the desk and reclined back in his chair. He laced his fingers behind his head. He closed his eyes and took several deep breaths. His eyes ached, and his breathing slowed; his chest rose and fell in a slow, rhythmic beat.

*****

Hailee and Tom boarded the plane. Tom stuffed their carry-on bags into the overhead compartment and directed her to take the window seat. She glanced out the window and hoped that takeoff wouldn't be delayed. She watched as the empty seats filled up. There were some perks to having an ex-cop escort her on the tour; check-in had been a breeze, and they were the first to board. She wondered how he managed to pull that off. The plane began its ascent, and she leaned back in the chair. Thankfully, Tom didn't engage in small talk; if he could say it in ten words or less, he did.

Her thoughts whirled. Is she in danger? How would Tom keep her fans safe?

"Miss Hollister."

She met Tom's questioning gaze. "I'm sorry. What did you say?"

"Who picks the locations for the book signings?"

"We base it on sales, and I always try to hit some of the more obscure places so everyone gets a chance to come out and see me."

"Do you revisit the same sites?"

"Sometimes, I like to mix it up. It's mind-numbing seeing the same places over and over."

"Do you go to Portland frequently?"

"Yes, it's not always because of work?"

"What is significant about Portland?"

She shifted to face Tom. "That's private and not relevant?"

Tom met her stare. "I'll be the judge of that."

"I won't let you bully me, Mr. Wilson. If it were work-related, I would tell you. It's not."

"I know you are not happy with me accompanying you, but it's necessary—"

"That's an understatement. I'm surprised you didn't speak to Kat about this."

Tom shifted in his seat. "The less time I spend with her, the better."

"Why is that?

He cleared his throat.

"She is an intelligent, organized, and highly motivated young woman. She is my friend and plays an important role in my writing career. She has pink hair and wears bright, vibrant clothes that best express her individuality. What's wrong with that?"

Tom shrugged. "Pink hair and pink flowered cowboy boots?"

"Do you have something against my friend?"

"No, I just prefer to deal with you directly."

"Yeah, whatever."

"I need the information. I'm not prying."

She blew out an exasperated breath. "After my parents died, I went to live with my Grandmother in

California, and we became inseparable. I had a better relationship with her than with my parents.

"Why the Meridian Hotel?"

"My grandmother and grandfather met there, and that's where he proposed. After my grandfather died, she went there every year on their anniversary. Now that she's dead, I'm keeping up the tradition. It keeps me close to her."

The questions had stopped. Hailee felt sorry for anyone who had to endure his inquisition. Tom found a way to get her to open up. Only Kat knew why she went to Portland. It was private and painful. In times like these, she missed her grandmother even more. She supported and loved Hailee more than her parents ever did. Their carefree and hippie mentality made it difficult to open up to them about her problems. The kids at school teased her mercilessly about her parents' lifestyle and their "free love" philosophy. Hailee's grandmother had repeatedly reminded her that her parents' choices had no bearing on her. It had been up to Hailee to remember who she wanted to be. Her grandmother had constantly given sage advice such as "follow your dreams, but keep your eyes wide open" and "restraint is key to respectability." What would her grandmother say about her tryst with Max after only knowing him for a few hours?

A heavy weight settled on her chest. Hailee couldn't do anything about it now. How would she get past the pain? She killed her parents, and she would, one day, burn in hell for it.

Hailee stared out the window and dreamt of what could have been. She snuck a peek at Tom; he appeared to be engaged in her agenda, or he might be plotting his next round of questions. She wasn't prepared to tell him anything else. The flight to New York had just begun; thankfully, it was nonstop. Hailee hoped Tom would be satisfied with her answers and would focus on the tour rather than her personal life. She extended her legs and crossed them at the ankles. She closed her eyes and drifted off to sleep.

Hailee felt a light tap behind her elbow. She opened her eyes. She watched Tom grab their bags; she squeezed behind him and headed toward the luggage carousel. While they waited, she could feel Tom's breath on her shoulders and his fingers on her waist. He quickly guided her through the airport and out to short-term parking. A tall, husky man in black jeans, a green sweater, and a leather jacket, with his hands crossed in front of him, waited by a grey Honda with dark windows. As they approached, the man opened the trunk. While she slid into the back seat, Tom loaded the luggage. They drove off without incident.

When Hailee traveled, she dressed down and wore no makeup. This made it easier to make her way through town undetected. Her reflection stared back at her; she cringed. Her face and neck were pale, and her characteristically vibrant eyes lacked luster. She had been blessed with a good complexion; still, she needed makeup to add some color. The driver maneuvered deftly through downtown New York City. The cars were backed up bumper-to-bumper. The man appeared unfazed as he whipped the car in and out of the lanes, finding the quickest route to the hotel. Hailee's annoyance with Tom turned to appreciation. He worked with her schedule without disrupting her routine. However, he changed her seat on the airplane to give himself an advantage in the event of an emergency. She sat back and watched the people on the sidewalk hurry to their destinations. They all marched together, as if in unison, and reminded her of ants.

After Hailee checked in, Tom ushered her to a private elevator and her suite. Typically, she never hired a bodyguard; she felt confident in her ability to handle any situation that came her way. An image of the media mob outside the Meridian Hotel flashed across her mind. She

146

could have used a bodyguard then, but everything turned out okay. Hailee wondered how far Tom would go to protect her. Did he have a gun? The man driving may have supplied him with any necessary weapons.

"Miss Hollister, I want to review the procedure for the book signings."

"Procedure?"

"Yes, you have to follow my directions."

"I thought we agreed you'd be as inconspicuous as possible."

"I didn't agree to that." With the itinerary in hand, Tom motioned for her to join him on the couch.

"How many changes did you make to my schedule?"

"None."

"I thought you said we were reviewing the book signing process."

"I did. I didn't say I made changes."

"Then what?"

Tom laid the schedule on the table. "You will have to follow some simple rules."

"How many and how simple?"

"A few. I will walk directly in front of you at all times. Do not stop and speak with anyone until I have cleared them. And pay attention to my hand signals. I may need you to run to a different location."

"I'm not running anywhere."

"I was making a point. Pay attention."

"Anything else?"

"Yes, I will leave you in a safe spot and secure the book signing area."

"Where will you be during the signing," Hailee asked?

"I will be standing a few feet from you—"

Hailee's mouth dropped open, "But—"

"I will be within reach and out of view."

147

"Good. What about my meals and time off?"

"I will go over your free time with you later. I have already made arrangements for our food to be delivered by an old friend."

"This cloak-and-dagger stuff isn't necessary."

Tom placed his shirts and pants in the bottom drawer and hung up his jackets. "I'll be the judge of that."

"I'm not trying to diminish your skill or efforts, but seriously, Tom. It's a little much. My life hasn't even been threatened," she closed his suitcase, forcing him to meet her steady gaze. "Has it?"

"No."

"I feel like I'm walking on eggshells."

"I said pay attention; don't be paranoid."

Hailee's frustration and annoyance with Tom soared. If he interferes with her book signings, there would be hell to pay. She unpacked and organized her makeup and hair accessories. In the vanity's mirror, she could see Tom's reflection; he set up his surveillance equipment. She stared at her face. How different she looked now. The stress must be getting to her. There were dark circles under her eyes, and they were red and puffy. It will take some creative makeup application and a good night's sleep to fix them.

Hailee sat on the couch and asked, "Why are you setting up your equipment here and not in your room?"

"I'm sleeping here."

"No, you're not. Get your own room."

"I have to be here in case of an emergency."

She knew there'd be no negotiating, so she grabbed her phone and dialed.

"Hang up."

Max's phone went straight to voicemail. She dialed again.

Hailee and Tom glared at each other.

"Max is busy. Don't bother him." He reached for her phone.

She backed up. "What makes you think you can tell me who I talk to?"

"I have the right if it involves your safety or Max."

"My personal life is off limits. You have no right to threaten me."

Tom let his hand drop. "I didn't mean to scare you."

"Since you are determined to invade my life, you have to remember it is *my* life."

"Until the murderer is caught, Max is off limits."

"That's my decision."

"No, it's not. Max doesn't need any more distractions, and that includes you."

Chapter 17

Hailee rolled over and covered her ears. The beeping pounded in her head. She dragged her arm out from under the comforter and slapped the clock radio. The noise stopped. She rubbed her neck, and a sharp pain shot between her shoulder blades. She sat up and stared at the wall, adjusting to her new surroundings. It took every ounce of strength Hailee could muster to get out of bed and shower. Her brain hurt, and her eyes stung. The tossing and turning added to her disheveled appearance, and the hot water did nothing to revive her. She cranked the faucet handle and jumped back as freezing water pelted her body. She lifted her chin and let the water hit her face. It worked. A few more minutes of this, and she would be as good as new.

Hailee twisted the handle and pushed the door open. Wrapped only in a towel, she peeked out. She forgot her clothes; it wouldn't usually be an issue, but with her unwanted visitor lurking around, she was trapped. Should she dash out or call out to Tom?

A confident rap interrupted her thoughts.

"Yes."

"I will be outside. You have ten minutes."

Tom shut the door loudly, and Hailee raced to the closet. She chose a red sweater and black slacks. She brushed her teeth and combed her hair. She slid her black ankle boots on as Tom entered. She breathed a sigh of relief. The shower invigorated her mind and body, giving her renewed energy. Her eyes were still puffy, and the dark circles were more predominant than before. Hailee applied concealer and sighed. This could take all day.

Tom had laid out a tray of pastries. Hailee grabbed a light jacket and a Danish. They went down the private elevator to a white Ford. The driver from the airport opened the door; she slid in and finished the sour cream Danish. Hailee brushed away a tiny crumb from her lip. It never ceased to amaze her how city life varied from one city to another. The weather and altitude played a significant role in it. New York City had busy streets and milder temperatures. It seemed natural that the pace would be quicker, almost erratic. The people hurried along, packed together like sardines in a can.

"Tom."

He glanced over the seat.

"Did you bring the extra books that Kat packed for me?"

"Yes."

"I told Carrie from Mysteries Galore we'd be there thirty minutes before they opened."

"I have it covered."

"I have special pens that I use. Did you bring them?"

"Yes."

"What about—"

"Relax."

She plopped back against the leather seat and tamed an unruly curl. They parked in the back, and she waited with the driver as Tom scoped out the bookstore. The driver, an unnerving and vigilant man, stood beside her door, blocking her view. She closed her eyes and prayed Tom wouldn't embarrass her or frighten her fans. This was getting old, and she hadn't signed one book yet.

She stepped out of the car and marched behind Tom. She followed so closely and could have been his shadow. Except he was six feet, and she wasn't. They made their way through the mall and to the employee entrance of Mysteries Galore. Carrie greeted Hailee with a tight hug and a welcoming smile. Hailee couldn't wait to see her fans; their encouraging Facebook posts cheered her up after the hospital disaster.

The first night at the Meridian, she couldn't catch anyone following her. Still, she had an uneasy feeling that someone had been lurking around in the dark. And now she knew somebody had been tracking her and had taken frightening, revealing pictures of her at the hospital. She never wanted anyone to see her like that. The pictures didn't depict what happened that night; they only showed the bloody results. Thankfully, her fans had reached out to her. Their support and concern had eased Hailee's pain; the girl had died, and it left her hollow and remorseful. Hailee squeezed her eyes shut, and the memory of that night vanished. Hailee opened her eyes and took a deep breath. She came here to celebrate with her fans and couldn't be more excited.

To accommodate all of Hailee's devoted fans, Mysteries Galore opened at eight instead of nine. The line wrapped around the top floor and continued onto the first floor. The mall hired more security officers, who worked hard to keep everyone in line and ensure no one hurt themselves. Hailee loved the one-on-one contact; she listened to stories about how her books entertained them and how they were motivated to write by her books. She loved that most, being the catalyst for someone's passion. As usual, and against Tom's advice, she stayed late.

The signing went well; everyone appeared to enjoy visiting with her. They expressed their gratitude that Hailee was safe. She wanted to stay and speak more with Carrie, but Tom bluntly reminded her that the ride from New York City to Albany took almost three hours, and she had to get up at four to make it on time for the signing the following day. Tom's regimen turned out to be more challenging than Kat's regarding her schedule; she didn't think that was possible. The driver from the airport dropped them off at the hotel.

At seven o'clock, Hailee asked Tom about dinner, and he arranged for a light meal to be brought to the room.

After Tom thoroughly inspected her meal, it had stopped resembling food, and Hailee wasn't sure she wanted to eat it. Despite that, she refused to let his overbearing habits ruin her trip and dug in. She plopped down on her bed and fell asleep in her clothes.

The aggravating beeping woke her; Hailee showered and ate an apple for breakfast. She checked her schedule to find the contact's name. Hailee had never been to Albany, and she wanted to make a good impression. A different, tall, husky man picked them up in a tan midsize truck. Although she asked several times, Tom refused to discuss anything about the man or the different vehicles they used. He caved in and told her it was on a need-to-know basis, and she didn't need to know. Hailee grabbed her purse and followed Tom to the elevator.

Although the trip typically took about three hours, they made it in two. Their driver had one goal: get them there fast. While Tom inspected the bookstore, she waited in the truck with the driver. When Tom waved them in, the driver escorted her to Tom's side. Just as she had yesterday, she shadowed him. Once in the bookstore, Hailee introduced herself to Sheila, the office manager. She apologized in advance for Tom's presence and any inconvenience he may cause. Sheila seemed to understand Tom's diligence.

The intimate crowd was just as enthusiastic as the larger New York fan base. A woman in her forties approached the table. Hailee smiled and reached for the book. The woman slammed it on the table. Tom stepped forward and grabbed the woman's arms; she screamed.

Hailee jumped up. "No!"

Tom had the lady bent over and pinned face down on the table. Her whimpers echoed in Hailee's ears.

"Get off her." Hailee tugged on Tom's arms; he loosened his grip. "Tom. Now!" She pulled harder on his muscular arms. "I mean it."

He relented and hovered close by.

Hailee pushed past Tom, reached down, and lifted the lady. The hushed chatter and clicking of camera phones made Hailee sick. She knew this would happen. The woman shrugged off Hailee's hands, reached into her purse, and dabbed at the streaks of brown and red streaming down her face.

"I'm so sorry. Here, let me help you."

With her tissue in hand, she tugged at the hem of her blouse and wiped off the front of her slacks. "Well, I never."

"I am so sorry. Are you okay?"

"I should have known you'd behave like a classless oaf."

Hailee stuttered, "What?"

"I came here to give you a piece of my mind," she said, picking up her copy of *Double Take* and waving it in Hailee's face. "You need to stop printing this garbage."

"Ma'am, I'd gladly give you a full refund if you'd like."

"I don't want my money back. You stole seventy-two hours of my life, and I'll never be able to get it back," she put her hands on her hips and shifted her weight forward. "How do you propose to refund that?"

"I, if you—"

Tom stepped forward, and the woman cringed. "Ma'am, you need to come with me." He gripped her left arm tightly, and the woman tightened her grip on her purse and pulled back.

"I'm not going anywhere with you." She swung her purse at Tom; he ducked. A mall security officer jumped in between them. He said, "That's enough, ma'am. Come with me." He guided her out of the store and down the steps.

As Hailee stared after them, cheers and laughs could be heard at the end of the line. Hailee glared at Tom and walked around the table. Her stomach tightened, and nausea welled up inside her. She blinked several times, plastered on a smile, and waved over the next in line. Methodically, she chatted and signed the books. Even though she had read about violence breaking out at events like this, she never experienced it firsthand. Several times during the day, she rubbed her temple and swallowed the acid creeping up her throat. Was the woman all right? Would they detain and interrogate her?

Hailee glanced at Tom, whose stiff posture and unmoving face indicated his displeasure with the entire process. After she signed the last book, she hurried to the back and begged Sheila for forgiveness.

Sheila laughed it off and said, "Although I feel terrible for what the poor woman went through, I won't lie. The publicity has been great. Some of the kids posted their videos online, and as a result, my sales doubled. So, thank you."

Hailee's eyes narrowed, and her nose crinkled up. How could anyone see a positive side to this?

She grabbed her purse and water bottle and let Tom lead her out the back and to the car. The ride back to the hotel was unbearably tense. Tom had crossed the line, and despite that, she would wait for them to be alone before confronting him. She didn't want anyone, not her fans or Sheila, to overhear what she planned on saying to Tom. After the driver stopped, she jumped out of the car. Tom chased after her.

"Stop."

"No, I've had about all I can take of you for one day." she brushed past him and waited for him in the elevator. "What's wrong with you?"

Tom's stony face didn't flinch. "I'm doing my job."

"Attacking innocent people is your job?"

"She swung at you, and I stopped her."

"She could have been hurt—."

"She wasn't."

"What if she sues me?"

"She won't."

They headed toward their suite. "And what makes you so sure?"

"She wasn't injured, no blood, no bruises."

"Tom, you scared her and embarrassed me." She threw her purse on the couch and headed for the mirror. The dark circles were back.

"She swung at you. I won't apologize."

Hailee whipped around. "She could have been hurt. I could be liable. I don't want my fans to think they'll be attacked if they want me to sign their books."

"Stuff happens."

She shook her head. "So... it was an incident to be swept under the rug, nothing more, nothing less?"

"Yes."

"What about dinner?" Tom asked.

Hailee threw her hands in the air and walked away.

*****

The night dragged on and on. Hailee tossed and turned. Images of the angry bookstore woman dominated her dreams. The dreams ended with her yelling at and firing Tom. If only...

She stayed in bed, and when the alarm went off, she shut it off and shoved it in the nightstand. Loud gurgling noises erupted from her stomach; she rolled over and tried to ignore them. Her hunger pains were getting worse, but she refused to leave the comfort of the bed. The morning sun peeked through the window, and Hailee pulled the comforter over her head. And just when her eyelids covered her eyes and a peaceful, warm feeling surrounded her, she heard Tom's voice. At first, she thought he had come back to ruin her dreams, but she realized Tom was calling her name.

She threw the comforter off and glanced around.

"Miss Hollister, the car's ready."

She stretched her arms above her head. "Car?"

"We're waiting for you."

"Oh, I'm staying here today. I'm tired."

"The driver is scheduled to take you around town."

"It's my day off, and I'm staying put. Tell him I'm sorry."

Hailee pulled the comforter over her head and waited for the door to close. She hurried to the table, grabbed a banana and a small package of cheese crackers, and jumped back into bed.

Hailee wolfed down the snacks and slid under the comforter.

She closed her eyes. A sinking feeling overwhelmed her. The same nagging, nauseating sensation that had consumed her after her parents died. She trusted her instincts; trouble was lurking just around the corner. She drank water, propped her head on her elbow, and stared out the window. She couldn't see the traffic or the people below; all she could see were the light, fluffy clouds sprinkled between the dark, ominous ones. Hailee hoped it would rain; she wanted to enjoy it from the comfort and safety of her suite. Yesterday's events replayed in her mind, and she wondered if she could have done anything differently to change the outcome. A fan, not a fan–an unhappy woman, came to speak her mind, to exercise her right to freedom of speech, and Tom tackled her. Why did Tom have to be so rigid and insensitive?

Sounds from The Cranberries rang out in the room. Hailee ran to her phone.

"Kat, I'm so glad you called."

"What's going on down there?"

"How did you find out?"

"It's all over the internet."

"Oh, no. Shelia mentioned something about that. I didn't realize the scope of it all."

"Well, right now, you are an internet sensation. There have been over four hundred thousand hits in just twenty-four hours. Not bad."

"Kat, this is serious. Tom roughed up a poor woman, and no one cares."

"I'm hurt...You know I care. You and your career are my priority."

"It's not my career I'm worried about; it's my reputation."

"You didn't make the woman do a face plant on the table; Tom, the caveman, did that."

"I'm no saint, and no one knows that better than you, but his actions are a reflection on me." She pushed her hair over her ears and switched sides. "He's not even sorry. He said he did his job, and that's that."

"Like I always say, what's done is done."

"So, how bad is it?" Hailee asked.

"Bad? We've only received positive comments. A lady from your fan club wrote that she has every one of your books and plans to buy the entire collection to support you. She thinks you're great."

"Sheila told me her sales doubled after the video went viral. I bet Rex is jumping for joy. Has he emailed me or left me any threatening messages?"

"No, he emailed twice that he needs to speak with you privately about the future. It's the same old blah blah blah."

"Good. I don't have time to worry about Rex now."

"So, how's the scrumptious Max doing?"

"I've been cut off. Max has more important things to do than talk to me."

"Just because Tom is right doesn't mean it doesn't hurt." Kat surmised.

A lump in her throat made it hard to speak, "I'm not sure how I feel about Max; however, I'm done with Tom ordering me around."

"Girl, you're on your own. I don't want him manhandling me again. My frail and expensive wardrobe won't survive another encounter with Tom."

At the sound of a loud click, she looked toward the door. "I have to go; he's back."

Chapter 18

Max's head bobbed and fell forward. His eyes popped open, and his crossed arms dropped to his side. He blinked several times, and his foot knocked over the empty coffee mug. Obscured by light, his office emitted an eerie glow. He massaged his aching neck. Great, he fell asleep again. He hadn't worked a case with such intensity in a long time. If he had to, he would spend all of his nights here until he captured the monster terrorizing his town. And he didn't want to go home until he knew Hailee was safe.

He turned on the light and the computer, took his mug to the lounge, and made coffee. Max searched the cabinets for a snack, but they were bare. Back in his office, he logged in and opened a browser. He had several people he wanted to check out.

Max started with the doctor's wife, Doreen Swisher. He checked for private bank accounts at home and abroad, looking for unexplained purchases or large transfers. He ran a background check on her educational and social activities before and after she married the doctor. An eruption in his stomach reminded him he hadn't eaten in hours. Max continued his hunt for a possible motive or at least a verifiable contradiction to her statement.

Doreen Swisher came from a modest background in Tennessee. Her father was the CEO of a construction company, and her mother was a retired dialysis nurse. She had no criminal history and no blemishes on her driving record. She had been an average student and a cheerleader. Her father took out a second mortgage on their family home so she could attend Vanderbilt University, where she initially entered the nursing program but dropped out after two years. She worked various odd jobs in Nashville until she secured a position as a certified nursing assistant in a luxury nursing home. She met the doctor while he was visiting his mother.

The doctor's mother passed away two months after Doreen had started working there. Doreen and the doctor were married four months later. Max didn't find anything unusual, except that she lied and turned pale when she spoke about her husband. On paper, she appeared to be clean.

While checking his emails, Max read Jake's email, which outlined the items they had discussed on the phone. Jake hadn't been able to shed any new light on the situation or come up with any new leads. Light-headed and unable to concentrate, Max shut down the computer and went home.

At home, he went to the kitchen and reheated something to eat. Generally, he liked living alone; he needed space and a safe place to unwind after work. It monopolized his waking hours, and he liked it that way. Max made his community safer and even saved a few lives. He knew his father had gone to his grave, not understanding why Max couldn't find a 'regular' job. Max had since made peace with his choices until he met Hailee. She had only been gone for a week, and it felt like an eternity.

His grandfather clock chimed four times. He had just enough time to eat and catch a few hours of sleep. He slid the casserole dish his mother had brought over into the microwave. He enjoyed the attention she showered on him. She still felt guilty about giving Hailee a ride to the airport. He should let her off the hook; if he did, then she wouldn't learn to stay out of his personal life. He decided to let her stew a little more. He ate and went straight to bed.

Max lay down and closed his eyes. He tried to relax, but sleep eluded him. He hadn't reached REM for quite a while, and his body and performance had paid the price. The first night he had spent with Hailee was the first night he had slept well in a long time. He had drifted to sleep in her arms–a deep, restful sleep.

The alarm's piping came too early, and the cold shower did nothing to revive him; Max hoped a cup of steaming, caffeine-filled coffee would. He grabbed a cup and headed to the station.

*****

Max nodded to Erma and hurried to his office. The caffeine kicked in; he knew the energy boost would be temporary, but he would take what he could get. As he pushed open the door, Max frowned. Keller was sprawled out in a chair and looking at his watch.

"You're up early; it's only seven," Max stated.

"I couldn't sleep, so I came in to get a jump on things. I thought you'd be here; I figured you'd burn the midnight oil, and we could compare notes."

"I did until three-thirty, then I went home for food and shut-eye. Have you found out anything?"

"No, just some preliminary information. "I scheduled four interviews for today," Keller glanced down at his notes. "I'm meeting the receptionist, Carol Baker; she's been with the doc for six years." I'm also meeting with three nurses. I haven't been able to reach two of the employees." He reread his notes. "I've left several messages for Janelle Clark, the patient file clerk; however, she hasn't called back. The other employee is Lindsay Mullins, part of the cleaning staff. Apparently, she is here at college and is on a short trip with her parents. They should be back tomorrow."

Max moved the stack of files to the right corner of his desk. "We really need to talk to the file clerk. She might know if the files were misplaced or when they went missing," he said, lifting the cup to his lips. "My search of the doc's wife hasn't turned up anything yet. I'm going to dig a little deeper. Maybe the employees will have some insight into the *real* Mrs. Swisher." He swallowed the coffee and leaned back in the chair. "We're lucky no one else has been hurt."

"Speaking of which, have you seen the news?"

"Is the media crucifying us?"

"No, we're not in the spotlight. Miss Hollister is."

"Why," Max asked?

"Tom had to subdue an angry woman at one of her book signings. Her fans taped it and posted it online. It's all over the internet, and Miss Hollister appears livid."

"I missed her call. She probably wanted me to get Tom to back off, as if anyone could."

"Well, at least you know she's safe."

"Yeah."

"Are you going to finish with the doc's wife, or do you want me to keep looking?"

"No, I'll finish it. Let me know if your interviews turn up anything."

Max glanced down at his phone and hit 'call back.' Before it rang, he ended the call.

*****

Hailee met Tom in the living area of the hotel suite. She managed a weak smile.

"Who was on the phone?" Tom demanded.

"Are you monitoring my calls now?"

"Only one."

"It wasn't Max. You made yourself crystal clear on that subject. Kat called to tell me about the fallout of your rash and unnecessary tactics."

"Stop pouting. It's over."

A few descriptive swear words hovered at the tip of her tongue; she held them at bay. "Is it? Or am I going to be haunted forever by your aggressive behavior?"

163

"That's up to you." Tom went to the kitchenette and washed an apple.

Hailee followed close behind. "It's all over the internet, and I can't do anything about it. It will be immortalized; how can I get over that?"

"Figure it out."

"You are incorrigible."

"Yes."

Hailee's frustrated groan ricocheted off the walls. She counted to ten.

"We need to talk."

The crunch of the crisp apple echoed in her ears.

He wiped his mouth. "Yes."

Her lips curved down. "Don't ever lay a hand on any of my fans ever again. Is that clear?"

He shrugged. "Fine."

"You're conceding?"

"If they don't try to harm you, I won't intervene."

"But—'

"We're done." He smirked.

"Done?"

"The conversation is over."

Tom turned on the television, sank back on the plush cushion, and flipped through the news channels. "Pack tonight. We leave at four-thirty."

Hailee grabbed a pear and more cheese crackers and retired to the bedroom. She put her dirty clothes in a bag and other miscellaneous items into one suitcase. She would pack her clean outfits and makeup after showering in the morning. Hailee plopped down on the bed; the bedspread rippled under her weight. Her dear, sweet Grandmother had scolded her when she had bounced on the bed, especially when they'd travel.

Hailee loved the structure and stability her grandparents gave her. She missed them daily, especially her grandmother. Her parents didn't believe in structure or

164

discipline. It was *cool* with them as long as it was *cool* with the cosmic universe. As a child, Hailee wondered what she could have done wrong that God would choose to put her in a home with two drug-induced bohemians.

A knot tightened in Hailee's stomach; the weight crushed her chest. Her heart raced. She sucked in hard. It didn't help; she couldn't breathe. She stumbled over to the dresser and grasped the edge. Hailee squeezed hard; her fingers turned white. Fear spread through her. Screams echoed in her mind. Pain shot through her hands; her fingers loosened their grip. She couldn't get any air. She dropped to her knees and leaned forward; her head hit the floor. Her body collapsed. A strange sound erupted in the room.

Strong arms shook her. Her eyes opened. Tom kneeled beside her, shaking and yelling at her; she couldn't hear him. She blinked and blinked. He kept shaking her.

Through dry lips, she asked, "What happened?"

"You had a panic attack?"

She rolled over, placed her hands on either side of her, and pushed up. Tom's fingers dug into her skin. She knocked them away. "I'm fine now."

He took in her watery eyes and flushed skin. "What were you doing right before you stopped breathing?"

"I was thinking about my parents." Hailee bit her lip; her quivering hand wiped off her pant legs.

Tom's eyes narrowed. "Tell me about your parents."

"No!"

"Why is it, Miss Hollister, that I can't find any record of you until eight years ago?"

Her eyes thinned. Heat scorched her chest and face. "Drop it, or I'll kick you to the curb. Got it?"

"Okay, Miss Hollister, I can take a hint."

Hailee didn't think he could; his facial expression made her believe he would try again. She sucked in a deep breath. She thought panic attacks were a part of her past.

Days after her parents died, Hailee started having episodes. Quick, painful occurrences of breathing issues and wild hysteria accompanied by mild vision loss. Her doctor had diagnosed her with panic disorder. There were times she had felt as if she were having a full-on heart attack. Her heart had pounded so loudly and painfully that she thought she might die. Her grandmother didn't know what Hailee needed, so she took her to a counselor. Until the panic episodes subsided, the counselor gave Hailee breathing techniques and other tips to get through them. The counselor had been kind and patient, encouraging Hailee to confide in others. The counselor said carrying around guilt, resentment, and self-hatred could be detrimental, and Hailee needed to get angry, grieve, and move on. She thought she had, at least, the best she could.

Tom lingered close by all night. Even though Hailee had been appalled at Tom's behavior at the bookstore, this was comical. Her lips curved up, and she stifled a laugh. He acted like a helicopter mom on steroids. Hailee tapped her finger on the mattress and gazed starry-eyed out the window. She hoped Tom wouldn't tell Max; she didn't want him to know. Hailee found it difficult to keep her situation with Rex from Max; she didn't want to break down and spill her guts. Max had a hold of her, and she wasn't sure how to break it or if she wanted to. She sighed. Tom glanced her way; she bit back a laugh.

Hailee washed her face, brushed her teeth and hair, and put her stuff away. She needed to get Tom to back off. Having him in the same suite bordered on absurd; there was no way in hell she wanted him hovering over her while she slept. She watched Tom pick up a magazine and stroll to the couch. Max hovered; when he did, it showed he cared about her. To Hailee, Tom's motives were unclear; it might

166

be his loyalty to Max or the fact that he enjoyed being in charge of everything. As Tom settled in for the night, she tried to sleep.

The tiny lights from airplanes ricocheted off the glass as they flew by. Hailee stared at the ceiling, then moved her eyes to the window. She would have to try harder to control her emotions; another incident like that and Tom would probably make her go home. Hailee couldn't let that happen. She had two more states and six more cities to hit.

The alarm went off. Hailee showered, dressed, and packed. It would take three hours to get to Bethel, New York. At the high rate of speed that the airport guy drove, they'd probably be there in two. Bethel had a colorful past. Many famous and infamous events took place there, including the Woodstock concert, and she couldn't wait to bask in its renowned musical history. In light of Hailee's apparent loathing of her parents' carefree lifestyle, Kat had balked at the idea that Hailee wanted to stop in Bethel. She warned Hailee that it might evoke powerful and painful childhood memories. Hailee insisted it would be fine; she wouldn't allow the past to ruin a great experience.

Hailee sat in the back of a silver Toyota. She hoped to visit the Catskill Mountains, with its rolling hills, dense forests, and picturesque lakes; however, she believed Tom had scratched that off the itinerary. Her mouth suddenly went dry; she swallowed hard. The sinking feeling returned. Tom had better be on his best behavior, or she would fire him. She wasn't sure how to get rid of him, but she'd find a way.

The book signing went great. Tom hovered at a comfortable distance. She took pictures with her fans, answered questions, and had a wonderful time. Her fans were supportive and understanding; Hailee had the best fan base in the world. Tom packed up, and they returned to the hotel. Their dinner was brought up the usual way, and after

167

Tom inspected it, they ate. She watched Tom deftly move around the suite, checking the windows and doors. Hailee wondered if he expected an enamored fan to jump out of the closet. She rolled her eyes; with Tom, one never knew. She settled in for the night.

Her head hit the pillow, and she closed her eyes. Hailee dreamed of her fans and her best friend. She owed Kat for stepping up and making her dream a reality. Kat's expertise and street smarts allowed her to live her dream and follow her passion. If she hadn't met her, she wouldn't have been able to pull herself together after her grandmother died. Kat, her rock, seemed to be able to smooth over any of life's challenges. The saying goes that some people come into your life for a reason or a season, and Hailee got lucky when Kat glided into her life. Kat had this unobstructed way of looking at life and relationships. Kat always told her the truth, no matter how much it hurt. She softened the blow, just like her grandmother did.

She rolled over and opened her eyes. Yellow and orange streaks raced across the sky. Hailee enjoyed how each sunset differed in color and intensity. Some were bright, featuring orange and reds, while others were softer, with pastel pinks and lilacs. Hailee wondered if Max had made any headway with the investigation. A warm feeling enveloped her. Max had tried to shield her from the world's atrocities, and she knew that if she needed him to, Max would protect her.

When the morning sun lit up the room, she showered, dressed, and ate an orange. She stuck to the tight plan Tom had created. Every day, they rode in a plain, nondescript car. The two things she could count on were the stony-faced driver and Tom's rigid schedule. They went to the airport, sped through the lines, and were the first to board. Hailee would have to ask Tom how he managed it, but for now, she would relax and let him handle it.

Touring was grueling; it kept her busy and gave her a much–needed break from her writing. She never brought her laptop on tour; she wanted to concentrate on the experience and live life, not shuffle through it. If inspired to write, she would record it on her phone and type it later. Rex consistently pressured her to finish her next manuscript and then the next. He refused to let her enjoy taking breaks in between her writing. At first, his greed surprised her, but then it became the norm, and it was just one more thing she despised him for.

Hailee and Tom departed from the airport with a new driver and another plain car. They made their way through the busy streets of Pennsylvania. Everything went according to plan; there were no more scared or angry fans, and Tom kept his distance while performing his self-proclaimed duties. Within five nights and three days, they visited Philadelphia and Pittsburgh, then headed to Illinois. Typically, Kat chose where Hailee toured, but occasionally Hailee selected locations that let her visit tourist attractions. Sometimes, Hailee would choose a place on a whim or where she wanted to research for her next novel. Hailee picked Chicago to experience Lincoln Park and the famous art museums.

As a child, Hailee aspired to create something mind-blowing, something meaningful. She envied the local artists in town; each had a style and sense of self. They were the happiest people she had ever met. They didn't care who her parents were or what they did. Hailee had inundated them with questions, trying to gauge their passion and creativity, and hoped it would rub off on her. No matter how many times she had tried, she failed.

She would try different ways to express her bottled-up resentment and her need for acceptance. Hailee had hoped that if she succeeded at something great, her classmates and neighbors would accept her for her accomplishments, despite what her parents did or how they lived. Her efforts to paint had resulted in a frightening display of spastic strokes and mismatched colors. No sign of life or passion could be found on the canvas. Hailee tried to sculpt, letting out a heavy sigh whenever her sculptures tumbled to the ground.

Her attempt at contemporary dance failed miserably; Hailee didn't understand the music or the story behind the elaborate moves. She struggled to play the piano, and while trying to learn Petzold's Minuet in G, she imagined she heard Chopin's Death March. That had been the last straw; she had given up all hope of becoming an artist. Frustration had filled her tiny frame. She had been trapped in the drug-induced, euphoric world of her parents, and she had wanted out.

Hailee firmly believed that her parents' choices had destroyed her childhood. She had been tormented by the school bully who'd called her parents hippies and sex maniacs. The bully had been right; they were hippies. Their clothes, their hair, their drug use, and their 'celebrations of life' parties made it evident to anyone who knew them that her childhood bully's assessment of them was spot on. They couldn't hold a job and rebelled against *the man,* the government, and society as a whole. Since her parents had no money, she had to wear hand-me-down seventies hip-huggers and used Birkenstock sandals. And instead of putting barrettes or fashionable combs in her hair, she had to use her mother's beads to pull her unruly locks away from her face. The other students had teased her about her clothes, and her classmates' parents wouldn't let their children visit Hailee's home or let her in theirs. She had been alone, and if it weren't for a kind and compassionate English teacher, she would have been swallowed up by darkness and solitude.

At night, Hailee had prayed for parents she could understand and be proud of. And then, one day, in the blink of an eye, they were gone. They had been horrible parents and weird individuals. Despite that, they didn't deserve to die. They were dead, and she caused it.

She closed her eyes, and her breathing quickened. Black dots flashed before her. Her skin tingled, and she shivered. Her heart beat wildly, and the sudden need to hurl overwhelmed her. She gripped the armrest tightly, digging her fingers into the material. She gulped for air—not *now, not here.*

She felt a painful punch, was knocked to the right, and fell against the window. She winced and rubbed her arm; her breathing slowed. She straightened out her blouse and shot an angry look at Tom.

Hailee and Tom had two hours before check-in. Hailee informed Tom she wanted a Chicago hot dog. While Tom instructed the new driver, she leaned against the cloth interior of yet another boring car. They drove leisurely, just a little faster than a Sunday drive, and pulled over. While Tom retrieved her snack, the driver kept the car running. Tom handed her a gigantic hot dog; her eyes widened, and she licked her lips.

The Vienna hot dog fit snugly in a twelve-inch poppy-seed bun. She sank her teeth into it; the snap of the hot dog surprised and elated her. An explosion of flavors erupted in her mouth: mustard, peppers, sweet relish, onions, tomatoes, and dill pickle. The tangy relish balanced out the sharpness of the mustard. Hailee finished the entire hot dog and wiped her mouth. The onions were fresh and pungent, and the vinegar from the pickles made her pucker. Her eyes watered, and her throat burned. She asked Tom for some gum; he handed her a breath mint.

After pulling up to the hotel, the driver waited for them to enter before driving off. They went up the private elevator to their suite. Hailee unpacked and then pulled out the brochures from the Roger Brown Museum. She would have to wait until after the book signing to start touring the sites. She would finally see the homes she had heard so much about. Famous artists, sculptors, and innovators had called the Lincoln Park area their home.

Hailee's childhood had been filled with long, lonely nights, torturous days at school, and the only glimmer of hope, the illuminating time she spent with the local artists. One day after school, Hailee decided to give sketching another try. She had gripped the charcoal, relaxed her shoulders and hand, and said a little prayer. She let the charcoal glide across the paper. Stroke after stroke filled the white canvas. Her forced and erratic strokes had become desperate and needy. The scraggy, gray, and black streaks resembled the ashes of a burned-down house. At that moment of defeat, the words of her English teacher resonated with her. 'Let your words speak for you.' From that moment on, she knew words would be her savior. She ditched the charcoal, and once she started writing, she couldn't stop. Her bent-up frustrations and fears had floated away.

Hailee leaned back on the headboard and gazed out the window. She pushed her childhood memories to the back of her mind and focused on the life she had built. She had been lucky: she had found the right agent at the right time. Rex had seemed knowledgeable, connected, and motivated. He had introduced her to a well-established, reputable publishing company, and they did a great job of marketing her first novel. Her first impression of Rex had been wrong. He turned out to be controlling, manipulative, malicious, and spiteful. He blackmailed her to succumb to his wishes, and she had been forced to comply or sacrifice her career.

Her passion for writing has been her outlet for creativity and emotion. Hailee had learned to put her feelings down on paper, and it saved her. The loss of her grandmother, the guilt over her parents' death, and her shame about her true parentage seemed to lessen with each novel she wrote. She continued to write and found that she had a knack for storytelling. She had found her true calling.

Although Hailee had planned to visit the WNDR Museum, Cloud Gate, and other local Chicago attractions, she would have to wait until the signing ended. Kat had picked a charming bookstore off Madison Street for her next event. They were getting into a comfortable rhythm: Tom stayed out of the way, and Hailee spent quality time with her fans. Everyone greeted her with open arms, and no one mentioned that Tom had accosted a woman in New York City. She felt physically and emotionally spent, and she couldn't wait to do it again.

As they approached the bookstore, Tom warned her that the narrow, winding stairs were dangerous and that they might need to use evasive maneuvers if an emergency arose. She signed books until her hand tingled, and her lips were stiff from smiling. Another successful signing. She had Kat to thank for that.

On their way out, Tom cautiously ushered her down the stairs and had her wait at the bottom while he scoped out the exit. A small group of enthusiastic fans stayed back at a respectable distance but followed them down. When Tom left to check the blocked exit, the fans descended on her. They pushed and shoved with outstretched hands, trying to touch her and have her sign their books. She stepped back and found herself trapped up against a wall. She took a couple of deep breaths and tried to regain control over the crowd by asking them to form a line. They shoved their books at her, touching her hair and grabbing at her clothes.

She felt strong fingers dig into her forearm. She was yanked sideways under the stairwell. A tall, lanky man with wavy, waist-length hair stared down at her. His long-sleeved V-neck shirt, raggedy velvet vest, and faint odor of weed reminded her of her childhood nightmare.

She pulled away and gasped. She couldn't believe it.

"Harmony, it's me."

"Don't call me that," She stared up at him – could it really be him? "Who are you?"

"Don't you remember me? Let your freak flag fly."

"Are you kidding me?" She turned and yelled for Tom.

She shook her head and backed away from the stranger. Tom, briefly sidetracked by mall security, came running with security in tow.

The stranger turned toward Tom and the approaching security team. "This is heavy—"
Tom rushed him. The stranger hit the floor with a thud. Tom and security subdued him.

"Not cool, man," he tried to wiggle out of the constraints. "The fuzz. What a downer." He continued to struggle. "I need a hit."

Security took the stranger to their office and waited for the police.

Hailee's stomach did somersaults. She felt faint. She did her best to act uninterested in the stranger. Had her past finally caught up with her?

"Did he hurt you?" Tom asked.

"No."

"Who is he?"

Hailee winced. She couldn't believe it herself. Could it really be him?

"My father."

Chapter 19

Max scoured the files and took extensive notes, comparing each victim and the circumstances surrounding their life right before they were murdered. If only he could find the patients' files, he could dig deeper and see what else they had in common. These young women seemed tortured by their perceived inadequacies. They had set themselves up to be victims of a dark, nefarious scheme. One that would prove fatal.

Keller came in at noon; dark circles encircled his eyes, and his creased suit had seen better days.

"Tell me you have good news," Max implored.

"It's too early to tell. The scheduler, Carol Baker, spilled her guts; she said the doc constantly made her rearrange the appointments to squeeze in his latest conquest. She said the doc threatened her and swore her to secrecy. He said that his wife must never find out, and if she did, Carol could look for another job."

"The wife's lying. Why?" Max mused.

"All three nurses confirmed what the scheduler told me. The doc was a cheating pig." Keller held up his hands. "Their words, not mine. The nurses stated that the women the doc cheated with needed little or no work, yet he still performed surgeries on them."

"The doc told me the first vic didn't need work, but she insisted. He didn't want to ruin a long-time friendship, so he scheduled the surgery. Were you able to review the patient files with the nurses?"

"Yeah, and from the looks of the pre-op photos, the nurses were right. The women the doc slept with didn't have any noticeable flaws and probably didn't need surgery. Maybe the doc convinced them they needed work, and he'd give them a big fat discount if they slept with him?"

"I don't know. The doc appeared to be telling the truth. What if it's another patient, one who physically needs surgery, one who was scarred or burned? Envy is a powerful motive." Max considered this new angle. "I need the vics' patient files. Have you located the file clerk yet?"

"No. The judge signed the warrant for her residence and car. Unfortunately, we can't find the car. The house is clean–no files–no sign of foul play–and no file clerk. The surgical nurse gave me some leads about where she hangs out. I'll check them out tonight. I'll brief you later."

Max nodded and dialed Erma's extension. "Get me dispatch."

The red light on his phone came on; he picked up the receiver.

"Toliver."

"Yes, Detective."

"Were you able to get me the address of where the two phone calls came from the night the third vic died?" Max asked the dispatcher.

"Yes, the first call was placed at approximately 2300 hours and originated from the Meridian."

"Damn!"

The dispatcher paused. "Do you want me to go on, sir?"

"Sorry, what about the second call?"

"It also originated from Meridian at 2310 hours."

"Did you check the tapes to verify the caller's instructions?"

"Yes, sir. The first call: the female caller stated she had information regarding the murders at the Meridian Hotel and to have you meet her at the concierge desk at the Meridian immediately. The second call: a female caller indicated she had given you the wrong hotel name. She was at the Sumpton Hotel on 5th Street and was to meet at the concierge desk. Both callers refused to give their names, and I don't know if the same person made the calls."

"Send me a copy of the tapes ASAP."

"Yes, sir."

Max wondered if the caller was a credible witness or an accessory to murder–did she concoct a ruse to lure him out of the hotel until after the murder took place? He had left with high hopes, his first real lead, but it hadn't panned out, and he had left Hailee completely vulnerable.

After reviewing the tapes, Max realized that he could not identify the caller and that the caller might be two different people. It could have been the file clerk or, perhaps, the doctor's cleaning staff woman, or both.

Erma burst into his office and turned on the TV.

A special report interrupted regular programming. The reporter, the same one who reported on the Meridian murders and the one who reminded Max of the *Dirty Laundry* song, flashed his immaculate smile and began speaking:

"Popular mystery writer and local favorite Hailee Hollister had been accosted at her latest book signing. We have footage of a man dragging Miss Hollister away from her fans, and it appears that he is threatening her—"

Max watched the footage of a dirty, disheveled older man yanking Hailee toward the stairs.

"…Fortunately, her security team warded off her attacker without injuring Miss Hollister." The footage showed Tom tackling the older man and then putting him into a half-nelson chokehold. The reporter continued: "We are relieved that Miss Hollister sustained no injuries. However, we at the station are concerned that this attack could be related to her involvement in the gruesome Meridian murders. We wonder if she is being targeted because, purportedly, she is the only living witness to these heinous crimes."

Max jumped up. "Get me, Pete. Now!"

*****

Hailee barely had time to think. After Tom tackled her aggressor, he steered her to the car, and they sped off. He had been in overdrive ever since, demanding that they change hotels, rearrange her book-signing schedule, and revamp his security measures.

After they settled into their new hotel, Tom relaxed a little; his pace slowed, and he stopped shooting dirt looks her way. It wasn't Hailee's fault her past had decided to rear its ugly head at one of her signings. She grabbed her phone and slipped into the bathroom. She turned on the tub faucet and dialed Kat's number.

"Kat," she whispered.

"Hailee!"

"I'm not hurt—"

"Who was that cretin?" Kat asked.

"He's the guy from my mom's picture. He might be my biological father."

"OMG!"

Kat had repeatedly told Hailee that if she continued to tempt fate, she would one day run into her biological father. She reminded Hailee it was *her* idea to choose locations for the book signings with a long history of the hippie lifestyle, including the place she decided to call home, Colorado. Hailee balked at the idea and remained adamant that she never wanted to meet the man in the picture, the one who had been labeled as 'Father.' Had she subconsciously been seeking out the man from the picture? The one who could explain what happened between him and the people she knew as her parents? It didn't matter now. She had to shake Tom.

"Tom's in a tizzy, and he's tightening his hold. I need to get back to Portland."

"To hunky Max and away from revolting Rex?"

"Yes."

"What's the plan?" Kat asked.

Hailee outlined a plan that required precise timing and execution. She needed enough time to get to the airport and board without Tom interfering. She knew she would need Job's patience to pull this off. She had no choice. Tom had become a dictator and needed to be stopped; her career and life must be preserved at all costs.

Hailee utilized her writing connections, primarily fans or other authors who were influential figures with connections in the right businesses, to get Kat a direct flight from Colorado to Chicago. The four-hour flight arrived at midnight. She wished she could see Kat's face when she read her text containing the flight information. Kat stuck to a tight sleep regimen, and the flight took off smack dab in the middle of her scheduled REM cycle.

Getting Kat to Chicago turned out to be the easiest part of her plan. Her repeated requests for unusual food or accommodations were met with an icy glare. Tom adamantly refused to leave her or the room unprotected. A crucial part of the plan required getting Tom out of the hotel. She needed time to get to the airport and take off safely. She knew he had connections, but she doubted he could stop a plane after it had taken off.

She lay low for the rest of the day, avoiding eye contact with Tom. She didn't want him to discover her escape plan, one that would make Houdini proud. She watched the news half-heartedly and mentally reviewed every step of her plan. It had to work.

At midnight, Hailee said good night to Tom, closed the bedroom door, and called Kat. Kat had just parked and was heading to the lobby. While she reviewed the plan with Kat, she packed and shoved her suitcase under the bed. Hailee secured her hair in a loose bun and dressed in a long-sleeve sweater and black dress pants. She put on her robe and slipped under the covers. And waited.

As she lay in the dark, she could hear the slow, methodical ticking of the wall clock. She closed her eyes and wondered whether Kat would succeed. Tom had to be caught off guard for her to make her getaway.

She waited with bated breath, then the fire alarm blared.

Tom burst into her room. "Get up! We have to get out."

She wrapped the robe tightly around her waist, slipped into her UGG booties, and scrambled out of bed. She hurried past Tom. He grabbed his 9MM, tucked it into his holster, and dragged her out of the suite. He pulled her up to his left side and clamped onto her right forearm. She winced. He led her to the private elevator and out onto the street.

Pandemonium broke out. The fire truck came roaring down the street and had just pulled up. The sirens and lights were ear-piercing and disorientating. Guests were huddling together, frantically searching for loved ones, and scrambling to keep the children calm. She swallowed hard. She was responsible for this. She prayed that no one would get hurt.

Tom steered her toward the fire truck and briefly spoke to the captain about the threat's validity. They were instructed to stay clear of the hotel so his men could assess the situation and locate the fire, if one existed. Tom steered her away from the crowd but stayed within earshot of the activity. He instructed her to stay there and wait for the driver, who would take her to a backup location. She nodded and kept her head down.

Tom returned to the front door and got lost in a sea of people. She shed her robe, shoved it into the trash, and quickly walked toward the alley. She turned the corner and ran to the car. Hailee jumped in, buckled up, and Kat punched it, speeding to the airport.

She glanced over at Kat, who smiled ear to ear.

180

"How'd I do?" Kat asked.

"Great. Now step on it."

Kat rambled on about how much she enjoyed the adventure. Although it was completely illegal, she would do anything for Hailee.

Hailee focused on Max. Until she knew Portland's citizens were free from danger, she had to push down any thoughts about consequences.

They made good time. Kat pulled up to the curb; Hailee handed her the hotel key card and hurried to Terminal 1. By the time she reached the counter, her side hurt, and she could barely breathe. She checked in and headed toward the security area. Hailee had no luggage and hoped that wouldn't be a problem.

The TSA agent refused to let her proceed and instead conducted a private pat-down. Hailee's heart beat loudly; her heart raced. Hailee tried to explain it was a life-or-death emergency and that she didn't have time to pack; despite that, the agent refused to back down. She made Hailee go through the X-ray machine twice. Hailee felt as if her heart would burst. Tom probably had realized by now that she was gone, and he and his goons would be hot on her trail. They'd split up to cover more ground. Tom would search the airline reservations, and the driver would investigate the rental cars. She tried to slow her breathing. She knew she looked guilty, and that's probably why the agent stopped her. The agent rechecked her ID and recognized her.

"Oh, you're the mystery writer." The agent mused.

"Yes, that's me. I'm sorry. I must get to my plane." Hailee looked over her shoulder and to both sides. "May I leave now?"

The agent nodded and handed her ID back. Hailee ran to the gate, scanned her ticket, and hurried down the jet bridge, finding a seat in the back. She buckled up and let out a sigh of relief. The plane was cleared for takeoff.

As the jet ascended into the clouds, Hailee settled into the seat and closed her eyes. She hoped Kat would be able to handle Tom's wrath. He would be furious, and Kat would be his target. She fell asleep, praying her friend would be okay.

Chapter 20

Before he left for the day, Max spoke with Pete and asked him to call the station to discuss an official statement. He didn't want the media speculating on the status of his case or his witness. He wished that Tom would call and update him on the incident; he probably wouldn't, but Max could hope. Tom's policy of needing to know annoyed Max. He figured he needed to know, especially if the perp could be connected to his murders.

While driving home, Max's thoughts inevitably returned to Hailee. She had shown him how driven and fearless she could be. Although she was thousands of miles away, she could still evoke strong sensual feelings. His work ethic demanded he investigate the case with his usual fervent intensity so he could make an arrest and figure out how he felt about Hailee.

He opened the refrigerator door, reached back, and pulled out a beer. He popped the top and headed upstairs. He rolled his neck and swiped his hand through his hair. He took a long, slow swallow of the ice-cold beer and breathed a sigh of relief. He took off his shirt and kicked off his shoes. He sat, leaning against the headboard, trying to relax.

The phone rang, shocking him out of reverie. "Toliver."

"It's Tom. Miss Hollister gave me the slip."

Max suppressed a laugh. "What happened?"

"Someone pulled the fire alarm, and she slipped away."

"Did anyone see where she went, or did she meet up with anyone?"

"Chaos erupted, and I could only speak to a few people. When the hotel was cleared for re-entry, the guests had dispersed quickly. On my way back to the room, I noticed the door had been propped open, and I found her friend waiting for me."

"Kat? She's harmless."

"Is she?" Tom asked. "She told me Miss Hollister was gone, and I couldn't get her back. That misfit grinned the whole damn time. I wanted to—"

"Easy… Kat is Hailee's good friend. What's she doing there?"

"She came to retrieve Miss Hollister's suitcase," Tom grunted. "I'll bet you she's the one who pulled the alarm. They knew I'd never leave her, so they had to get us outside."

Tom's angry tone clearly indicated he disapproved of Kat and her actions.

"What did you do?"

Max waited and waited.

"Nothing."

Max knew Tom nothing meant something, but he wouldn't spill.

"Did Kat tell you where Hailee's going?"

"She's headed back to the danger zone."

Max hoped Hailee would return. Tom was right; if she came back to Portland, she could be in harm's way. Tom informed him that he had booked a flight to Portland and should be landing the following morning at ten. He'd arrange for his guys to meet him there to start the search for Hailee.

After they hung up, excitement briefly filled Max's being, and then reality sank in. Why would she come back? A serious threat loomed in his precinct, and Hailee might be the next target.

He called Keller. He put a BOLO out on Hailee and told Keller to intercept her at the airport and take her into custody. He would hold her as a material witness so he could keep an eye on her; she would fight him. At least she'd be safe. He downed the last of his beer and settled in for the night. He stared at the ceiling, waiting for Keller's call.

*****

Hailee sprinted past the baggage carousel, glad Kat would send her things after her. She headed toward the exit where a car would be waiting. She scanned the lot for a black SUV and rushed to it. Hailee reached for the handle. A hand gripped her elbow tightly. She winced, tugged at her arm, and looked directly into Detective Keller's eyes.

"Miss Hollister, please come with me."

She tugged at her arm again, to no avail. "I'm sorry; I'm in a hurry."

"Please, Miss Hollister, don't make a scene."

"Why would I—"

Keller cleared his throat. "You're being detained as a material witness. Come with me."

Keller guided her to an unmarked car, opened the door, and slid beside her.

The seatbelt cut into Hailee's neck; she yanked it down and released it with a snap. "This isn't necessary. I'd planned to see Max, um, Detective Toliver."

Keller directed the officer to go to HQ straightaway. He reached into his jacket pocket and pulled out his phone.

Hailee watched and waited. She guessed he would call Max and let him know they were on their way to the station. Tom had ratted her out; how else would Max have known of her escape? Did she honestly think she could return undetected, meet Max, explain, and then everything would be alright?

She anxiously looked out the window. She felt deflated; she needed the element of surprise. She didn't have a plan B. Her hope that Tom would be too proud to call Max and inform him that he failed was fleeting and naïve. She dreaded their reunion. Would Max welcome her back and into his arms, or would he be in cop mode and reprimand her for leaving and jeopardizing the case? Maybe a little of both? She hoped it would be the former. Haile had left to give him space so he could concentrate on the case and make an arrest. She also went to confront Rex and get back to work. She felt horrible for taking off without a word to anyone, and she wondered if Sophia would forgive her for using her to sneak away.

At the precinct, the officer pulled up and parked near the door. She scanned the area for Max's car and swallowed hard when she spotted his silver Cadillac parked in the front row. Excitement and anxiety engulfed her; her stomach turned, and she trembled. On the plane, she had replayed dozens of scenarios of her homecoming, analyzing each one for viability. Right now, she could only concentrate on walking to the front door.

A hush fell over the squad room as she and Keller walked down the hall toward Max's office. Keller held the door open. She walked past him, and he closed the door behind her. Max stood by the window, gazing out at the morning sky. She waited nervously by the door.

"Please have a seat." Max requested.

So, he chose cop. "Max—"

Max turned from the window and went to his desk. He stood looming over her for a moment, then said, "Miss Hollister, in light of your recent decision to leave without consulting Detective Keller or me, I am placing you in protective custody until this case is resolved—"

She jumped up. "You can't do that."

"I can, and I am. You are a material witness, my only witness, to a brutal attack that led to the death of a young woman. You could be in danger, and I need you here and safe so that you can testify at the trial."

"What trial? Did you arrest anyone? Who?"

Max scowled. "As I've told you, I cannot discuss an ongoing investigation with you."

"I have a lot to offer. I can be useful."

"No, thanks."

They glared at each other.

Hailee's gaze fell. So, this is how he wanted to play it fine with her.

"How can you hold me when you don't even have a suspect. You know I'll show up for the trial, and I'm not a flight risk. Can't you depose me and call it a day?"

"No."

"No? I'm not guilty of anything." She squared her shoulders and held her chin high. "Are you going to arrest me?"

"No, a team of specialized officers will be assigned to protect you, and you will be taken to a secure location until I deem it necessary."

"Am I under arrest, or are you putting me in protective custody?"

"What difference does it make? You're not leaving."

"It matters because I don't want you trampling on my rights."

"I'm not going to violate your rights. I have every right to ensure you are safe and can testify, when needed, at the trial."

"How can you justify holding me until such a time that an arrest might be made? Am I supposed to stay here forever, waiting for due process?"

"Four people are dead, and the city is in a state of chaos. We are still piecing together the evidence and trying to prevent more bloodshed. I'd appreciate your cooperation in this matter."

Hailee wasn't ready to give up her freedom on the chance that the police might apprehend someone. "I want to call my attorney."

"You're not being arrested."

"Then I'm leaving."

"You are being detained."

"I'm not well-versed in Oregon laws. I'm pretty sure you can't hold me until there's a trial. And it's a judge who determines whether my testimony is material and necessary."

"That's True. I've decided to detain you until such a time as I feel that your life and safety are no longer at risk."

"Sounds fishy."

"I can assure you that your rights will not be violated."

Hailee felt drained. "Am I going back to the Meridian?"

"No."

She plopped down on the chair. "Then where?"

"You'll be staying here tonight, and we'll find you a safe place in the morning. Where's your luggage?"

"You're putting me in a holding cell?"

Max came to her side and gently brushed her cheek. She looked up and studied his face. She felt him relax, and then he pulled away.

"No. Detective Keller set up a makeshift room for you down the hall. Two of my officers will watch over you until the security team arrives and your accommodations have been verified."

"Max, aren't you overreacting just a little?"

His lips thinned. "No."

Hailee joined him on the other side of the desk. She reached up and caressed the frown lines on his forehead. "Can't we talk about this?"

"Miss Hollister, please don't make this more difficult than it needs to be. You are not trustworthy, and I am willing to take extraordinary measures to ensure the integrity of my investigation. I will not have you become a victim of the fiend that is terrorizing my precinct."

"I'm as honest as they come." Her hand dropped to her side.

One lie. One Max doesn't even know about, and he thought she couldn't be trusted. She had been one hundred percent open with Max. It had been liberating to share her passion with him. Since her one colossal lie, she had made it her mission to be completely honest with everyone, a penance of sorts. Maybe it was too little too late, and her past wrongdoings had finally caught up with her.

Her attempts to ease the tension backfired, and instead of breaking the ice, he refused to budge. She couldn't find a way out of this situation, and Max's professional demeanor cut her to the core. Did he choose to forget everything that had happened? Had she meant anything to him at all, or was she just a convenient distraction?

*****

As the sun slowly descended, darkness fell on the brisk Portland night. Max waited for Keller's call. With Hailee's sudden return, Keller had to postpone his search for the file clerk. Now, he was back on her trail. Keller had been instructed to visit the stomping grounds of the elusive file clerk. He had located her car and had been waiting for her to exit the building so he could bring her in. The clerk's coworkers had given a detailed description of her: long black hair, olive skin tone, and surgically enhanced features. She had breast augmentation and cheek and buttock implants; apparently, she had also been a patient of the late Dr. Swisher.

Keller radioed in and let Max know that he and Miss Clark had arrived and were heading to the interrogation room.

Max stopped at the interrogation room door and instructed Keller to oversee Hailee's needs. He reminded Keller not to allow visitors or permit her to make or receive phone calls. Max strolled in, his step lighter, his attitude brighter. Finally, something had panned out, and he planned to capitalize on it.

He took a seat directly across from the file clerk. "I'm Detective Max Toliver. I'm the lead detective on the Meridian Hotel murders. Time is of the essence, so I will get right to the point."

Miss Clark stared blankly at him. He wondered if she'd been drinking. "I need the patient files of the three murdered girls. Where are they?"

She continued to fixate on Max as if he had two heads. "Did you hear me? Have you been drinking?"

"No."

Max noticed the file clerk's rumpled appearance, her tousled hair, and wrinkled clothes. Did she struggle with Keller or try to flee? Miss Clark's hair and skin tone gave her an exotic appeal, and he wondered if the doctor had convinced her, too, that she needed work done to be happy. The file clerk kept her cloudy gaze affixed on him. Max leaned in and examined her eyes; Hailee had been right. The perp who attacked the third victim had a birthmark on her left eye, and she sat right across from him.

"Did Detective Keller read you your rights, and did you understand them?"

"Are you arresting me?"

"We have a warrant to obtain the patient files; if you have them, you must turn them over to us immediately. I have specific questions about one of the murders. I want to make sure your rights are being upheld." When she didn't respond, he continued, "Where are the files?"

"They're in my trunk. It won't do you any good, though. He's smarter than you. He's everywhere and nowhere. You'll never catch him. Our mission is almost complete."

"Who is he?"

"It doesn't matter now."

"Why did you kill Brenda Jacobs? Why did you kill a young, innocent woman?"

"They weren't innocent; they were slaves to their own beauty. They were guilty."

"Is he planning to kill anyone else? What do you mean, our mission is almost complete? Miss Clark. Tell me. Help me save the next young girl."

She laid her head down on the table and spoke. Her words were barely audible. "Your girlfriend should have stayed out of it."

She closed her eyes.

"Hailee? Is he going after Hailee? Why? Miss Clark?"

Her body convulsed, and foam oozed from her lips. Max yelled for an ambulance and ran to her. He laid her on the floor, rubbed his knuckle on her breastbone, and shouted again for an ambulance. "Who is he? Where is he?" Max started chest compressions. "Stay with me. Stay with me." He heard footsteps approaching. "Is he going after Hailee? Answer me!"

Keller ran to Max's side; they took turns performing chest compressions. Max's heart raced, and fear spread through his body like wildfire. The one person who could save Hailee had to live.

"Don't die. Hang in there." Max took over. His heart felt as if it would burst. "Who is he? Where is he?" Max's hope of saving the girl plummeted with each compression. "Is Hailee in danger? Tell me!"

The EMTs arrived and took over, starting rescue breathing. They administered an opioid antidote. Nothing happened. Her body continued to spasm. Maybe her partner poisoned her, and the medication wouldn't work. They continued CPR. They worked harder and faster, trying to revive her and get a pulse.

The contractions slowed and then stopped...

The EMTs declared her DOA.

Max remained crouched down on the floor. He gasped to catch his breath. It served him right. He came in all cocky, thinking he would finally solve the case, and his best lead just died. He wouldn't know from what until he received the ME's report. Before she died, she had confirmed what Max had feared all along: Hailee was in danger.

"Miss Hollister is asking for you," Keller informed Max.

Max nodded, dragged himself up, and went down the hall. He put on his cop face and hoped he could hide his emotions.

He reached her impromptu quarters, knocked, and entered. She stood, wringing her hands nervously. She looked up when the door opened.

Hailee moved closer, then suddenly stopped. "Max, what happened? What's going on?"

He took a deep breath. He couldn't discuss the case with her; Hailee looked frightened and deserved to be told something. "An incident occurred, and the paramedics were called. It's over now. Nothing to worry about."

"I heard yelling. Is the person alright?"

Max stared past her, contemplating Janelle's admission, 'Our mission is almost complete.' What mission?

"Max, what's going on. Tell me, please."

Fear, anger, and frustration exploded all at once. "Hailee, what do you want!"

She recoiled.

"I needed to see you before I left. I'd hoped you might want to see me too."

Max watched her. Her slumped shoulders spoke volumes. He had hurt her. A loud rap on the door interrupted his train of thought. The security team arrived to get Hailee. Max looked around, "Where's your luggage?"

"Kat has it. I'll have her send it to you, and you can forward it to me." She glanced around, grabbed her purse, and hurried out the door.

Max stared after her. He blew it. He knew he would. His dad had always predicted this type of future for him: to be alone. It exasperated him to admit that his dad had been right. At times, he had doubts about his decision to pursue a career in law enforcement, and this was one of them. His mother begged him to quit, settle down, and give her grandchildren. She didn't want her youngest son to die on the job.

"The team left with Miss Hollister, and they're heading to an undisclosed location. They'll wait for further instructions. What do you want to do now?" Keller asked.

"I want to catch the murdering bastard!"

Chapter 21

Max pored through the murdered victims' files. The files contained information on blood type, type of surgery, victims' overall health, age, and identifying details. It seemed that he already had all the pertinent information on the girls. Max rubbed his aching eyes; he needed a break and some food. He ordered Chinese takeout, and when the food arrived, he tossed a file on his desk. His stomach grumbled, and Max devoured the food with vigor. After he finished, he felt stuffed and lethargic, regretting his impulse to gorge himself. He washed down the Kung Pao Chicken and rice with an ice-cold soda and began scouring the files again.

He took his time reading the same information over and over; it had become repetitive and annoying. Max flung the file on his desk, cutting his index finger on the file folder. He wiped off the blood and discarded the tissue. Blood! He re-read all the files. He buzzed Keller, who hurried to his office.

"Max, what did you find?"

"It's where the blood came from, not the type. Look at page four. All the vics had donated to the same location, the Blood Systems Donation Center. That's another link. Look who volunteered at the donation center."

Keller skimmed the information, and a smile hovered on his lips. "Damn. Miss Clark. She worked at the doctor's office and at the donation center. She helped the vics throughout the entire process. I wonder if she chose the vics, and if so, why?"

"When I asked her why innocent girls were being murdered, she said they were guilty because they were slaves to their own beauty. Didn't you tell me that Miss Clark had been a patient of the doc, too?"

"Yes, she had several procedures done. Maybe her partner found out and offed her, too?"

"That's my guess; we need to concentrate on finding her partner now. Miss Clark had said, 'He's smarter than you…You'll never catch him.' I'm guessing they were lovers. Let's start there. I'll check her social media, and I was hoping you could revisit her coworkers and find out who she dated. We're getting close. I can feel it."

Keller hesitated at the door. "Do you want me to pressure the ME to get the report on Miss Clark?"

"Yeah, I need to know if the perp poisoned her or if she did it herself. Suicide may have been her solution to a murder charge. When you brought her in, did she resist? She looked like she'd been roughed up."

"No, she seemed defeated. Maybe her accomplice got to her, forced down a poison or drug, and scrammed."

Great cops relied on evidence and hard work and had to trust their guts. After years of dealing with suspects, victims, and lawyers, Max had trained himself to listen and act on his instincts. At times, they were all he had. They never let him down before, and Max hoped they wouldn't now. He pulled up Facebook on his computer.

It never ceased to surprise Max the type of content people would post – all in the name of getting likes. Janelle had several social media accounts and appeared to have been quite popular. She had numerous posts and comments about her body's enhancements. Max studied her before-and-after pics. His first impression turned out to be spot on. He couldn't see any significant improvement from the surgeries. Her breasts were slightly larger and maybe more symmetrical, and her cheekbones and nose appeared more defined. Overall, she had retained the same beauty she was born with. Max scoured her posts for a male family member, a boyfriend, or someone who might be her partner and possibly her killer.

Janelle had a copious male following, and Max reviewed hundreds of male pictures. The redundancy made him nauseous: the men were mesmerized by her natural and newfound beauty. None of the men captured Janelle's attention, except one. She responded to all of his comments. Max scrutinized the pics. The guy's roguish good looks and goatee were familiar: Simon, the ice guy.

Max's heart pounded loudly; he found another link. Hailee had great instincts. She advised him to check out Simon because he showed up at the crime scene and because something about him didn't sit well with her. If she had stayed and assisted with the case, would she have discovered more information? Information that could have prevented more killings.

He now knew that the wet spots at the crime scenes were melted ice. Why would Simon leave ice in the victim's rooms? Did he want to get caught, or was he taunting the police? Max clicked on Simon's link and searched for an address or number he could trace. He couldn't access Simon's account, so he needed a warrant. He googled the Glacier Palace site, dialed the number, and waited. He checked the time: ten p.m. The site claimed the company delivered ice 24/7; a recording requested delivery information and stated that someone would be paged. Max hung up and buzzed Keller.

He waited, and when Keller didn't show up, he rushed to his office. Keller covered the receiver and waved Max in.

"You're sure. There's no evidence to connect the widow Swisher to Mrs. Swisher's untimely demise in the nursing home. Did they do a tox screen before the cremation? Yeah, thanks."

"What did the Tennessee PD turn up," Max asked?

"The doc's mother's death had been ruled undetermined. The police statements indicate the nurses were genuinely surprised when the doc's mother died. She had been in good health; she only needed assistance with daily chores."

"So, Mrs. Swisher died prematurely, and there's no way to pin it on Widow Swisher."

"Maybe she didn't do it, and Widow Swisher didn't kill the doc. It could've been the Meridian killer."

Max considered the possibility. Other than lying about the money, they had no evidence linking Widow Swisher to the crime. "Good point, and speaking of the devil. It appears that Simon, the ice delivery guy, knew the doc's file clerk. In fact, from their posts, they were pretty chummy. His company is closed, so I need to get a warrant for his media and other accounts so we can pick him up."

"Get me a warrant ASAP. I want Simon in custody."

Keller nodded and dialed the judge.

*****

Hailee struggled to see out the blacked-out car windows and hoped they weren't leaving the state. Typically, her worst security issue was an over-enthusiastic fan who wouldn't respect her space. Now, she might be the target of a serial killer. She had difficulty believing that Max would go into cop mode and disregard her entire life on the likelihood that she *might* be in danger. Hailee would need to be careful.

Sitting in the back of a massive, nondescript SUV reminded her of her time with Tom. Every city meant another monotonous, no-frills car, driven by a large, capable driver. While with Tom, Hailee remembered seeing one of the anonymous driver's weapons. It had been larger than her purse. Even though she appreciated the perks of having a well-oiled security team, she would never admit it to Max or Tom. After Max arrests the killer, Hailee would speak to Kat about hiring security, at the very least, part-time.

The car swerved, throwing her against the door. Hailee reached out to steady herself. She flew forward as the vehicle screeched to a halt. The squealing tires echoed in her ears. The seatbelt cut into her throat. She gripped it tight, trying to hold on. The driver and front passenger swore and drew their weapons. Fear rose quickly, and Hailee hunched down behind the seat. Her heart pounded loudly. One of the team members yelled. Shots rang out. Smoke filled the SUV. Her eyes, lungs, and skin were on fire. Hailee fought to breathe. She tried to unlatch the seatbelt but froze. Fear engulfed her.

Lord help me…

More shots rang out. Long, muscular fingers dug into Hailee's arm and yanked her out of the SUV. Her ears were ringing. She struggled to get control. Dark smoke stung her eyes. Panic set in. Despite Hailee stumbling, the assailant dragged her to the nearest cove. The streets had cleared quickly, probably as the first shots rang out. Hailee felt dizzy, and an overwhelming sense of Déjà vu engulfed her. *Not now!* To survive, she must stay calm.

Her breath came in jagged intervals, and she struggled to free herself from the man who held her captive.

Hailee landed face-first into a smelly van. The driver punched it, tossing her around like a rag doll. She bounced off the walls and equipment piled high in the back.

As the van sped away, Hailee could hear shouting and tires squealing. She tried to sit up, but the driver's erratic, evasive moves made her dizzy. As she lay immobile on the grimy mat, her eyes and throat burned. She inhaled, gasping for air. The van reeked of paint or thinner.

A knot in Hailee's stomach tightened. She had been weakened and injured by tear gas or some other chemical agent. Were the police following her, and were they going to fire at her captor's car? The tear gas dulled her senses, and she couldn't think clearly. Hailee had never been so scared.

The driver slammed on the brakes; she slid across the filthy floor and slammed into the back of the passenger seat.

She lay gasping for breath and was jerked back to the middle of the van, where her wrists were securely tied above her head. Her arms and shoulders were stretched to the limit. The intense pain ravaged her body. With each moment, her fear increased. Dread consumed her. If the Meridian killer had taken her, she would need every ounce of energy and courage she could muster.

With each new kill, the Meridian killer had become increasingly brazen, and he never let his victims live. Did he choose her because she could be linked to Max or because she screwed up his third kill?

She pulled on the zip ties that bound her wrist and struggled to stand to get a better view of her kidnapper. She slipped on the greasy floor, bashing her knee into the wall and pulling down tighter on the ties, tearing her skin. She cried out. Blood dripped down her wrists and onto her sweater.

"Stop moving!"

Hailee felt woozy from the chemicals and strained to listen. She couldn't be sure if she had heard his voice before; it appeared he was a stranger–no identifiable characteristics or habits.

She had never felt so vulnerable; Hailee had been literally kept in the dark by the police, and when the SUV had been under siege, her entire world imploded. No one knew where she was, including herself. She realized she had to be her own savior. A sinking, nauseating sensation threatened to spill out and ruin her bravado. Knowing what to do and actually doing it were completely different things.

Hailee would focus on getting out alive and with as few injuries as possible.

From her research, Hailee knew to look for landmarks or anything that stood out so she could give the police a description of her location. That would prove impossible. All windows, except the front windshield, were painted black, which would explain the sickening smell.

The driver took a sharp right and pulled into an empty lot that appeared to be an industrial park. The van slowed, and a roll-up garage door creaked open, granting it access to the bay. The driver backed in slowly.

They were stopping. Hailee's heart pounded. Would he leave her there and return later or move her to another location? Neither was a viable option. Would he hide his identity to increase her fear? Forcing her to deal with a masked madman with no hope of making a connection. And if he showed his face, she knew that she wouldn't be able to testify against him. *She'd be dead.*

The van door opened, and she took a deep, frightened breath. In her current condition, she wouldn't be able to fight an infant and win. Hailee braced for the worst.

"You should've stayed out of it. Did you think I wouldn't come after you? Just because you're a celebrity?"

"Well," he asked?

She swallowed hard; her throat throbbed. "No."

"Really?"

Her words were strained, and it took a monumental effort to speak. "The girls deserved justice."

"Justice!" He spat.

Hailee had hit his hot spot; she needed to tread carefully.

He stared at her as if he expected an answer.

"Nothing I say will ease your pain or give you solace. You have to be accountable for your actions."

Whack!

She moaned and licked the blood from her swollen lip. Hailee's face tingled, nausea filled her core, and bile threatened to spill out. She tried to keep her eyes open; it was an exhausting feat. Her head fell forward, and darkness surrounded her.

*****

Max and Keller assembled their team and waited outside Simon's single-story house. His house was a typical Cape Cod-style home, featuring a central front door and French doors at the back that led to the patio, making it easier to see the living room and kitchen. Max gave the signal, Keller knocked loudly and identified himself, and when Simon didn't respond, the battering ram pummeled the front door.

The team rushed in and cleared each room throughout the entire house. Max slapped a copy of the warrant on the coffee table, and the forensic team went to work.

The entire precinct wanted this guy, and after hours of scouring the house with no results, and even though he knew they were tired, Max pushed his men harder and harder. Max owed it to his community, family, and Hailee to catch this guy.

Discouraged, Max called off the search and instructed everyone to pack up and return to the station. On his way out, he heard a loud whooping noise.

Keller yelled, "Johnson found a trap door leading to a basement. Come see."

Max hurried to the trap door in the spare bedroom; it had been hidden under an area rug glued to the floor. Johnson had climbed down first, made the discovery, and let out a hoot. Max squeezed into the two-by-two-foot opening, clung to the rickety ladder, and made his descent. A lone cot with crumpled, smelly bedding leaned against the wall in the furthest corner. Food containers and boxes were thrown haphazardly on the floor. Dirty clothes and towels were rolled up and shoved under the cot. Max held his breath as he inspected the rest of the small bunker-type room. Max followed Johnson to a corner of the room, which was now fragmented.

The south wall had been plastered with pictures of the victims in different poses and locations. There were even pictures of Janelle Clark, Dr. Swisher's file clerk. Max wondered if she knew that Simon had placed her on his kill list. The north wall contained calendars and surgery schedules that looked to be from Dr. Swisher's office. Max examined the wall more closely; a picture of another young woman —a redhead — stared back at him. Max didn't recognize her; she wasn't from the Meridian. Did Simon already kill, or was she next? His pulse quickened. He had to find her and protect her from Simon.

Max took several shots of the unidentified woman and sent them to his email. "Johnson, get pictures of this entire wall and bring me the pics of the redhead. I need them now. She may be the next victim."

With Keller on his heels, Max sprinted to the car. On the way back to the station, Max received a frantic call from his secretary. She patched through a call from Sean, the security team leader.

"Toliver."

"We lost her?"

Max pulled over at the first available side street. Through clenched teeth, he ground out. "You lost Miss Hollister?" Before the officer could respond, Max boomed. "What the hell happened?"

"A disabled vehicle blocked our way. Although we approached it cautiously, using evasive measures, it rammed us. A boom erupted, and the SUV filled with tear gas. Shots were fired; we returned fire. Two were hit and went down. We all succumbed to the gas, and Miss

Hollister was forcibly removed from the SUV. We sustained severe damage to the SUV and were unable to pursue the van. We called for backup. The other vehicle had vanished. Miss Hollister and the perp were gone."

"What about witnesses? Did anyone get a look at the perp?" Max asked.

"Just a basic description: tall, one-seventy, maybe Caucasian. He wore a black ninja outfit. He could be anybody."

"It's the Merdian Hotel killer, and he's abducted my only witness." Max pounded on the steering wheel. "Have your commander call me. He'd better have good news!"

Max hit the gas and spun out. He raced to the station. His head throbbed. His anger rivaled only his fear. Hailee had stepped up and now could be the next to die. His well-formulated plan just imploded. Everything had to be reworked.

"Did anyone get a look at the perp?" Keller asked.

"Possibly a white male in a ninja suit; tall, one seventy. It's Simon. I can feel it in my bones."

Max had no idea if Hailee was still alive. Simon's propensity for blood made him an unconscionable and vicious killer. Hailee didn't stand a chance. Visions of her brutal demise flashed across his mind. Why couldn't she let Tom keep her safe?

Think, damn it, think! Max had to get Hailee away from Simon. "We need to find the redhead. If she's alive, she might lead us to Simon."

*****

Back at headquarters, Max waited impatiently for his computer to load. He didn't know what he would do if Hailee died. Could she fight Simon and win? He sent the redhead's pic to Jake, updated him on Hailee's status, and asked him to contact his friend at NCIC to confirm the redhead's identity and obtain an in-depth report on Simon Adkins. Max expected another wacky book or movie quote from Jake, but didn't get it.

"If the redhead knew the doc, why wasn't she killed at the Meridian? And if she wasn't killed, where is she," Keller asked?

Max shook his head, " I don't know. I don't have time to sit around here waiting for intel. The redhead has to know something. We need to find her."

Max's hand shook, part from fear and part from anger. He delved into Simon's media accounts again and couldn't find one picture of the redhead. He combed through Simon's high school and college information with the same disappointing result. After searching the doctor's file clerk's Facebook, he found a throwback picture of Janelle and her high school cheer squad. There was the elusive redhead. He contacted his go-to judge to get a warrant.

Judge Abbott had always gone the extra mile for Max. She followed the letter of the law, respected the spirit in which it had been created, and gave law enforcement the benefit of the doubt, providing they had probable cause. Based on the evidence found in Simon's home and his belief that the woman could probably be the next victim of a serial killer, the judge granted the search warrant, which included all of the girls in the picture. He bolted down the hallway and out to his car. He called Keller from the car and instructed him to wait for Johnson and the crew to return with the evidence from Simon's home.

Max's stomach relaxed a little. He had hope, which he didn't have five minutes ago. If he could save the redhead, he could save Hailee. She had nothing to do with Simon except for the fact that she tried to stop the brutal murder of an innocent woman. It happened in his town, his precinct, and his hotel. He knew tenacity and hard work usually paid off. Now, he was working on hope and prayer.

On his way to the high school, Max left an emergency message for the principal, letting her know to expect him. He hoped to be there before the office closed; time was of the essence.

Max sped through town, watching for kids and cars. He whipped into the front parking lot and saw Principal Danes waiting for him at the front door. Max jumped out, closing the door behind him. He willed himself not to run; he didn't want to alarm her. He smiled and extended his hand.

"I'm Detective Toliver. Thank you for waiting."

Principal Danes waved him to come in. "Your message sounded urgent; you said you have a warrant. What can I do for you?"

Max followed her into her office and sat down. "I'm working on a case and have come across a picture. I need to get the girls' names and contact information in the photo," Max handed her the picture.

"I'll give it to the yearbook staff to get the names and then get the other information from the registrar's office. This could take a while; do you want to wait?"

"I'll wait."

She nodded and headed toward the main office area.

His heart seemed to race constantly. If he lost Hailee, he would be a failure. He hoped the girl could lead him to Simon and then to Hailee. His patience was running low, and he was suffering from physical and mental fatigue. No matter what it took, he would find a way to take down Simon.

While he waited, Max paced. He thought back to his high school days. He welcomed the distraction. He'd played football, participated in two track and field events, and had been a good student, so he only had one experience reporting to the principal's office. At the time, he had skipped Spanish class and had been caught kissing Tiffany Butler behind the bleachers. At that moment, he had felt maybe she had been the one; as it turned out, the next day, Tiffany had moved on to another jock. The principal had issued a warning and sent him back to class.

After several long minutes, the principal returned, and when she did, she was smiling. He hoped it meant she found what he needed. When she re-entered the office, Max stood. Principal Danes handed him a file folder and sat down.

Max thumbed through the folder, "It looks like some contact information is missing. Were you unable to find it?"

"No. Beanie Harper passed away on graduation night–a drunk driver."

An unexpected sadness engulfed Max. Losing someone so young was tragic; her life had just begun. A reckless, irresponsible party-goer took her life. It took him a moment to gather himself. Her death hit him hard. Her death paralleled the events at the Meridian Hotel–young, vibrant lives were being deplorably snuffed out.

"Were you able to identify the redhead?" Max asked.

"Rain Whitlock. She had been the head cheerleader and had been voted most likely to succeed. She modeled for a few years before opening her own modeling agency. She's doing rather well."

A light. A bright light came on in Max's overtaxed mind. Model–perfect bodies–perfect hair… It finally all fell into place.

He thanked Principal Danes and headed toward the car. His strides were deliberate. He buckled up and called Keller to give him his ETA. Max drove cautiously down the road. Once he cleared the school zone, he floored it, heading for HQ.

Chapter 22

For the first time since the murders began, Max had real hope that he would be able to end them once and for all. Principal Danes' identification of the redhead had been invaluable. Hopefully, Rain would be alive, and she could provide insight into where Simon and Hailee were. Before Hailee's abduction, finding Simon had been his number one priority; now, saving Hailee and possibly Rain took precedence.

Max pulled into the parking space at headquarters and bolted down the hall to his office. He turned on his computer and gritted his teeth while it powered on. He pulled up Rain's modeling agency website and dialed the contact number.

They spoke briefly. Rain had dated Simon throughout high school, and they had a great relationship. When her career took off, he had become jealous and suspicious. His behavior had become violent, and he would confront any guy who dared to look at her. She had no choice but to break it off; she hadn't heard from him for a few months, and then she had started dating a male model. After that, her life took a drastic turn. She had received threatening calls and letters and had applied for and received a TRO against Simon. The threats stopped. She didn't know where Simon was. However, she knew his father owned an ice delivery company. She gave Max Mr. Adkins' phone number.

Max dialed Glacier Ice and anxiously waited for someone to answer. He held his breath as the receptionist went to get Mr. Adkins. If Simon's father cooperated, he might be able to bring Hailee home tonight. If not, he might have to drag him down to the station and grill him. Hailee didn't have time for that.

"This is Benjamin Adkins."

"Mr. Adkins, this is Detective Toliver. I need to reach your son immediately. Do you know where he is?"

"What's he done? What's this about?"

"Time is of the essence. A young woman's life is at stake. Where is he?"

"I don't know what you think he's done; he's changed since Rain served him with the TRO. He hasn't been in trouble since."

Max blew out an exasperated breath, "He is our number one person of interest, and we believe he has kidnapped a witness to a murder. If you tell me where he is, we can straighten this all out. I don't want anyone else to get hurt. Please, tell me."

"He didn't come in today, so I'm not sure where he is. He might be at our cottage at Cannon Beach. He likes to take pictures there. It's off Highway 101. You could try there."

"Please text me the address." Max hung up.

Max sprinted to the car. He left a message for Keller informing him to expect a text with an address and to meet him there.

Max floored it. He took the 26 to the 101 and headed toward Cannon Beach. He pulled over when Mr. Adkins texted him the address. He called Judge Abbott, requested a search warrant for the Adkins cottage, forwarded the address to Keller with a nine-one-one, and requested backup. He redialed, and when Mr. Adkins answered, he thanked him for the address and assured him he would do everything possible to ensure his son's safety. Before he hung up, he asked one last question.

"Mr. Adkins, is it possible to forge a weapon out of ice strong enough to kill someone?"

"I'm no expert on weapons, and I don't know how much force it would take to kill someone; still, if somebody were to create an ice knife, the knife would break before it could penetrate the skin. If someone were to create a large block of ice, it could be used as a substitute for a rock. If you keep ice in liquid nitrogen, it would be as strong as steel but extremely brittle and likely to shatter."

"Thanks again."

"My son—"

"I'll do my best. It's up to him."

Max cursed as he sped down the road. His initial lead on the murder weapons just went down the drain, and he didn't have any other leads.

He called Keller to update him on the weapons and to get his ETA for Cannon Beach. Keller informed him that he was ninety minutes out and that the team had no further news regarding Miss Hollister.

If traffic permitted and only if he pushed it, Max would arrive fifteen minutes after Keller. He hit the sirens and rocketed down the highway. Due to exigent circumstances, Max knew he didn't need a warrant. Still, he would prefer to have one. If Simon wasn't there, he didn't want any evidence they discovered thrown out.

Simon had to pay for his crimes. The murdered women had suffered unimaginable pain, and the thought of Hailee enduring that kind of torture made his stomach turn. He focused on the road while perfecting a plan to get Hailee back and finally capture the fiend terrorizing his town.

Max cranked the radio, choosing 105.9 The Brew for classic rock. He felt the gas pedal resting on the floor and looked down at the speedometer. He hadn't realized that as the music intensity increased, so did his speed. He checked the GPS; he was still twenty minutes out. He continued to floor it, speeding past the other cars.

Keller's call interrupted his thoughts.

"Toliver."

"I'm at the cottage; the Adkins' cottage faces the beach and is south of Haystack Rock. I drove past the target and parked behind a cluster of cottages. I canvassed the area. As far as I can tell, no one seems to be inside. I can't get close enough to be sure." Keller paused. "Backup just arrived. What's your ETA?"

"I'll be there in ten. Hang back. Don't let anyone in or out of that cottage, and if you see Simon, don't let him get away."

Max followed Highway 101 junction and took it south for about five minutes. He coasted up behind Keller's car and nodded to his team. He exited the vehicle, secured his Kevlar vest, and checked his weapon; he had four mags with seventeen rounds each. His pulse raced as it always did right before a takedown. He hoped Simon's dad hadn't tipped him off; they needed the element of surprise to be successful. He didn't want a hostage situation where Hailee would become the bargaining chip.

The team had a clear view of the house, beachfront, and ocean. However, the windows and doors were closed and had reflective window film, which made it difficult to see through during the day. Max signaled, and the team advanced toward the cottage.

Max had to decide whether to take the house or wait it out. Since no cars were visible, he only had Mr. Adkins' statement that Simon might be there. A team member found a small opening and inserted the tactical snake camera to get a visual on the perp or his hostage; the living room and front door were clear.

Max and Keller crouched as they approached the front entry. The team swept the outside perimeter and then converged on the front door. Max knocked loudly, identified himself, and waited for a response. When none came, he had the team break down the door, and they swarmed the front room. After clearing each room, they checked for hidden rooms, trapdoors, and any other areas where Simon might have stashed Hailee. They came up empty. Max was torn: happy that he hadn't found Hailee dead or severely wounded and disappointed that she wasn't there. Max instructed the team to wait outside until the search warrant arrived. In their separate cars, he and Keller sped off toward Portland.

*****

Hailee glanced around, taking in her surroundings. The dark and dank cargo space smelled of gasoline and paint thinner. Her arms felt tight, stretched to the breaking point. Her wrists were numb and latched to a hook near the side window.

She felt like a protagonist in one of her books, experiencing the 'all is lost' moment. This wasn't a story, and Hailee couldn't choose the ending. She had been thrust into this nightmare because she had decided to do the right thing. She couldn't stand by idly while someone suffered, and she wished she had listened to Max and been more prudent in her decisions. Hindsight is twenty-twenty. *Next time…*

A loud thud startled her. The van rocked from side to side. Hailee heard screeching, followed by the clank of a chain being hoisted. Did her captor hook up the van for towing? Where were they going? Wherever it was, she guessed it was in the opposite direction from Max and his team. Hailee wondered if she had been allowed to participate in the investigation, if she might know the identity of her kidnapper, and where he might be taking her.

The door banged open; she feigned sleep and waited until the perp entered the van. When she could feel breath on her cheek, she kicked out several times, making contact with a thigh. Her face stung, and her head whipped to the left as something made contact with her cheek.

"Stop it!" He screamed.

Her head reeled with pain, and blood dripped down from her lip. She winced as she straightened up. The ties dug deeper into her wrist. Her foot had made contact with a groin, and she heard a male voice. It was a start; she could devise a plan from there.

"If you want to live, don't do that again." He growled.

"You're going to let me go if I follow instructions?" Hailee asked sarcastically.

"Probably not. I would advise you not to fight me. You'll die sooner." He reached up and tugged on her restraints. "Don't move around; you could slice through your wrist and bleed to death." He snickered. "We wouldn't want that now, would we?"

Hailee focused on his face; if she lived through this, she wanted to give the police a good description of him. She took in his textured and spiked hair, disconnected goatee, and piercing blue eyes. He seemed familiar; maybe she had met him at a signing. He didn't fit her target audience. Hailee thought a moment; perhaps he had a girlfriend or wife. She waited patiently while he tinkered in the van. She mulled it over. Her assumption just didn't fit.

She cleared her throat, "So," she started, "have you read any of my books?"

He laughed. "Don't flatter yourself. This isn't about you."

Her fan theory just imploded. Chills ran down her back, and her arm hair stood up. The Merdian Hotel killer. Hailee licked her lips; she could taste the dried blood and swallowed hard. A fan, she could persuade to let her go. Hailee would promise him full access to her and her life, only to renege on it when she was long gone. A cold, calculating killer wouldn't be impressed or interested in anything she had to offer.

The longer she stared at him, the more frustrated she became. Hailee prided herself on her ability to remember details, and his face had distinct features. His rugged good looks and intense blue eyes were stunning, and his oval face and goatee were strangely familiar. She berated herself; now was not the time to choke. Her senses screamed for her to figure it out, but she couldn't put her finger on it.

The man jumped over the middle console and landed in the driver's seat. He sat staring at the windshield. She wondered where they were–probably an abandoned warehouse or a mechanics shop. As the man stared silently out the window, she studied the back of his head. His well-kept, light brown hair looked familiar. Hailee felt light-headed and extremely weak. The intense fumes made her sick; she felt as if she would pass out. *Not now.* She was on the verge of remembering where they had met.

"I need water."

"Really?"

"The chemicals are strong, and my throat is dry. So, yes. I need water." She choked out, "I'm guessing you're waiting for someone or possibly reevaluating your plan, and it may be a while before I can get anything to drink."

Hailee watched him climb over the console and open a large ice chest. He moved deliberately and confidently, reaching into the chest and pulling out a bottle. He handed it to her and met her gaze. It was friendly and professional. She swallowed. *The ice guy…*

"You're Simon, right? You supply the Meridian with ice?"

"So, you're not just another pretty face. Most celebrities are too self-absorbed and don't notice the little guy. I guess in your profession, it pays to pay attention." He laughed at his own pun.

"Alex, the bartender at the Meridian, is a good friend; he introduced us a couple of weeks ago. Of course, I would remember you." She yanked on the zip ties, trying to revive her cramped and aching fingers. "Why did you start killing? Why now?"

"Wow, straight to the point–I like a woman who speaks her mind. You don't sound as if you're afraid; doesn't it bother you that I've killed before, and you're here with me, at my mercy?"

"Honestly, I'm still woozy from the tear gas, so the gravity of the situation hasn't fully sunk in."

Hailee would never let it show, but every fiber of her being screamed with fear. Every hostage situation was unique. Staying calm meant staying alive. Under different circumstances, she might want to delve into his mind and try to figure out what made him tick and what set off his killing spree. For now, she would settle for not being tortured or brutally murdered.

"I had no choice; the cops had you under tight supervision. Lucky for me, you are constantly being watched by someone, and a few dollars here and a few dollars there, and I was given your exact location. It did take some planning, though. Your security team was top-notch."

"I'm still being followed?" Hailee asked.

"Don't act so surprised. You should be used to it by now."

Hailee blinked; her eyes were growing accustomed to the poor lighting. She took in his dark outfit and gasped. He wore a black ninja suit, similar to the one worn by the woman who attacked the third victim. His face wasn't covered, and that meant he had every intention of killing her–leave no witnesses…

"Are you going to kill me here, or are we going somewhere else?" Hailee asked.

"What makes you think I'm going to kill you?"

"I can identify your face, your voice, your van…"

"True. Initially, I had no intention of harming you– you don't fit my MO." He laughed.

214

"Did you study law? I'd peg you for a model."

Simon glared at her, then slapped her.

Blood oozed from Hailee's nose. She coughed and spat blood on the wall.

"Now, why would you think that?"

She struggled to speak and think clearly; her lips were swollen, and her head spun. The tear gas had worn off, although the physical abuse started to take its toll.

So, something about being a model or having a perfect body offended him. She would keep that in mind.

She swallowed. "I could really use some water now."

Simon opened the bottle and held it to her lips. "Lean back." He tipped the bottle.

Hailee gulped and then coughed. She spat the excess water out.

"So you think I'm a mindless zombie with a perfect body and face?"

"No, you're tall, in good shape, handsome—"

Pain shot through Hailee's jaw, and she groaned. Maybe she should let him do the talking, at least until her body recovered from the shock of being punched.

"What's the matter? Did I hurt you?" Simon smirked.

His comments worried her. Hailee thought he had a goal: murdering specific women for a particular reason. It seems he wants to hurt as many people as possible. He may not have started as a sadistic and homicidal lunatic. Killing three people must have pushed him over the edge, and he seemed to take pleasure in it. Her hope of surviving just plummeted.

"Yes, I'm not used to being a punching bag."

Simon moved closer, inspected her face, and lifted his hand.

Hailee recoiled.

Simon dropped his hand, moved to the center console, and pulled out some tissue. He wet the tip of a tissue and cleaned Hailee's face.

She looked into his eyes as he methodically wiped the blood from her face. He seemed detached yet compassionate. His contrasting actions made it harder for Hailee to determine her best course of action.

Hailee wanted to learn more about his contempt for the fashion industry, "Alex never mentioned anything about you modeling, I guessed."

He dropped his hand and threw the crimson-stained tissue toward the back of the van. "You're right. This whole bloody mess stemmed from the pursuit of fashion and perfection. My girl was ripped away from me with the lure of big money and fame. She forgot that she loved me and we were meant to be together." Simon started at the back window, a dejected look on his face.

Hailee wondered whether the victims were models and why he had chosen them; if so, the media would have pounced on that angle. None of the reports mentioned anything about fashion or models. Did he target women who resembled the woman he lost? Or did he single out perfect women who could've been models?

She had to choose her words carefully. If she dug too deep, it could backfire. She felt Simon wanted to open up about this, and she would listen for as long as it took to break free. "I'm sorry you lost your girlfriend; it hurts to lose someone you love, no matter the reason."

"What do you know about loss? You have looks, money, and fame. All the things that most people want and never have. Tell me why I shouldn't just end you right now."

Hailee hoped that apologizing and recognizing his loss would help them connect.

"I worked for everything that I've achieved," She paused. She didn't want to relive it; perhaps it could save

216

her life. "My parents were dope-smoking, free-sexing hippies. I endured a revolving door of unwanted sexual advances and attempts to convert me to my parents' beatnik lifestyle. My classmates brutalized me at school because of it; I grew up friendless and lonely. After my parents' sudden death, my grandmother took me in and away from the horror of my childhood. That's when I began to feel loved–like a cherished human being."

The disappointment and pain came rushing back. Saying it out loud, remembering the lonely days and nights, and the feeling of despair, knowing she had been the reason her parents had died, amplified her feelings of guilt and regret. She needed a moment; confession was supposed to be good for the soul, apparently not all at once.

"So, you didn't have a picture-perfect childhood. None of us did. You want me to feel sorry for you?"

"No, my pain is just as important to me as yours is to you. We all suffer pain and loss; we have to learn to grieve and then deal with it."

"What are you saying? I chose the wrong outlet for my grief?" He countered.

"Taking someone's life is never the answer. So, yes, you chose the wrong path."

Hailee instantly regretted it. Simon poised to strike, then let his hand fall.

"There's nothing I can do about that now. I have to finish what I've started. It's the only way."

"The only way to what? To show the world you're hurting? You can stop this. Don't take another life." Hailee pleaded.

"You're just saying that because it's your life you're trying to save."

"No, it's not. I tried to rescue the third victim. I didn't know her. I did everything I could, and it still wasn't enough."

217

Sadness flooded through Hailee. She would never forget the fear or the relief in the woman's eyes when she came to her aid. It hadn't been enough, and it devastated Hailee, knowing she had promised the girl she would be alright. In the end, the girl had lost the battle.

"You did the right and brave thing. I can see that you are still visibly upset. You're not what I envisioned you to be. I'm glad we had this talk—"

Panic engulfed her. "Are we leaving? Are you going to kill me now?"

He seemed to be in deep thought, weighing his options. "No. Not now. Good night." He wound up and made contact with Hailee's face.

Chapter 23

Back at the precinct, Max waited for Simon's dad to arrive. His phone rang. Keller called to report a five-minute ETA, and Max instructed him to contact Detective Reece at the cottage to obtain the search results.

A few minutes later, Erma escorted Mr. Adkins to the interrogation room and asked him to take a seat. Max stared across at the fifty-year-old father, who appeared scared and tired. How many times had he been forced to defend his son? Max examined Mr. Adkins' features and determined Simon must take after his mom. Mr. Adkins shifted nervously under Max's scrutiny.

"Why am I here? Did you find Simon?"

"No, and that's why you're here. We didn't find him at the cottage, and time is running out for the kidnapped victim. Please think about where Simon might be. Somewhere quiet, desolate. Do you own any property that is abandoned or out of town?"

"Just the cottage. It's only used a few months a year; if Simon's not there, I don't know where he is."

Max slammed his fist on the table. "A woman's life is at stake."

"Are you sure Simon has her?"

"He is our only suspect, and we believe he is going to kill her."

"Simon learned his lesson. He's not stalking or killing anyone. He has no reason to. He doesn't even know how to—"

"To what? Kill?"

At the sound of an insistent rap, Max waved in Keller. Keller hovered in the door jamb and motioned for Max to meet him outside the room. Max jumped up and pointed his finger at Mr. Adkins. "Don't leave."

Keller closed the door. "We got another break. Reece found a sword and a couple of bloody knives buried in the sand near Haystack Rock. Reece is on his way to the lab to check the blood to see if it matches any of our victims' blood."

Max stifled a smile. "If we can pinpoint when the low tide rolled in, we can determine if they were buried after the murders. Do you have pics of the weapons? I want to show Mr. Adkins and see if he can ID them as Simon's."

Keller nodded and forwarded the pics. Keller's phone rang, and he returned to his office.

Armed with his only evidence, Max closed the door with a bang. Mr. Adkins jolted upright.

"Look at these photos and tell me if you've seen them before?" Max handed him the phone.

Max watched intently as Mr. Adkins thumbed through the photos.

"I can't be sure; these look like throwbacks of Simon's Comic-Con days. He gave that all up after he pleaded guilty to stalking Rain," he frowned. "He's not supposed to have these. Are they real?"

"Yes, and deadly. A woman is in danger; are you sure you don't know of any place Simon might run to, or go to think or hide?"

"We don't have unlimited resources. I can't think of anywhere Simon would go."

Max stood, knocking the chair over. His balled fists supported his weight as he leaned across the table and glared into Adkins' eyes.

"I need you to think hard. Someone is in danger and might die, and it might be your son."

Adkins' shaking hands covered his face. "I swear I don't know where he is?"

"Think, man!" Max slammed his fist on the table. "Do you have any company cars or vans he could hide in?"

"A van," Adkins perked up, "A delivery van. We have an old maintenance shop in the Pearl District. It's about ten minutes from here. He might go there if he's in trouble."

Max jumped up and slammed the door shut. He rushed into Keller's office and instructed him to get backup, head out to the Pearl District, and wait for orders. Max bolted down the hall to get the location from Adkins and told him to stay put and not to call anyone, specifically Simon. He texted Keller and sprinted to his car.

Simon had no soul and proved to be highly unpredictable. Max knew Hailee would do everything in her power to survive. It may not be enough. It was his responsibility to bring Hailee home safely. She wouldn't be in this mess if she hadn't gotten involved with him.

He darted in and out of the lanes, his speed increasing with each passing minute. He took SW 4th Ave., then side streets. Keller and the team would surround the repair shop from all sides and be out of view until they were ready to converge on the building and extract Hailee.

*****

The throbbing woke Hailee. Her mouth and jaw were stiff and swollen. She blinked furiously as she tried to focus on her surroundings. Darkness surrounded her, and her wrists were still tethered together and hung from a hook. She swallowed painfully; she felt fatigued, and her dry throat ached. A loud squeaking pulled her from her examination.

Simon, who crouched on his knees, reached out and yanked on her forearms; she cried out as the zip ties tightened.

"Where are we?" Hailee asked?

"Does it really matter? Your fate was sealed long ago." He moved closer and stared into her eyes. "You should've stayed out of it."

"I tried to rescue an injured woman."

"No, you interfered with my plan, and now it's time for you to pay."

Hailee knew that most serial killers have been victims of physical or sexual abuse, or they come from a dysfunctional situation or from a family with absent parents. She didn't know why Simon had killed; it couldn't hurt to find out. She needed time to plan her getaway.

"Why did you kill those girls? What did they do to you?"

"If things were different, we could be friends. I already told you I like your candor." He glared at her with pursed lips. "They represent evil, and evil must be eradicated."

"Evil? They were barely adults; they hadn't been given a chance to live or love."

"Love is not a worthy goal. Besides, they chose the wrong path, and I delivered them from themselves."

"They weren't evil; they were young, intelligent, beautiful women—"

Hailee inhaled sharply. Simon's obsession with beauty is why four people had to die. "When I mentioned you were attractive, you snapped at me. Why do you find beauty offensive?"

"Natural beauty is commendable; what people will do to achieve perfection is what makes them evil."

Pain erupted when she tried to speak; if she didn't get something to drink soon, she'd fall victim to severe dehydration and may lose consciousness. "May I have some water?"

He smiled. "I know what you're doing, and it won't work. Even if you stall for another two hours, your lover won't find you. We're hidden far, far away. No one will come to your rescue." He opened a water bottle and put it up to her cracked lips.

She drank greedily. The warm water burned her throat and then quenched her thirst. She started to feel better. Simon sat uncomfortably close; she could smell his sweat. The odor began to consume her. She turned away. She had hoped to examine him more closely; however, the funk originating from his body was more than she could bear.

"Did she do this to you?" Hailee asked sincerely.

"Who?"

"The woman who broke your heart and made you feel like you weren't good or attractive enough."

"My own vanity sent me down the path to hell. I recognize that now, and it's my job to save others from falling from grace, too."

"Is she still alive, or did you kill her too?"

"She forced me into submission, then rejected me. She died the day she turned her back on me."

Hailee knew that serial killers rarely kill the target of their anger or desire; she wondered if Simon had imprisoned the poor girl or if she even knew her ex had a taste for killing. "So," Hailee started, "she marginalized your efforts to fit into her world, and then you decided to go on a killing spree to save the world from your mistake." She regretted it instantly. Simon raised his hand to strike her, and she braced for impact. He let it fall.

"So brutally honest. Where have you been all my life?" He grinned devilishly.

His volatility frightened her, and she didn't want any unwanted attention from Simon, so she continued interrogating him. "You seem to have good bones and be naturally good-looking. What did she do to you?"

"She stole my soul. She robbed me of my self-confidence, self-respect, and dignity. She forced me to believe that I had to be better to be with her. It still wasn't enough."

"Tell me what she did to you."

Simon ripped off his shirt and lifted his arms high. "See?"

She leaned closer to him; Hailee's wrists slipped off the hook. A low gasp escaped from her lips. She kept her arms above her head, and her eyes darted from side to side, searching for a weapon to overpower him with.

Nothing.

She inspected his chest and then his armpits. Tiny incisions were barely visible. "Pec implants? She coerced you into having plastic surgery? Why?"

"That's not all." He lifted his chin and pointed to the skin that separates the nostrils.

"Rhinoplasty?" Pain shot through Hailee's wrists and arms. She'd be damned if she let him know she was one step closer to freedom.

"You really don't know, do you?"

At the moment, she really didn't care. Thirst scorched her parched throat. She swallowed hard. "Can I have more water?"

He held the bottle for her, and she drank the remaining water.

"She had an anatomically perfect body. She said she loved me and wished that we were the same, perfect. She had a modeling job and wanted me to join her. When I didn't make the cut, she introduced me to Dr. Swisher, and the rest is history."

"Dr. Swisher? Did you kill him?"

Simon laughed explosively.

Hailee scanned the area again and smiled in the darkness. Something long and hard lay a few inches from her.

"No. The doctor's bitchy wife did that."

"Why?" Hailee inched closer.

224

"He was a vile pig. Or maybe his greedy wife wanted all the money. Who knows? Who cares? He's dead, and it saved me from having to do it myself."

"How do you know his wife murdered him?" She asked breathlessly.

"I went to his office to do the deed myself and retrieve the patient files he promised to give to the police. Imagine my surprise when I saw the life drain from his eyes, and I didn't have to lift a finger." He smirked. "I didn't know the doc's wife had it in her."

Hailee lunged toward the object and pushed Simon down. He screamed as his ankle buckled. Her nails scraped along the floor and came in contact with a hammer. She grabbed it. Simon pushed her down and jumped on top of her. She moaned and swung the hammer. It made contact with his shoulder; he recoiled, swung wildly, and missed. She gripped the hammer tight and swung with all her strength, striking him in the chest. He flew out of the van.

She scrambled to her knees and struggled to close and lock the door. She climbed over the console and into the driver's seat. She searched for the keys and found them closed in the visor. She looked out the open driver's window. Blood oozed from Simon's head. She turned the keys in the ignition.

Hailee couldn't find the opener in the van, so she inched closer to the rollup door and found a release button on the wall. She hit it several times. The door got stuck halfway up. Hailee clung to the top of the steering wheel with her bound hands and hit the gas. The bottom of the metal door crunched outward as the van crashed through it. The van continued forward and smashed into a light pole. She hit her head on the steering wheel. She flew forward, then back. Blood oozed from her face, and she blacked out.

*****

The team waited in the standby position; Max waited for Keller at the back of his car. The repair shop appeared abandoned. Adkins had assured Max that he still used it and that the company's vans were stored there. Keller lifted his hand and then heard a grinding noise. He motioned for the team to hold their position. The right bay door partially opened, then bowed outward, producing a loud, grating sound. A white van with dark windows rammed through the door, then accelerated directly into a pole.

Max and his team drew their weapons. Max ordered the driver to exit the van with his hands in the air. He shouted the command again, and then the door opened slowly. The driver slid out of the van, hands in the air, and crumpled to the ground.

Max raced to Hailee's side and pulled her out of the line of fire. Blood dripped from her nose and mouth. Her lips moved, but nothing came out. He cut the zip ties and called for an ambulance; his team checked the van for Simon and then advanced into the building.

The EMTs put Hailee onto a stretcher and loaded her into the ambulance. Max watched as the paramedics checked her vitals and hooked up an IV line.

"Can you tell the extent of her injuries?" Max asked.

"She's dehydrated and may have sustained broken bones from the accident; the doctors will be able to give you a better diagnosis after she's been examined."

"H u r t." She croaked through swollen lips.

Max moved closer. "Hailee, don't talk. You're safe now. You did great."

She lifted her head. "Simon's." Her head dropped onto the pillow. "Hurt."

Max climbed into the back, and the ambulance sped down the road, flying through the stop lights. Max watched Hailee struggle to breathe and hoped her injuries weren't life-threatening. What terrors did she suffer at the hands of Simon, and how did she get free?

Max called Keller for an update on Simon's whereabouts and the repair shop's search. He listened as Keller relayed the evidence they found, starting with the pool of blood in the first bay and other traces of Simon's DNA found throughout the shop. Keller detailed his theory on Simon's departure: while Hailee crashed through the bay door, wounded and disoriented, Simon limped out to the employee entrance to a waiting car, possibly another company van. Simon's blood had been found leading out of the bay and stopped outside in the first parking spot. Then, as if Simon had never been there, the trail went cold. Max directed Keller to return to headquarters so the team could finish up and find out where Simon had gone.

The ambulance stopped at the ER entrance; Max jumped out, and the paramedics rushed inside with the stretcher. The ER nurses moved Hailee onto a gurney and hurried to a stall, where they drew the curtains closed. Max paced; a knot formed in his gut. He'd been so close to bringing Simon in. If only Adkins had been forthcoming sooner, Hailee may not have suffered at the hands of his psycho son. Keller texted Max to notify him that he had arrived at the station and that he had an update regarding Dr. Swisher's murder.

Max could not leave Hailee alone and vulnerable, so he arranged for two uniformed officers to protect her. While he waited for them to arrive, a nurse peeked out of the stall where Hailee was receiving treatment and waved him in. Max strode quickly to the stall and hesitated before going in. He took a deep breath and prepared himself for the worst: the worst-case scenario would have been that Hailee turned up dead. She had fought well and had survived a serial killer. The nurse motioned for him to come closer.

"She's asking for you." The nurse stated as she exited the stall.

Max bent down. "I'm here."

Hailee tried to raise her head.

"Hailee, you need to rest. You're safe now."

"Doctor's wife—" she licked her lips. "Killed doctor."

"Don't worry about the case. I've got it under control."

Hailee nodded and closed her eyes.

Max waited for the uniformed officers to arrive and ordered them not to leave Hailee's side for any reason. Max knew Hailee would be safe, so he headed back to the precinct.

The drive back was riddled with questions. How did Hailee know the doctor's wife murdered him? What was the emergency back at the station? Would Simon kill again?

He drove fast, and when he arrived at the precinct, he parked and rushed to Keller's office. He scanned the room and found Mrs. Swisher sitting facing Keller. Her eyes were red and swollen, and she wiped away the constant flow of tears.

"The killer has threatened Mrs. Swisher, and she wants our protection," Keller stated.

"Mrs. Swisher, why would you need our protection?"

She whipped her head around to face Max, who stood in the doorway, "Because the lunatic killing women called to tell me I was next. I want protection."

"When did he call, and what exactly did he say?"

"What difference does it make? That psycho is after me. You have to keep him away from me."

"Mrs. Swisher, I understand you are frightened. If you tell me what happened, I might be able to find him quicker and get him off the streets. Then everyone will be safe." Max assured her.

Mrs. Swisher dabbed at her eyes and brushed a wayward hair back into place. "I arrived home this afternoon at two p.m. I got a call from an unknown number." She angled her seat to face Max. "When I answered, a low, growling voice said, 'You're next, prepare to die.'"

"Did he say anything else or give you a clue to his identity?" Max asked.

"He just told me he wanted to kill me; nothing mattered after that. I hung up and drove right here." She handed Max her phone. "Here's the call history from the call. It only lasted thirty seconds."

"Thirty seconds," Max mused, "he must have said something else. It would only take about 5 seconds to say what you allege he said."

Mrs. Swisher huffed. "You don't believe me?"

"I don't have time to waste on someone who won't tell the truth. I am trying to catch a killer and keep my town safe. What else did he say?" Max demanded.

Mrs. Swisher shuffled her purse from side to side. "That's all."

"If you don't tell me the truth, why should I offer you protection?"

Mrs. Swisher stared at Max with mouth wide open. "I'm a resident of Portland, a prominent one. That's why you need to help me. I'm telling you the truth."

"I don't believe you." Max motioned for Keller to follow him. "Stay here, we'll be back. I want the truth, so don't waste my time."

Max closed the door firmly, and they moved further down the hall. Max asked Keller if they had any leads on who had murdered the doctor. Keller said that the M.E.

believed the murder weapon to be a surgical scalpel. Unfortunately, there were dozens of them in the office. Everyone, including patients and employees, had access to them. Keller told Max that they had found financial discrepancies that might serve as a motive. Mrs. Swisher had been moving money from their joint accounts into her private account, and our legal advisor said that the money in her personal account would not be subject to the doctor's children's inheritance.

"Even though she could barely speak, Hailee told me before I left that the doctor's wife had killed him, not Simon. I don't know how she knows, but I believe her." Max said.

"So, Mrs. Swisher was siphoning the marital money into her accounts, then offs the doc, blames the serial killer, and then doesn't have to share the spoils with his kids." Keller nodded. "Good plan. Except, for now, she's claiming Simon's after her. Do you believe her?"

"I do; she's scared. She doesn't know that we suspect her of killing her husband. Have we searched her house?"

"We couldn't get a warrant until now. Do you want me to hold Mrs. Swisher or move her somewhere?" Keller asked.

"No, I'll take care of her. Call the judge and get a team out there. Maybe we'll get lucky and find the murder weapon or at least some documents that we can use to hold her."

Max headed to Keller's office, where Mrs. Swisher waited. She slouched in the chair and looked peaked. Max ushered her to the lounge, gave her water, and had her lie on the couch. He instructed Officer Thornton to keep a close eye on her and detain her at the station. Max figured she would feel safe here and wouldn't leave, but just in case.

Max dialed Mr. Adkins' number and drummed his fingers impatiently on the desk. If Mr. Adkins encouraged his son to flee and he hurt anyone else, Max would throw the book at him.

Mr. Adkins answered timidly. "Yes."

"It's Detective Toliver. Where's Simon?"

"I told you everything I know. I saw the news—"

"Your son," Max gritted his teeth, "Beat my witness and then got away. I want you to tell me where he is, or else!"

"I didn't hurt anybody—"

"Maybe not; if you had been forthcoming sooner, no one else would've gotten hurt. Think hard. Your son is in trouble, and he's wounded. Where would he go–who would he ask for help?"

"I really don't know. Simon's changed. Really, I can't—"

Max slammed his fist on his desk. Hailee barely made it out alive. Now, Simon was on the loose and, like an injured animal, would be extremely dangerous.

"He's a killer, and if you don't tell me, I'll lock you up and throw away the key!"

"His mother, she's—"

Max stood up. "Where is he?"

"Try the bartender at The Meridian Hotel. I think they're friends."

Max asked, "Alex?"

"Yes, Simon talks about him, so ask Alex."

Max called Carrington and got Alex's contact information. He dialed the number and prayed that Alex would answer—it went straight to voicemail. Max's stomach clenched; this could get ugly really fast. Either Alex was an accessory to murder, or he might be Simon's next victim.

Max dialed again.

"Hello."

"Alex, it's Detective Toliver. I need to reach Simon Adkins; do you know how to reach him?"

"Yeah, he just called for a ride; I told him I'd pick him up in thirty minutes."

"I'm trying to get Simon off the streets. I have a plan; it's going to be dangerous. I'll be there to back you up."

"What's going on? Is Hailee in danger?"

"Yes, and she's hurt. You in?"

"Hell yeah!"

Alex told Max that he'd arranged to meet Simon at a local tavern in the Pearl District and then would take Simon to his Aunt's house in Cedar Hills–fifteen minutes from the tavern.

Max filled Alex in on the basics: Simon killed several people, and now that he had been wounded, he would be extremely dangerous. Max had always liked Alex; he was a great bartender and great with the customers and vendors. When Alex confronted Max, potentially risking his job, Max came to appreciate Alex more.

Chapter 24

Hailee moved her arm and winced; her entire body ached. Her wrists were bandaged, and her head throbbed. She must have hit the steering wheel when she plowed into the pole. Her lips and eyes were swollen; she could still feel the sting of the tear gas. She had gauze stuffed up her nose. All in all, she felt pretty good. No, she felt damn good to be alive.

She searched for the emergency buzzer to alert a nurse. She fumbled for it and moaned.

"What do you need?"

Hailee looked up to see a familiar face. She smiled; her bulging lips stretched painfully across her bruised face. "T o m." She squeaked.

"Easy now." He leaned closer to hear what she said.

"Good to see you."

"Liar."

Hailee laughed, then moaned.

"Take it easy."

"M a x?"

"He's working. I'll keep you safe." He smiled. "This time, I know you'll stay put."

When she tried to roll her eyes, pain shot through her temple. For now, she would have to believe Tom about Max. If only she could say the same for herself. Hailee's physical injuries were excruciating; she couldn't feel anything emotionally, not fear or relief. It could be shock, or maybe the medicine that dulled her pain numbed her emotions as well.

Tom sat near the door, and Hailee closed her eyes, saying a silent prayer of thanks.

Hailee's swollen eyes stung, and she couldn't see the clock. The medicine was a welcome relief from the pain; her entire face felt dislocated. She wondered how severe her injuries were and if surgery would be necessary. If she needed surgery, what would she think about her body and the results, and how would it affect her relationships? Simon's words were affecting her.

Hailee knew the cosmetic surgery industry was growing and realized that it had two sides: medical and aesthetic. She hadn't delved into its non-medical side. Simon's obsession with perfection skewed his ability to make good choices. He resorted to drastic measures to boost his self-confidence and sense of belonging, but ultimately failed.

Hailee believed that physical improvements were a choice, but at what cost? Self-esteem and confidence stem from experiences, both good and bad. Simon underwent surgery to enhance perceived physical flaws. The surgeries did nothing to increase his emotional confidence. He allowed a woman to convince him he didn't deserve her love. After Simon made the surgical changes, the woman he loved left him, stealing his heart, identity, and feelings of security.

Reflecting on her time spent with Simon made Hailee's head hurt. She motioned to Tom. He strode to her side.

"What can I get you?" Tom asked.

Hailee cleared her throat, and she strained to speak. "Find my Father."

Tom shook his head. "We'll worry about him later. You need to heal."

Hailee shook her head. "Please."

Tom gently patted her forearm. "Get some rest."

"No. Please." Hailee tried to sit up.

Tom carefully eased her back down. "Miss Hollister, I know you're probably worried that you'll never see him again. Give yourself a break. What you need right now is sleep. Let the staff take care of you."

Deflated, she closed her eyes. She heard Tom's chair scrape on the floor as he sat. She opened her eyes and strained to see him. He opened his computer and started typing.

She smiled; what a softy.

*****

Two blocks surrounding the tavern were closed off. Swat, Max, and Keller surrounded and secured the tavern's perimeter. Max signaled to Alex, who exited his car. Alex headed toward the back parking lot. Max noticed that Alex's strides were confident at first; however, as he neared Simon, his steps slowed and became timid. Simon leaned forward against the tavern's back fence. Max held his breath. If Alex showed signs of fear, Simon might smell a trap, and there could be substantial casualties. Max didn't care about Simon; if he got shot or killed, he deserved it. Alex, a decent, hardworking guy, could be injured or worse.

Max watched with bated breath as Alex picked up the pace and strode casually to the block fence. Max had warned Alex that if he got too close to Simon, he might be his next victim, and Max didn't want Simon to find the wire on Alex.

Everyone held their positions. The takedown loomed.

Max's heart raced as Alex approached Simon. Alex and Simon fist-pumped; Alex kept his distance. Max pulled out his Glock, racked it, and waited with his finger on the trigger. Max listened as Alex chatted. The takedown seemed to be playing out in slow motion. Alex rambled on. If Alex didn't move soon, Max felt his heart might burst. Simon's impending capture was palpable.

Max watched as Alex smiled and nodded. Alex started walking and motioned for Simon to follow. Simon straightened up and stepped forward, faltering as his ankle twisted outward. Alex continued talking.

Simon fell behind.

Alex turned.

Simon looked around wildly.

Alex sprinted toward the tavern.

Simon twirled and looked around.

Max shouted, "Down on the ground!"

Simon fell to his knees.

"Hands above your head! Face on the ground!" Max ordered.

Simon slowly lifted his hands.

"Now! Hands above your head." Max shouted.

Simon hesitated; a look of defiance crossed his face. He shook his head no.

"Face on the ground!" Max screamed.

Simon reached into his waistband, pulled out a gun, and smiled.

Shots rang out.

Multiple rounds struck Simon. His body convulsed and fell forward. His gun dropped near his bullet-riddled body; blood stained the ground.

Max, Keller, and the team rushed to Simon. Max pointed his Glock at Simon's head, kicked his gun away, and rolled him over. Simon's lifeless eyes stared up into the sky.

*****

After much-needed sleep, Hailee woke to raised voices. She opened her eyes and squinted. She could clearly hear Tom but not the other voice. She struggled to sit up, wincing. Both parties looked in her direction. *Max.* Her heart pounded; her hand instinctively flew to her hair to tame her unruly locks. Hailee frowned. What a sight she must be.

236

Max went to her side.

He smiled at her, then turned and walked away.

Tom rushed over and asked if she needed assistance. She shook her head no. Max hadn't been able to look Hailee in the eye; her injuries must be horrifying. Her mind had concocted this hideous, bloody face, and based on Max's reaction, her assessment had been correct.

Hailee watched Max; he seemed to be debating with himself. She smiled, and her skin tightened and throbbed.

Max returned to her side. "Hailee."

Her name rolled off his tongue; she imagined him caressing her, and right now, she really needed that; unfortunately, her bruised and battered flesh wouldn't allow it.

"Hailee, I got him. Simon has been neutralized and won't hurt anyone again."

She closed her eyes briefly. Finally, Portland was safe.

"I know you're hurting," Max started, "but I need to know how you know that Dr. Swisher's wife killed him."

Tom interrupted. "Toliver. Look at her. She needs to rest."

Tom had started as an unwelcome nuisance, but then he morphed into Hailee's biggest supporter. Hailee lifted her hand to signal to Tom; it felt heavy and dropped back down.

"Simon went to the doctor's office." Pain erupted in her throat. "To get files and kill the doctor." She wavered. "Mrs. Swisher arrived first and killed her husband. Simon watched."

Max softly stroked Hailee's hand. "That's my girl. Get some rest. I have one more murderer to catch. Tom will be here if you need anything."

Max hurried to the door; Hailee couldn't be sure. She thought she saw him wink and blow her a kiss. That didn't seem like Max; she must have imagined it.

237

Tom hovered for a while, checking her pillow, her tubes, and her monitors. He acted like a nursemaid. It gave her much-needed entertainment, and now, Hailee had something to hold over him the next time he tried to act the 'tough guy.'

She napped throughout the day; knowing that Simon wouldn't hurt anyone again made sleeping easier, well, so did the pain medicine. Now that the victims had received justice, Hailee realized she could concentrate on herself and start to heal. She wondered if luck, skill, or fate had allowed her to survive while the other victims had not. Did Simon plan on torturing her, but let her live? Or, because she interfered with his plan, did she make herself his next victim? A sad, profound, sinking feeling overwhelmed Hailee. She couldn't shake it off. It consumed her, drowning her in a pool of regret and guilt.

Even though she felt guilty for surviving, deep down, she knew it wasn't her fault that the other girls had died. Hailee hadn't fought any harder than the third victim, yet she survived, and the other girl died. Nausea swelled and threatened to spill. Simon's crimes were senseless and horrific, and they hurt so many people. How did killing three young women make Simon's life better–did he get his girl back? Did his self-esteem return, giving him confidence and increasing his self-worth? Did robbing these women of their lives and potential do a damn thing for him?

Hailee felt a tightening in her chest and a burning in her throat. She tried to squash it. Anger coursed through her being. Feelings of shame and unworthiness boiled over, and she swung out with her arm, knocking over the food cart.

It crashed to the ground.

Tom flew up and rushed to her side.

"Miss Hollister, what's wrong?"

Hailee didn't realize she'd hit the cart so hard.

"I—" she started to say, then whispered, "Why did they have to die?"

"I don't know," Tom's features softened, "It's not your fault."

"Why me?"

"Don't try to figure out the motives of a madman. It will drive you insane."

Tom picked up the cart and buzzed for the nurse. The nurse came in, checked Hailee's IV line and heart monitor, smiled reassuringly, and left.

Tom returned to his seat and continued working on his computer. Hailee closed her eyes and prayed for sleep.

*****

On the way back to the precinct, Max called Keller to get an update on the search of Mrs. Swisher's property. They were looking for a scalpel, hopefully, one that contained traces of the doctor's DNA or blood. After taking Simon down, Max went straight to the hospital to check on Hailee and share the good news. He hadn't had time to decompress and was still pumped up on adrenaline. Hailee looked worse than he remembered; her bruises had turned into hematomas, and the swelling had increased. He hated seeing her that way. It would haunt him. He knew she came back because of him; if only she hadn't been so stubborn, she might not have been hurt. But if she weren't so confident, she wouldn't be Hailee. Her tenacity and good heart made her the woman he respected.

Max pulled into the front parking space and checked his phone—no word from Keller.

Max nodded to Erma, who waved him down.

"You have a visitor," Erma said.

"Rex?"

"No, a young woman. She wouldn't give me her name. She's quite upset. I put her in interrogation room 1."

Max grabbed two bottles of water and headed down the hall. He paused outside the interrogation room, peered in, and then pushed the door open.

A young woman with long, pink hair, a purple see-through blouse, and a plunging black bralette looked up when Max entered the room. Her deep plum lipstick accentuated her olive skin and brown eyes. She had been biting her lower lip when Max came in.

Max extended his hand, "I'm Detective Toliver. What can I do for you?"

The young woman smiled, flashed her pink stiletto nails, and extended her hand to Max. "Oh, you're the yummy Max," she eyed him up and down a couple of times. "I'm Kat. Hailee's bestie."

Kat was everything that he had envisioned her to be. Now he knew why Tom had such a problem with her clothes. She wore bold, vibrant clothing. Her nails could be deemed dangerous weapons, and her smile could melt a man's heart.

"The hospital and that Neanderthal Tom won't let me visit Hailee."

Max suppressed a grin, so the feeling *was* mutual; Kat and Tom definitely disliked each other. "Hailee's recovering in the hospital, and even though the threat to her life has been eliminated, I asked Tom to make sure she's safe."

Kat drummed her razor-sharp nails on the table, "When can I see her? I have to see with my own eyes that she's okay."

Max shook his head, "That's not a good idea; she needs to rest."

Kat bolted up, exposing her gold lamé belt and bright-orange pleated miniskirt. "How bad is she hurt?" She met Max's steady gaze.

"Kat, a serial killer, held her captive, and then she hit a pole trying to escape." He let that sink in and then

240

said, "Hailee is doing remarkably well, and as you know, she is strong. She's going to get through this. It will take time; time to heal and time to reflect."

Kat's lips pursed downward, and she plopped down in the chair. Her eyes narrowed, and her brows furrowed. "She's my boss, my friend. She needs me."

"She speaks highly of you. I know she is worried about you and misses you too."

"Why would Hailee be worried about me?" she asked.

Max took a drink of water and offered Kat the other bottle. "She thought Tom had hurt you, or worse."

She scoffed, "We reached an agreement, and as far as I know, he was just blowing smoke. Of course, I wouldn't want to test that theory. We're good."

"Does Tom know?"

Kat cracked a smile. "Sure."

"Hailee can't have visitors for a while. Is there anything else I can do for you?"

Kat sat tall, shoulders tense, "I'm glad you offered. I need help with Rex."

At the sound of Rex's name, Max's face heated up, and his jaw tensed. He wished Rex would disappear. "What's he doing now?"

Kat visibly relaxed, "He's been inundating her emails with veiled threats. He doesn't believe she's in danger. He thinks she is avoiding him and is threatening to come forward with her secrets and destroy her life and her career. We can't let that happen."

Max swore under his breath. He didn't have time for Rex. He would be damned if he let him ruin Hailee while she lay hurt and vulnerable in a hospital bed. "What is he threatening to reveal–what secret?"

Kat stared back at Max. He waited for a response. Kat tilted her head and examined her perfectly manicured fingers.

Max blew out a hard breath, "Really?"

"Not my secret to tell, so yeah, really."

"There's not much I can do if I don't know what I'm up against."

"He's a bully and a greedy, despicable man."

"And," Max asked?

"And I can't tell you anymore. Just arrest Rex and throw away the key." Kat grinned widely; she looked like the cat that swallowed the canary.

If it were only that easy, Max would've already done it. And it couldn't happen to a nicer guy. He preyed on Hailee's insecurities and guilt. He forced her to endure his illegal behavior, all in the name of business. Max would bet his badge that Hailee hadn't done anything legally or morally wrong. She had convinced herself that she had done something terrible and would put up with Rex's overtures and constant threats.

Max checked his phone; he still hadn't heard from Keller. Max sent a quick text asking for an update on the Swisher search. He would brainstorm with Kat to come up with a short-term solution until he resolved Doctor Swisher's murder. Once he wrapped that up, he would focus solely on Hailee's problem. Blackmailers were a tricky breed. They preyed on other people's fears and doubts, using any method they could to achieve their goals. Most blackmailers wanted money. Unfortunately, Rex wanted Hailee to control and manipulate her. Rex would need to be dealt with carefully. Hailee had repetitively told him that her career, everything she loved, would be devastated if her secret got out.

Max ran his fingers through his hair, excused himself, and headed to the lounge. Mrs. Swisher jumped up when he entered the room.

"Did you get him? Am I safe?" She asked nervously.

Max poured himself some coffee, added cream and sugar, and turned to face her. "I am not able to discuss an ongoing case. Rest assured, we are going to apprehend all guilty parties." With that, he left and returned to the interrogation room.

Kat paced vigorously. Max hadn't noticed her shoes before; she wore pink-flowered cowboy boots, and when she walked, she flitted across the floor. Kat made bold and vivid choices and was interesting, loyal, and strong. Hailee thought the world of her. Seeing Kat would significantly improve Hailee's mood and temperament. Regrettably, Hailee's physical condition and appearance shocked even Max, and he had seen a multitude of serious injuries. He had a hard time looking at her, and he didn't want to alarm her. She had survived what most people couldn't even fathom, and to make matters worse, her escape included crashing head-on into a pole.

Kat stopped pacing when Max entered the room. "Is Hailee alright?"

"Hailee's condition hasn't changed," Max rolled his neck. "I needed caffeine."

"What about Rex?" Kat asked.

"The best way for Hailee to get rid of Rex permanently is to come clean. Whatever he has on her, she needs to come out with it first–beat him to the punch so he can't hold it over her." Max knew that the fear of being found out might be worse than what would actually happen. Typically, the victims would convince themselves that their secret would destroy them if they told.

Kat pouted, "I've been telling Hailee to do just that. She won't. She thinks her world will end and that Rex will win, so she refuses to come forward."

"There's got to be a way to make her understand; she has support, and if she confesses her alleged sins, it will be cathartic. And Rex won't be able to hurt her anymore."

Max's phone dinged. He checked his messages. Keller texted to say they had found the scalpel. It had traces of blood, and Keller would drop it off at the lab before returning to HQ. He sent Max a picture of the scalpel and would be back in forty minutes. The second message was from Erma, stating that she had spoken to Rex Chandler and that he anxiously awaited a callback from Max.

Max stood and smirked. Rex's timing couldn't have been better. He had been mentally working on a plan to hold Rex off, and Max was ready to put it into action. "I'll be back in a few minutes. Please wait here. Do you need more water?"

Kat shook her head no and then asked, "Is it about Hailee?"

Max nodded, went to his office, and closed the door. He pulled Rex's card from his wallet and dialed. Rex picked up on the first ring.

"Mr. Chandler, it's Detective Toliver. What can I do for you?"

"Is Hailee alright? Where is she?"

"Miss Hollister is safe and recovering nicely." Rex had no legal right to Hailee's medical information, and Max refused to give him any hint about her condition.

"I've called the hospital several times, and they refuse to let me speak to her. I need to know she's okay."

"Mr. Chandler, Miss Hollister's health and safety is our number one priority; I can assure you she's safe."

"Safe?" Rex squeaked. "A killer kidnapped her. You call that safe?"

Max held his tongue. Rex knew how to push his buttons; he wouldn't let that smug, self-righteous prick get the best of him.

"Miss Hollister came back to Portland to get away from you and, in doing so, put herself in harm's way. Do not place blame, Mr. Chandler; there's plenty of that to go around."

Rex remained quiet for a few minutes; Max thought he had hung up, but then he heard Rex's labored breathing and figured he must be scrambling to find the right words.

"Well, um, I'm sorry. I didn't mean to imply you aren't doing your job; I'm just frightened for Hailee. She needs guidance and support; I've always tried to give that to her."

Max thought about many different ways he would like to get rid of Rex. None of them were legal, so he decided to stick to his plan. "Mr. Chandler, Hailee is healing nicely and should be able to make a statement in a week or so." Max's plan morphed a little; thankfully, it still had merit, "I know she loves her fans and wants to reassure them that she is alright. Let's set up a press conference where she can address their concerns. What do you think?"

"Press conference? At the hospital," Rex asked?

"No, we'll make sure she's healthy enough to speak in public. However, it should be in a controlled environment—"

"I agree. I'll be in attendance; I'll invite Hailee's favorite news correspondents and her assistant."

Rex seemed to be a willing participant in Max's plan; he swallowed it hook, line, and sinker. "That's great. Why don't you set it up for a week from today? I'll get you the location, and if anything changes, I'll call you."

"It will be a relief to see Hailee."

Max worked with criminals of varying offenses, and he knew his personal relationship with Hailee colored his views of Rex. Still, the guy rubbed him the wrong way. Rex's hold on Hailee was about to come to an abrupt end. Max smiled as he considered how to implement the rest of his plan.

Chapter 25

While Max waited for Keller to return, he called Alex, the bartender. Partaking in a SWAT take-down requires courage and timing. For a brief moment, right before Simon challenged the team, Max felt that perhaps he had asked too much of Alex. Alex had hesitated, and Max doubted his decision to use a civilian. Alex handled himself like a pro, and the perp went down.

Alex suffered no injuries and seemed to be in great spirits. He expressed his gratitude to Max for allowing him to participate and assist the police. Alex said facing off with a killer had been thrilling and more exciting than bungee jumping. Alex asked about Hailee and expressed his concern for her well-being. Alex proved to be a loyal friend to Hailee, an invaluable employee, and an asset to the investigation.

Max was thankful that Alex had sustained no injuries and that he appeared to be handling the emotional side of it well. Max had been on the force for so long that he had forgotten the surge of adrenaline he used to get from taking down the perp. Alex had a fresh, untainted view of police work, which reminded Max why he had chosen law enforcement over the family business.

Max escorted Mrs. Swisher to the interrogation room. Her anxiety over being threatened seemed to have increased with each passing hour. Keller wouldn't arrive for five minutes, so Max decided to get started without him. Mrs. Swisher kept looking over her shoulder. Max wondered if she thought Simon might waltz into the station, then burst into the room and bludgeon her right in front of him. Max knew that wouldn't happen. Simon was dead, and good riddance. Fortunately, Simon's death hadn't been publicized, and Max would use that to his advantage.

Max offered Mrs. Swisher some coffee; she sipped it and grimaced. Max guessed it was too strong; she looked like the cappuccino type. Keller came in and whispered to Max, who nodded and checked his phone.

"Did you get him?" Mrs. Swisher asked breathlessly.

Max looked across at her before putting his phone on the table.

"Mrs. Swisher, I appreciate your patience."

"I didn't have a choice. A madman threatened to kill me. I figured this would be the safest place in town."

"Yes, it is." Max nodded. "I have some questions regarding your husband's death. Do you know anyone who might want him dead?"

"You mean besides the guy butchering those poor young women?"

"We're not sure that his death is related to the Meridian murders. We have to pursue all leads." Max picked up his phone and scrolled through his texts. "How often did you visit your husband's office?"

"I only went there to drop off or pick something up. It was my husband's domain, not mine."

"You benefited from it. He provided you with a good life: beautiful house, money, expensive cars."

"Well, yes, he did. I'm not the guilty one; he committed adultery, not me. Why are we rehashing his extracurricular activities? Anyone, an old flame or angry boyfriend, could have killed him. He deserved it!"

Max shook his head. "He deserved to die because he couldn't keep his zipper up?"

Mrs. Swisher huffed and examined her nails.

Max opened the text Keller had sent of the bloodied scalpel. He pointed the screen toward Mrs. Swisher. "Can you identify this piece of equipment?"

She leaned forward and gasped. "It's a surgical scalpel, and it's stained. Is that blood?"

"We believe it is," Max confirmed.

"Whose?"

"We are testing it now. Is this one of your husband's?"

She stammered, "I can't be sure. My husband did dozens of surgeries every week."

Max put the phone down. "Mrs. Swisher, I'm exhausted. I don't want to play games. So I'm going to lay out what I believe happened." Max paused. "You were tired of the doc's sleeping around with beautiful, young women. He said he would be discreet, and you counted on that. When his patients started dying, and it became national news, you flipped out. You confronted him and demanded he stop, and when he wouldn't, you stabbed him in his office and left him to bleed out."

When Mrs. Swisher didn't respond, Max continued. "We found the alleged murder weapon in your house. Are you denying that you put it there?"

She smirked and said, "If I killed him, why would I take the murder weapon back to my house? It would be the first place you looked."

"True. Most criminals make at least one mistake that usually leads to their capture."

"I'm not sure I like you comparing me to a criminal, much less a killer." She huffed.

"I'm stating facts. If you killed your husband in the heat of the moment, it would seem reasonable that you were not thinking clearly and wanted to flee the scene before you were caught."

"You're assuming that I killed my husband. Why would I do that? Besides, I didn't know when he would be in his office, especially the night he was killed. I didn't know you had asked for his patients' files."

Mrs. Swisher took a sip of water. She spoke slowly and clearly, looking Max directly in the eye. "What if the Meridian killer did it? He had already killed three people.

248

He knew my husband had the patient's files and that something in the files might point to him. It seems more likely that he would kill my husband to keep his identity hidden and to evade jail time and then plant the weapon in my home to divert suspicion from him."

Max paid close attention to Mrs. Swisher's body language and word choice. She had chosen her words carefully. He wondered how she would react if she thought Simon was still alive and might be looking for her. He planned to use that to his advantage. Her earlier behavior and desire to stay at the precinct clearly indicated she knew she would be the next victim. What would she trade for her safety?

"You could be right. Even so, I need to pursue all leads, and as the spouse of one of the victims, you are naturally a person of interest. Besides, we would need to arrest the Meridian killer and get his statement to find out if he had any involvement in your husband's murder."

She scooted her chair closer to the table and leaned forward. "Do you know where he is? Am I safe?"

"I can't comment on the case. Don't worry. You should be safe. You don't fit the killer's MO."

She jumped from the chair. "He threatened me. He said I was next!"

Max waved her down, and when she sat, he said, "We are doing everything we can to stop his reign of terror and to stop innocent people from dying."

She shook her head violently, sending her glasses flying across the room. "What about me? Because I'm a person of interest, you don't think I'm worth saving?"

Max suppressed a smile. She didn't say anything about being innocent.

"Mrs. Swisher, I don't want anyone else, guilty or not, to die. We are working hard to find out who killed your husband. It takes time. The evidence we collected at your home is being processed. We have to wait for the results and see what our next move is."

She chewed her bottom lip. "Evidence? What Evidence?"

"I told you. We found a stained scalpel, and the lab is processing it–"

"What else did you find?"

"I can't share that with you. I told you about the scalpel because I needed an identification. Otherwise, all information is classified."

"What am I supposed to do now?" Mrs. Swisher asked.

"Go home–"

"Home!" She shrieked. "I can't go home. A psychopath wants me dead. You have to protect me."

"I know you're scared. Since we don't have any proof that you are being threatened. I need to devote all of my resources to ridding my town of a ruthless killer. You do understand?"

She stared at him, mouth open.

Max envisioned his words whirling around in her head as she tried to figure out her next move. He met her frightened gaze with a compassionate nod.

"But, I—" Mrs. Swisher's body trembled, and her lips quivered.

"I'm sorry. I need to get back to work."

Max stood and raised his hand in a sweeping motion to usher her out.

"You can't. He'll kill me!" She jumped up and grabbed Max's arm. She squeezed hard as if holding on to a life preserver. "He'll hunt me down and butcher me just like he did those young women and my husband."

Max uncurled her fingers and brushed them away. "We haven't determined who killed your husband. That's why I need to get back to work, I have another psycho to find." He moved toward the door.

"Wait!"

Max swirled around, his lips curved up into a slow, deliberate smile. His plan worked.

"Yes?"

"I know who killed my husband, that cheating pig. If I talk, I want protection."

"I would need proof, evidence of your claim. I can't rely on your word alone."

She faltered and stared at the ground. She grasped her trembling hands together and said, "I know whose fingerprints will be on the scalpel." She slumped down onto the chair and continued, "Mine."

"Mrs. Swisher, do you want to consult with your attorney?" Max asked.

Her face contorted, and she went pale. She paused as if weighing her options.

Max's cell phone rang. He checked the number and said, "I'll be back. Let me know if you want your lawyer."

"Wait! What about my protection?"

"I'll be back. You'll be safe here."

Max shut the door and instructed Thornton to detain Mrs. Swisher until he returned.

Max answered the phone. "What's up?"

"It's Hailee." Tom began, "She—"

Max hung up, sprinted down the hall toward the exit, and jumped into his car.

*****

Max burst into Hailee's room. The bed was empty. Tom had been giving him status updates. Nothing indicated that Hailee's health had taken a turn for the worse. He searched the room for Tom, who sat rigidly on his chair near the door.

"Where is she? What happened?" Max's heart pounded painfully in his chest.

"She had a mild reaction to the painkiller. The nurse took her to the ICU for observation."

"When did this happen? What's her status?" Max demanded.

Tom walked over to Max and said, "Easy, Toliver. She'll be fine?'

"She suffered torture at the hands of a serial killer and then ran headfirst into a pole. I hardly call that fine."

"She is a strong, determined woman. She's made it this far; I hardly think a skin rash and some itching will do her in."

Max did not find that amusing. Anything could go wrong in a hospital, and it sometimes did. His father's doctor had once told him that hospitals were scary places. That hadn't instilled any faith in Max at the time, and his dad had died in a hospital. Now, as Hailee struggled to recover, fear and despair started to creep in, and he knew if anything happened to her, it would be his fault.

Tom clapped Max on the shoulder, interrupting his thoughts. "The nurse told me she's doing better and should be back in her room tomorrow."

"You sounded troubled when you called; why?"

Tom turned and headed to his laptop. "I wanted to show you this." He sat and pulled up a mugshot.

"What are you working on?" Max looked at the picture again. "Wait a minute. That's the guy you tackled in Chicago."

"That's right. Hailee believes he is her biological father and asked me to find him."

"She told me that her parents died. She's not a liar. Why would she say that?"

Max refused to believe that Hailee had lied to him. She had been forthcoming about everything: her virginity, her problems with Rex, her passion. Why would she hide this from him?

Tom pulled up a rap sheet and said, "I didn't get a chance to tell you; I ran a check on Miss Hollister, and I found that she didn't exist until eight years ago. When I called her out on it, she shut down and threatened to 'kick me to the curb.'"

Max grinned. That sounded like Hailee. "That's strange. I wonder why she would have to 'reinvent' herself. Perhaps her scumbag agent is responsible. He's been blackmailing her for years, and her attorney has been collecting evidence to break her contract."

"Did she tell you what he had on her?"

"No, she freaked out when I mentioned that she should leave his company or refuse his demands."

"What did he want?" Tom swiveled around toward Max. "What kind of demands?"

Max's skin heated up. Hailee's fear that Rex would end her career, or worse, angered him. Max couldn't convince Hailee to share her secret; he knew the mere thought of it coming to light terrified her.

"I don't know. It's extremely personal, and it is consuming her."

Tom nodded. "Here's the man I stopped in Chicago. His name is Raymond Bayard. He goes by Buzz, which is fitting because all of his arrests have been minor and for drug use or possession."

"Where is he now," Max asked?

"After the incident at the Chicago mall, the police detained him for two days, then released him. Since I couldn't rule him out as a threat, I had my guys in Chicago watch him." Tom pulled up a picture of a small hippie compound on the outskirts of Chicago. "This is where he is staying, at least for the moment. He has an eclectic array of arrests; he tends to gravitate to locations known for the nonconformist lifestyles, like California, Colorado, Oregon, Vermont, and Pennsylvania."

"So he doesn't have a steady income or permanent residence?"

"No. As far as I can tell, Buzz wanders from place to place, getting high and apparently scaring the daylights out of his alleged daughter."

Max wondered why Hailee believed that this man could be her father. If only she would open up to him, Max could rid her of the scourge that was Rex. *Rex.* He totally spaced it out. Mrs. Swisher's soon-to-be forthcoming confession had temporarily distracted him.

"Tom, I am planning a Rex takedown. I told him that I'd have Hailee give a press conference with a few of her closest friends and media personalities so she could show everyone she was doing fine. I didn't tell him that her attorney and my entire team would be there to pounce on him."

Tom smiled.

"I would love to have it at the Keller Auditorium. I want a venue that's worthy of Hailee's celebrity status. Unless there's a cancellation, we won't have a snowball's chance in hell of booking it. Can you check for me? If it's booked, I'll call the mayor and schedule it for City Hall. Please convince Hailee to do the press conference. If the idea comes from me, she'll know I'm trying to trap Rex." Excitement and hope built inside of Max. "Make sure she is physically and emotionally ready. I don't want to rush her. I did tell Rex it would take place about a week from now. Do you think Hailee will be ready?"

"She should be—"

"Did I hear my name being used in vain?" Hailee laughed.

The nurse wheeled Hailee into the room and steadied her as she helped her climb into bed.

Hailee straightened the sheets and looked toward Tom. Her breath caught. "Max."

He hurried to her side. "How are you feeling?"

254

"The swelling has gone down, and I feel better, so that's a start."

"Did you come to see Tom or me?"

"Both–my two favorite people in one room."

Tom grunted. Hailee smiled.

"Have you been able to find the doctor's wife—"

"Hailee, you know I can't discuss the case with you. Concentrate on getting better." Max smoothed out her rumpled hair and said, "Tom, I'm leaving Hailee in your capable hands. I have to go. I have one more arrest to make."

"The wife—"

Max shook his head. "Tom, brief me when you capture the other target. I'd love to speak with him."

Max insisted that Hailee be on the top of her game so she could convince Rex that she would resume her tour. Rex had to believe he still had control over Hailee, and then Max would swoop in and take him down. Max hurried to the door. He smiled at Hailee, shot Tom a knowing look, and left.

Chapter 26

Max rushed back to the precinct, zigzagging through traffic. Keller had called to inform him that Mrs. Swisher had gone into a hysterical frenzy and wanted to speak with him. Max hoped she would be scared enough to make a full confession, and then he could concentrate on setting Hailee free.

At the station, Max parked and headed straight for the lounge. Thornton stood guard and nodded to Max as he entered. Mrs. Swisher jumped out of her seat and ran to Max.

"Did you catch him?" She asked breathlessly.

"Catch who?"

"The maniac who wants to slice me up and throw away my body parts."

"Is that what he told you he would do?"

She chewed her bottom lip and stared at the door. "That maniac said he would hang me from the Oak tree in my backyard, cut off my limbs with a chainsaw, and then take my head as a trophy."

Her hand flew to her mouth, and she sucked in air. "He knows where I live. He's going to kill me. You have to help me."

Max walked her over to the sofa and eased her onto it. He poured a cup of coffee and offered it to her. She waved it away.

"I will do my best, but you have to cooperate. Do you want a lawyer?"

"No! There's nothing he can do."

"Don't let your fear interfere with your rights. You have a right to an attorney. Do you have one?

"Of course I do. I need police protection."

"Very well. I need you to tell me everything." Max sat at the round table and pulled out a mini-recorder. "Do you mind if I tape this?"

"No, please don't let him kill me."

"Calm down and tell me everything. Start with why you killed your husband and how. Max hit start and waited.

"My husband thought that I didn't know he screwed his patients. What a weasel. After the first girl died, he became extremely anxious and paranoid. I asked him about it; he just blew me off. He didn't tell me that he knew her." She reached for her water and said, "When the second young woman died, he jumped at every sound; he had started sweating profusely, and he couldn't sleep."

She took a drink and laughed. "At first, I found it amusing. I thought that Karma had finally caught up with him. It got worse. He couldn't concentrate or focus. He told me that he had canceled most of his surgeries. That's when I knew it was serious. If he didn't work, how would he support his employees or me?"

"So, you were worried about your lavish lifestyle and less concerned about the women being butchered?"

She cleared her throat. "I didn't kill anyone, and I didn't know they were my husband's patients until after the third girl died. He told me he planned on visiting you to tell you about the girls. He packed a bag and told me he didn't know when he would be back."

"Did he think his life was in danger?" Max asked.

Mrs. Swisher shrugged, "Who knows. By the time he came to see you, he could barely keep it together."

Max wondered what pushed her over the edge, the cheating or the lack of income. "So, when did you decide to kill him, and why?"

"He promised me a grand life. A life of prestige and luxury. Instead, he made me miserable and a laughingstock. Everyone knew that he cheated. His entire office knew. They covered for him. When he decided to pack it in and leave. I had had enough." She finished off the water and said, "I followed him to the office and waited outside the filing room. Once he found the patient files, he put them in his briefcase and then started to lock up the cabinet. I stabbed him in the back with the scalpel, and when he turned and fell forward. I sliced his throat." She stared at her hands. "Blood sprayed everywhere. It took forever to get it out. I took the files to make it look like the serial killer had been there and took his revenge on my husband."

Max studied her face. She showed no real emotion. He knew from the first time he met her that there was something off about her. After investigating her background, he wondered if she had offed the doctor's mother to insinuate herself into his life and bank account. He knew the doctor's wife could be just as dangerous as Simon.

Mrs. Swisher leaned forward. "Is that all? Is that what you needed to get me protection?"

"Your story doesn't back up the evidence. We already have the patient files."

"I took them. They were in my husband's briefcase. He had just finished pulling them out before I um— before I stabbed him. I stashed the briefcase in the floor safe in my closet. It's in the right-hand corner; lift the twine folded over the edge of the carpet. The combination and key are taped to the underside of the carpet about four inches from the wall."

"Why would the doctor have two copies of the patients' files?"

"Maybe the killer made copies before the girls started to die. Maybe that's how he chose them. How would I know?"

Max impatiently tapped the table, "Don't you feel any sense of remorse or regret for taking a life, your husband's life?"

"He took advantage of his patients and violated our marriage vows. And when his patients started dying, he didn't come forward. He's inherently a coward. He could have tried to save their lives. He didn't. Why should I feel sorry that he is gone?"

Good point. If the doctor had come forward, Max might have been able to save at least one life, the one life that Hailee had tried so desperately to save. The doctor's actions lacked courage, but did he deserve to die at the hands of his gold-digging, apathetic wife?

Max turned off the recorder and placed it in his jacket pocket. He headed toward the door and stopped.

"Wait. What about me?"

"I'll be back with a typed version of your confession. If you want to consult your lawyer before signing, call him now."

"No. I'll sign. You have to keep that maniac away from me."

Max slammed the door shut, strode to Keller's office, and plopped down on the chair across from Keller.

"Did you get it?"

"I did, and I'm looking forward to seeing her face when I tell her she's not in danger. By the way, Mrs. Swisher said that the deceased patients' files are in a safe in her closet. Did you find them?"

"We did—nice little setup. Mrs. Swisher had over $300,000 stashed there. I guess she didn't trust the bank, or she didn't want a paper trail."

"That's a lot of cash. Why didn't she transfer it to an offshore account?"

"Based on the clothes in her closet, the woman loved to shop. We also found some high-end jewelry. I guess she needed a little spending money."

"My wife would kill to have the clothes in her closet." Keller grimaced. "Too soon?"

259

"It's always too soon." Max stretched out his legs. "It's been a long case. I'll get this to Erma so she can type it up. The doc's wife is still refusing an attorney. Should be a slam dunk."

Max walked down the hall to Erma's desk, and when she hung up the phone, he said, "Transcribe this, and I need it yesterday."

Erma nodded and began typing.

The investigation and his fraught nerves were finally winding down. Simon had been neutralized, Mrs. Swisher had confessed to killing her husband, and Rex was about to get the biggest surprise of his despicable life.

Max thumbed through his texts as Erma finished up the doctor's wife's confession. He grabbed the two-page report and hurried to the lounge, where Thornton remained constantly vigilant, standing guard at the door.

He pushed open the door and found Mrs. Swisher on the couch, leisurely sipping coffee as if she didn't have a care in the world. As if she hadn't committed a heinous murder and would stand trial and hopefully go to prison for the rest of her life. He closed the door and watched her eyes light up.

"It's about time. I thought you had forgotten me. Have you arranged my security?"

Max waved her over to the chair and said, "Please sit and read this carefully. If this is a true representation of your statement, please print your name, sign, and date it."

Mrs. Swisher grabbed it from Max and quickly read through it. She held out her hand, and Max gave her a pen. She signed her name with determined strokes. "It's done."

Max examined her signature, and a relieved smile swept across his face.

"Well, how do you propose to keep me safe?"

Max yelled out. "Thornton."

The door opened, and Max waved Thornton in.

"Mrs. Swisher, Detective Thornton will escort you to your cell."

"Cell!"

"Thornton, don't forget to read her rights. She has already waived the right to an attorney; go through them again."

"No! Wait!" She stumbled as Thornton secured her hands in the cuffs. "What's going on? I thought you were going to protect me."

"You declined the right to speak to a lawyer, and you confessed to the cold-blooded murder of your husband. You committed a heinous crime, and you will have your day in court."

"You said you were too busy to protect me and that you were trying to catch a murderer."

"I told you I had to get another psycho off the streets. Mrs. Swisher, that psycho is you." Max gripped the confession tightly. "Thornton will take good care of you," Max smirked. "Make sure she gets the deluxe suite."

"You can't," she shrieked. "Wait!"

Thornton guided her down the hall for a pat-down and fingerprinting.

Max gave Mrs. Swisher's confession to Erma for processing. Max blew out a heavy breath. This case had been especially draining, and his involvement with Hailee had made it more difficult.

Now that the four murders had been solved, Max could concentrate on Hailee and getting her life back on track. Tom worked diligently to find her biological father and would oversee Hailee's recovery. Max's plan would trap Rex and take him down once and for good.

Chapter 27

Hailee could finally roll over without any pain. She extended her legs, stretched her ankles, and moved her head from side to side. She tested her arms, wrists, and fingers. Everything worked, and the swelling had completely gone down. She glanced over at Tom, who pounded furiously on his keyboard. She wondered what had captured his attention the past few days. He had kept to himself, checking on her only if she moaned or tried to move. She appreciated all that he had done for her. Hailee hoped that he had been able to locate the man she believed to be her biological father.

The man she encountered in Chicago eerily resembled the man in the picture with the people she had known as her parents. When he called her Harmony, a familiar knot tightened in her stomach, and she had been filled with dread, and she knew in that instant that he was the one labeled 'father."

Although Haliee didn't want to interrupt Tom, she tried to speak with him to get an update on Max and the murders. He seemed enormously pleased with himself and his progress. Hailee had heard him chuckle a few times and then grunt, so maybe it wasn't going as well as he had hoped. The man in the picture and the man in Chicago didn't fit her image of the father she wanted. She had had enough of the bohemian lifestyle. In fact, remembering all the pain and confusion she had endured as a child, she wanted to stay as far away as possible from anyone or anything that could threaten or destroy her life, the one she had built and had worked so hard to achieve in the past few years.

A feeling of desperation overwhelmed her. Hailee had been in the hospital for six days, and her recovery took precedence over everything else. She had pushed thoughts of Rex and his constant threats and innuendos completely out of her mind. Hailee felt healthier and stronger and needed to contact her attorney, Carl, to get an update on her case. Did he find a loophole so she could break her contract, or did he have enough evidence to get Rex out of her life?

She looked up when she heard a loud click. Tom marched quickly over to her side. An uncharacteristic smile hovered on his lips.

"Did you find him?" Hailee asked.

"Yes, and he's on his way to Portland."

"Here? He's coming here?" Hailee's stomach did somersaults. She only wanted to find him; she didn't know how she would feel about seeing him again. Perhaps Kat had been right all along; she had purposely visited locations known for their alternative lifestyles and had been secretly hoping to run into her biological father unintentionally.

"Yes. I invited Buzz to be my guest."

"I heard you tell Max he had been arrested."

"He had been held for a couple of days and subsequently released. My man in Chicago tracked him down and made him an offer."

"I wanted to find out who he was. I didn't want to see him again. Why would you force him to come here?"

Tom arched his brow and said, "I didn't say anything about forcing him."

Hailee gave him a stern look. "Most people can't say no to you."

"True. I can be very persuasive."

Hailee smoothed out the sheets with one hand and ran her fingers across the cold rail with the other. "What's his name?"

"Raymond Bayard. They call him Buzz."

Hailee burst out laughing. The laughter rolled off her tongue and wouldn't stop. Her side hurt, and tears rolled down her cheek. After all the years of loathing the hippie reality of her parents' life and wishing she knew more about the man who had created her, she laughed hysterically. All the pent-up frustration, anger, and disappointment came spilling out, seeming to shock Tom. He stared at her with a look of deep concern.

"I'm sorry," she said, grabbing her side and continuing to giggle. "I—"

"Do you want me to call the nurse?" Tom asked.

"No," she wiped away the tears. "It's just that after all this time, I assumed my real father's name would be Bob or Joe, and he wouldn't be a part of the life that I desperately tried to escape from."

"Max asked me—"

"Max," Hailee whispered.

Tom continued, "Max has a plan to get Mr. Chandler out of your life."

At the mention of Rex, Hailee began to shake. An uncontrollable, involuntary movement that had been the norm since she had fallen prey to Rex's blackmail.

"No, he can't. Rex will destroy me!"

"Miss Hollister, Max has a solid plan, and it will work. We need your cooperation and some information."

"My lawyer, Carl, is handling it. He will take care of it. He needs a little more time."

Tom stood stoically by Hailee's side and looked down on her with that 'my way or the highway' look. "It's settled, and we are moving forward." Tom paused, then said, "It will be easier if you join us. Either way, it's a go."

From the moment that Max heard about Rex and his hold on Hailee, she knew Max wouldn't let it go. He would intervene and try to fix her problem. Except that would only make matters worse. Rex would feel betrayed, unleash her secret to the world, and she would be finished. And her dream, her passion, would be gone forever.

"Tom, I know you and Max are just trying to do the right thing, but Carl and I can do this. We are building a solid case against Rex, and when Carl is ready, he will proceed with it. Any premature actions could severely damage my professional reputation. I won't have it."

Hailee waited. She wanted Tom to understand the precarious position she found herself in. She didn't want Max and Tom to barge in with guns blazing. It would take time and finesse to wrangle herself away from Rex, his greed, and his romantic obsession.

"I appreciate everything that you have done for me, especially after…" Hailee gently touched her face and said, "Simon kidnapped me and the accident. I'm begging you. Let it be. Let me handle it."

"I'm sorry, Miss Hollister. It's not my decision, and Max has made up his mind. So buck up and accept it." Tom strode back to his computer.

Tom's words echoed in her ears. They didn't care about her future. Max and Tom wanted to catch a crook, not help save her career. Hailee felt sick. She had two choices: one, try to fight, and probably lose. Both Max and Tom were formidable opponents; together, they would be invincible. Two, trust that they would remove Rex from her life with the least amount of damage to her reputation and career.

She had hoped to rid herself of Rex herself; he was a parasite that needed to be exterminated. Carl had worked diligently and faithfully to use the law to break the contract and force Rex to remain silent. Carl made no promises; he had told her when she hired him that it would be a battle that would eventually lead to victory. However, it would take time and patience to achieve the desired results—Rex completely out of her life. Carl had been on her side from the beginning and not just for the money. He despised how Rex used his position to threaten Hailee and vowed to stop him.

Everything, all the promises and threats Rex had made to her, spun around in her head like a cyclone. She tried to stop the fear that had begun engulfing her as it always did when she considered even for a moment to stand up to Rex. He had somehow come across her private things and found a picture of her parents, the man she now knew as Ray, and her grandmother's will, which granted her the rights to her best-selling novel. The one that launched her into stardom. Rex used this information against her and forced her to give him thirty percent of her royalties instead of the traditional fifteen percent. He tried to force her into marriage and into his bed. Carl had been working hard to build a solid case; he would need more evidence to legally break her contract. Maybe Max should stop Rex.

She eased herself into a sitting position and watched Tom key angrily on his laptop. She knew he didn't like his decisions to be questioned. It might not be a good idea to interrupt him.

"Uncle," Hailee said hesitantly.

Tom looked back, "What?"

"I surrender. What do you need from me?"

Tom's impatience turned to a relieved smirk. "Tell me everything."

"It will take a while." Hailee sighed.

"Fine. I'll order lunch, then we'll get started."

Hailee needed the brief reprieve. It would take her a moment to gather strength and organize her muddled thoughts.

Tom pulled up his chair and sat uncomfortably close. Hailee guessed he didn't want to miss anything, and it would be more discreet if someone happened to come in.

"My parents, the ones who raised me, were the epitome of the Bohemian life: drugs, sex, and hatred toward the establishment. They didn't work, and even today, I don't know how they paid for anything; maybe they were drug dealers." Hailee cringed. "I spent my childhood wishing I had normal parents, parents who cared enough to ground me and to come to parent-teacher conferences, and as I got older, I began to hate my parents and the barrage of people that came and went. Our house had a reputation as a smelly party house. I had no friends and no discernible talents."

She didn't know if this information could be used; he did say 'everything.'

"When I was sixteen, my parents and I were fighting. They wanted to go away for a few weeks to visit a compound in Vermont. Under normal circumstances, it would have been a godsend to get away from them. I had no money, no food, no friends, and strange men kept showing up at the house at all hours of the day and night; I didn't want to stay there alone."

Hailee closed her eyes; she regretted the next part of the story. She hoped she would be able to get it out before she had another panic attack. If she did, it would be a miracle.

"I screamed at my parents, calling them names and telling them how much I hated them and that I wished I had different parents. When they told me I was 'blowing their mind' and when they responded with a hippie quote, I lost it and told them I wished they were dead."

She waited for it to come, the nausea, the dizziness, the pain, and the fear that usually gripped her tight and caused her to double over. It didn't come. Perhaps years of regret and guilt had built a barrier to the pain, and she had finally accepted the truth. What she said had been mean-spirited, spoken out of fear and disappointment; nothing she said could have caused what came next.

"My parents left that day and died in a car accident on their way out of town. After they died, I went through their belongings, and I found two items that changed my life forever. One, a picture of the people I thought were my parents, and a man I now know could be my biological father. Second, an old address book of my mother's. I went through it and found my grandmother's phone number. I called her, and she arranged for me to come to California. She saved me. She loved and took care of me, everything that my parents didn't know how to do."

"Is this what Rex is using against you, that your parents were drugged-up hippies?"

Hailee shook her head no and said, "My parentage is a part of it. Rex and I had numerous conversations about my dissatisfaction with my childhood. The reason he is blackmailing has to do with my grandmother."

"What did she do to make Rex blackmail you?" Tom asked.

Here it goes. Hailee's entire life was about to be blown to pieces. Her secret would finally be revealed, and she struggled to tell him the truth. Tom looked at her with questioning eyes.

She swallowed hard and tried to speak. Nothing came out. She couldn't do it. Her dreams and her career hung in the balance. She had kept this secret for over eight years, and now, a few words would implode her world.

Hailee sat up taller, looked Tom straight in the eyes, and said, "I'm a fraud."

A numbing sensation enveloped Hailee, and she trembled. She waited for Tom to respond. Instead, he maintained eye contact with her, his questioning eyes boring into hers. What now? Was he judging her or planning a way to minimize the blow when he told her he had to inform Max that they couldn't resolve her problem with Rex because she had committed a crime? Maybe Max would have to arrest them both.

Her mind wandered to strange places; thankfully, Tom broke the silence.

"What kind of fraud?"

It could take a while to defend her position and provide Tom with all the details, so she decided to discuss the key points. "After my mother left to join a hippie compound, my grandmother started writing a book, and when I came to live with her, we worked on it together. After she died, she willed the first rights to me, which allowed me to finish it and claim it as my own."

Tom frowned, "Where's the fraud?"

"It's my grandmother's story. I only finished a small portion of it."

"I'm not seeing the problem. It's yours legally. You can do whatever you want with it. There's no crime in that."

"My grandmother's novel, *Something Dark*, was a best seller. It paved the way for me to write more novels and to enjoy a good life. My fans don't know that I didn't write it. I have been lying to them this whole time. That novel made me a household name. I took my grandmother's idea and finished it."

"Seems like you're splitting hairs."

"No, I'm not. Do you like being lied to?"

He shrugged.

"I don't, and I bet most people don't. When you trust someone, you expect them to be honest with you. I've betrayed my fans, and if it comes out that I lied, they will jump ship and never forgive me."

"Miss Hollister, I can see that this topic upsets you. I've dealt with many bad people, some of whom I would even call evil. This alleged transgression can be easily fixed, and that's how we plan to ensnare Rex. Max is setting up a press conference, so we will need you to contact your lawyer and your friend with the cowboy boots."

Hailee smiled when she thought of Kat. She missed her something fierce. Since Simon abducted her after she ditched Tom, Hailee hadn't had an opportunity to regroup with Kat and find out how she evaded Tom's anger. She would love to hear how that ended.

"Max wants to hold a press conference? Where? What good would that do?"

"We'll get all the major players to attend on the pretense of giving them a status update on your health. Instead, you will come clean with your perceived crimes and call Rex out for the blackmailing scum that he is. Max will take him down."

Hailee violently shook her head. "Not happening. I won't do it."

"Miss Hollister—"

"No way. I agreed to tell you because I thought you had a plan to get Rex out of my life and off of my back, not humiliate me in front of my fans. I can't."

"Have faith. Max will—"

"I want to speak to Max!"

Chapter 28

Max answered Tom's call. "What's up?"

"It's Miss Hollister. She refuses to do the press conference. She wants to see you now."

Tom hung up, leaving Max feeling unsettled. He knew Hailee would be against the idea. Max had been sure Tom could convince her to do it. Max dialed and headed out to his car.

When the phone rang, Max said, "Meet me at the hospital in Hailee's room." He hung up and pulled out of the lot.

The chaotic drive to the hospital annoyed him. Traffic, an accident, and his racing thoughts all made it worse. Max hoped that by calling Kat, she would convince Hailee to do the right thing and let them put Rex away for good. He liked Kat and could see why Hailee trusted her. She was younger than Hailee, had a unique perspective on the world, and could put a positive spin on anything. Kat would be the last attempt to persuade Hailee. If she refused, he would be forced to take other actions, which could permanently change their relationship.

*****

Hailee heard Tom call Max. She hoped he would come so that they could straighten this out. She had, at least in the past, been able to persuade Max to let her resolve the issue. Since the Meridian murders had been solved, he had time to invest in her life and her dilemma, and it would be harder for him to see that she should hold off until Carl could take Rex to court.

Tom's chair squeaked as it rolled. Hailee looked up, and relief flooded her. Kat…

"Hailee, OMG! It's so good to see you." Kat stepped in and glanced toward Tom. He nodded.

Hailee guessed that Kat had been able to win over grumpy Tom. She was glad; Tom had grown on her, too.

Hailee sat up and said, "Kat. I'm so glad you're here. Come here."

Kat glided over to Hailee's bed and gave it the once-over. "Hmmm. Is this the best they could do?"

"Oh, don't be a snob. It's not like you."

Kat's shoulders relaxed. "I've been so worried about you. This whole sordid situation has messed with my REM sleep, and I'm getting premature wrinkles. See." Kat pointed to the corner of her eye.

Hailee played along. "Maybe you need better eye cream."

"Or maybe you need to listen to Max more and stay out of harm's way."

Kat's words rang true; sadly, she couldn't change the past. Hailee nodded.

"What are you doing here? Are they finally letting me have visitors?"

"Don't be silly. I'm your bestie, not a visitor."

They both laughed. It felt good. Hailee hadn't laughed in a while, and it only took sharing the same room with Kat for five minutes to melt away all her tension.

"I don't care why; I'm happy you're here." Hailee motioned for Kat to sit; Tom grabbed a chair and set it next to the bed. "What did you tell my fans? Are they worried? I bet they're worried. They are the best fans in the world."

Kat looked at the chair and cocked her head. "My outfit won't survive that. I'll stand."

Hailee and Tom laughed. Kat glared at Tom, then grinned. "I guess it will work. I hope it doesn't snag my leggings."

Kat wore clothes that made her look and feel good. Today's outfit consisted of neon green leggings, stone-washed cut-off denim shorts, a sexy hot-pink off-the-shoulder t-shirt with a fishnet cover, and her signature pink, flowered boots. She wore neon-orange eyeliner, black-glitter mascara, and matte plum lipstick.

"I spoke to Carl, who prepared a statement. I wanted to make sure I didn't say too much."

"Carl?" Tom asked.

"My attorney. The one who built a case to take Rex down, legally."

Tom grunted. Kat swiveled in the chair and then grimaced.

"Hailee, we've been besties for years now, and you know I will always have your back. I always tell you the truth, no matter how painful."

"I know." Hailee leaned toward Kat. "What's happened. Tell me."

"I didn't mean to scare you. I'm going to tell you what I've always told you."

Hailee shook her head, "Don't."

"You, your career, and my livelihood are at stake. If you continue this way, Rex will win. He holds all the cards, and even though Carl is working hard, he has to wait for Rex to screw up." Kat tapped her boot loudly. "Rex has been straddling the law to force you to do what he wants. It must stop now. Let them do this." Kat put her hands on her hips. "If you go down, so do I."

Hailee hadn't even considered that outcome before. If Rex takes her down and discloses her secret, Kat will lose her job, too. Hailee felt defeated and deflated. "Okay."

Kat gently squeezed her arm. Hailee flinched. "I'm sorry."

Kat sprinted over to Tom and said, "I thought she was healthy. If she's not one hundred percent, she can't face Rex."

"Kat, I'm good. Really."

"If you're not strong enough, Rex will eat you alive—"

Tom cleared his throat. Hailee looked up.

Max.

Max nodded to Tom and Kat and went over to Hailee. He looked tired and had a healthy five o'clock shadow.

"How's my girl?"

Hailee's pulse quickened, and her hands started to sweat. She had almost forgotten how strongly she reacted to Max. She smoothed out a flyaway strand of hair and tugged on her gown. When she heard a clacking sound, she looked toward Kat and Tom, who were making a quick exit into the hall.

"I hear you've arrested the doctor's wife. I'm glad you were able to give the victims justice."

Hailee could have kicked herself. She hadn't seen Max in a few days, and all she could think to do was to regurgitate redundant information about the case.

"We're still tying up some loose ends, but Simon killed the first two girls, and the third girl appeared to be killed by Simon and the doctor's file clerk. The file clerk stole the doctor's key to his suite at the Meridian and gave it to Simon. They used it to kill the girls and hide the bodies until they could discreetly move them. We're not sure if Simon poisoned the file clerk or if she committed suicide; she died at the precinct. She's the reason we called nine-one-one the night you were there."

Max heard giggling and glanced toward Kat and Tom. They were deep in conversation. "The doctor's wife gave a full confession. She thought Simon wanted her dead, and by the time she confessed, we had already taken him down."

Hailee felt a huge weight lift off her shoulders. It had been dragging her down since she fought with the ninja file clerk. She couldn't save the young girl, and despite

274

everything that she endured, Max had been able to stop the monster from hurting anyone else.

"Hailee, it's time to deal with Rex head-on. Are you ready for that?"

"Kat gave me the pep talk and convinced me you two know what you're doing. I guess that's the way it's going to be."

"You and your attorney have done all you can. The ball's in Rex's court. It's time to play hardball. Can you do that?"

She sat up straight, squared her shoulders, and said, "I'm ready."

He swooped in and gave Hailee a gentle kiss. "Good. If we are going to win, I need you to be ready and to be brave." He paused, "I know you're brave. You took on a serial killer and won. Now, let's rid your life of the bloodsucker you call an agent.

Hailee listened intently as Max outlined the plan. He reserved the city hall auditorium and invited Kat, Tom, Carl, Rex, and her favorite media personalities and news anchors. Once Hailee began speaking, the auditorium would be locked down, and Max's team would block all the exits. The event would be televised locally and nationally. Rex's scheming, blackmailing, and deviant behavior would finally come to light.

Hailee liked the plan. Max could control the invitees and could control when they left.

"It sounds good on paper. What if something goes wrong? How do we make sure that everyone knows what Rex did to me and that it was mostly his fault and not mine?"

Max shook his head and said, "It's never been your fault. Rex is the blackmailer. He's a criminal. Tom agrees with me. You told him how and why you came into this career, and as Carl said, it's all legal."

"I lied. No one, especially me, likes to be lied to. Do you?"

"No, but I believe your fans will understand. Carl wants you to be careful when calling out Rex." Max handed her a few typed pages. "Read them, get familiar with them, and call Carl if you have any questions."

Hailee nodded. "This is going to work. Right?"

"Absolutely."

"What is your plan for Rex? What's going to happen to him?"

"Do you care?"

"Not especially. I just don't want my fans to associate me with repeated acts of violence."

"The only thing your fans will remember is how you triumphed over an obsessed, petty man and how you were strong for coming forward after everything that you have been through."

Hailee glanced at her typed speech and cringed. She didn't do well with public speaking. She would study and practice until it flowed freely. She wanted to do justice to Carl's meticulously worded speech.

"I hope you're right. My career and Kat's are depending on it."

Max kissed her again and whispered, "I can't wait to get you alone." He smiled and headed to the door.

"Wait, what's going to happen to your hotel, the Meridian? What about Carrington and Alex?

"I'm tearing it down—"

"No…"

"I'm rebuilding and renaming it. I know you and your grandmother made special memories there. It may feel like you are losing a part of her or that your connection to your grandmother is no longer there, but she will always be with you."

"I don't want my hotel or the memories of the victims to become a True Crime fanatic's vacation spot. I want to do something in memory of the victims. I just haven't figured out what, and don't worry, Carrington and Alex are being taken care of."

*****

Max believed that, at last, his dad would be proud of him. He had kept his family and town safe and still had time for a personal life. He would speak to his mom about boundaries, but he doubted that she'd listen. She wanted more grandchildren and hoped that Hailee would give them to her. He smiled when he thought about Hailee. He didn't know where their relationship was headed; he just knew that he wanted her in his life.

He headed back to the office; Max had some details to iron out. He wanted Hailee's speech to go without a hitch. Rex's arrogance and entitlement would be his undoing. Max hoped he could take Rex down without incident. He didn't want Hailee to feel guilty if her fans were upset or felt threatened by the situation.

Chapter 29

A week later, and with a fair amount of make-up, Hailee stood solemnly in front of the camera. Her stomach clenched, and a wave of dizziness hit her. Failed attempts to find her niche in childhood flashed in her mind. She had long struggled with confidence and self-worth. Now, standing before her friends, fans, and Max, she yearned for success. Everything led to this: her admission of guilt and confession of her sins. This could end her career and life as she knew it. Hailee straightened her shoulders, standing as tall as she could muster. She had survived a serial killer; this should be a piece of cake.

Hailee's well-rehearsed and heartfelt speech had taken days to learn and prepare for, and she hoped it would be enough. Carl knew her heart and her fears and did an excellent job conveying her feelings, all while legally protecting her against any claim Rex may make.

Making amends would be difficult and a multiphase process, and this would be the first of many painful stages. The first one, the one that would reveal Hailee's most profound and regrettable pain, would be the hardest to admit. She looked straight into the camera and suddenly felt dizzy. She couldn't have prepared herself for the barrage of emotions overwhelming her.

"First, I want to say welcome to everyone and thank you for all of your love and support these past few weeks. I have recovered nicely, and I am proud to be able to speak to you today." Hailee looked out into the audience. Carl, Alex, and Carrington all met her gaze with supportive smiles. "Eight years ago, after my parents' sudden demise, my grandmother took me in. I was sixteen and filled with anger and angst. At that time, I foolishly believed that my hateful words to my parents had caused their car accident, and I have lived in fear and in a dark place of grief and regret. I'd wanted to blame someone for their death, and I was a convenient scapegoat."

Hailee swallowed hard and scanned the audience for Max. He stood to the right of the main exit. He nodded, and she continued, "My parents had an affinity for drugs and a no-boundary way of life that took their lives. The man that I knew as my dad had been high when he got behind the wheel, and his recklessness took their lives. I pray that my harsh and cruel words didn't faze them and that they felt no pain from what I said. I feel horrible. It was spiteful, and I have suffered the consequences of my actions my entire adult life. That tragic accident led me to my savior, my grandmother. When she took me in, I changed my name to Hollister, her maiden name, to extricate myself from my parents and their lifestyle. My grandmother gave me two of the greatest gifts of my life: unconditional love and the support to pursue my dream of becoming an author.

She took a deep, cathartic breath; it cleansed her soul of the burden she had voluntarily carried around. Hailee scanned the room again, looking for Rex. She made two sweeps of the audience before she laid eyes on him. He stood tall, his face creased with a silly grin. He seemed proud, as if any of her accomplishments were in part due to him.

"What I'm about to say may shock and even offend some of you, and for that, I'm truly sorry. I hope that you can forgive me; please believe me, I had no malice in my heart, only fear. Fear of losing what I loved most in this world." Hailee's heart pounded loudly, and she could barely hear herself speak. "I have deceived you." At the loud gasps, she paused.

Hailee spoke louder, trying to be heard over the flustered chatter. "My grandmother wrote two-thirds of *Something Dark*. She willed the publishing rights to me and told me to finish the story and make it mine, and I did."

Hailee searched the crowd for Rex. He turned ghostly white. "My agent, Rex Chandler, has been blackmailing me for years. I should have done the right thing and come clean at the beginning, but I didn't, and I've regretted it every day."

Hailee looked up from her notes and saw Rex darting across the room, trying to reach the exit. Max intercepted him and pushed him up against the wall. Cameras were flashing as Max cuffed Rex and escorted him outside.

The chattering in the auditorium got louder. Hailee stopped. Everyone had focused on Max, and she lost their attention. She had to finish so that things could be set straight. Panic surrounded her. She had to make them understand. She spoke loudly. "Rex Chandler is being arrested. Please, let the police do their jobs."

Several minutes later, the audience returned their attention to Hailee. "I should have given my grandmother credit for her work on the novel, and I regret that I didn't. Due to her love and generosity, I have been able to pursue my dream." She stopped and waited until everyone listened. "I want to assure you that the following five books are all mine, my ideas, my characters, and my plot. I have worked hard to earn your loyalty and will continue to work even harder to maintain it. I have learned my lesson. Please forgive me."

Carl nodded.

Someone in the crowd yelled, "Go, Hailee!" She thought it might be Alex, but she couldn't be sure.

Hailee had one more item to address, and it might be the most gut-wrenching. She motioned to the man standing to her right to come to the microphone. He looked different from when she last saw him. His long hair had been washed, trimmed, and pulled back into a ponytail. He wore a clean, long-sleeve shirt and denim jeans. She looked down at his feet, which were adorned by a well-used pair of Birkenstock sandals.

Never in a million years could she have imagined that she would be willing to accept anyone, especially the man who had essentially abandoned her, who voluntarily participated in the lifestyle she had spent her entire childhood running from. As she studied him and his clothes, she felt an unexpected sense of pride and wonder. This man gave her life. She didn't know why he had left. Perhaps her mom had decided to get married, and he had other plans or no plans at all. Either way, he now stood by her side. Hailee decided she would not waste one more minute rehashing her ill feelings about her childhood or about her disappointment with the people who had raised her. She would make the most of their time together.

"I want to thank you for coming and for allowing me to share my secret with you. I hope you will accept my sincere apology. I hope you can find it in your heart to forgive me."

She breathed a sigh of relief. She did it, and as far as she could tell, neither the world nor her career had ended.

"Before I go, I would like to introduce you to a man who made all of this possible. He is the man who created me, and without him and the gift of life, none of this would have been possible." Hailee grasped his hand in hers and said, "This is my father, Raymond Buzz Bayard."

Clapping and whooping erupted in the hall.

Buzz said, "Cool, man."

Hailee replied, "Yeah."

The End